The War in Venice

Glenn Haybittle

Published by Cheyne Walk 2022

Published by Cheyne Walk

www.cheynewalk.co

ISBN paperback: 978-1-9999682-8-1
ISBN ebook: 978-1-9999682-9-8

For my mother and father

Destiny may take thy part,
And may thy fears fulfil;
But think that we
Are but turn'd aside to sleep;
They who one another keep
Alive, n'er parted be

John Donne

Part One

1

Venice 2007

Kate stands outside the once-upon-a-time door with its blistered green paint. She takes a deep breath. Momentarily she feels the weight of all the unfinished stories she carries within her lift. She is outside of time for a moment. No longer a sixty-one year old woman with most of her life behind her. There are one or two places in the world that know our secrets. On the other side of this door in a narrow backstreet of the San Polo district of Venice there are ghosts with knowledge of her. But this is a threshold she will never cross again. That time is past. There is a different world behind this door now. She is standing as close as she can get in physical space to the happiest moments of her life.

2

"Are you a fairy or a fool? Are you a cat or a coward?"

It was something her father said to her. Sometimes he crouched down in front of her to deliver his mantra. Other times he kept his hands in his pockets. It was as if he couldn't think of anything else to say to her. She remembers him as a shy awkward man, a solitary walker in the world. She still, in disarming moments of loneliness, finds herself wishing she could talk to him. But he has been dead for fifteen years. Now another formative person in her life has died. And as was the case with her father she can't help feeling it is her responsibility to make sure Elisabetta Del Monaco isn't forgotten. The last task of love is to protect remembrance.

She feels history ought to be interested in Elisabetta Del Monaco. She was a unique figure. Probably the only woman in the second half of the twentieth century overseeing atelier training in the tradition of Renaissance Italy. She has helped keep alive a heritage of portrait and figure oil painting in Venice which dates back to Titian and Tintoretto. Her name should be remembered; her work needs to be preserved.

Kate stands at the helm of the vaporetto, fancying herself for a laconic moment a heraldic figurehead. The reflections in the water seem like the last lingering trace of a magical dream. The palaces along the Grand Canal appear ghosted with nostalgia. Or perhaps she is imposing her own mood on them. There's no denying her life has fallen short of the promises Venice made to her when she was a young woman. How could it not? It is an ever more frequent pastime of hers nowadays to climb into photographs of distant times when she was less lonely and take up residence there for as long as she can sustain the effort of imagination.

She remembers the first time she arrived in Venice. Descending the steps outside the station of Santa Lucia she felt as though she was walking out onto a stage. She experienced a sweeping hush of expectation. As if the moment had arrived for her to audition the part she was to play in life. She quickly learned that the sight of Venice at given moments can root you in your deepest longings. It can also make you realise your identity too is built on shifting water, consists of rising and falling tides, countless ephemeral reflections and refractions. Venice can wash through you the love you have never made, the battles you have never fought, the beauty you have never created. It can flood to the surface everything you have lost and everything you have never known. It can reveal you to yourself without your carnival masks.

She is on her way to meet a distant relative of her former art teacher. Signora Berti, she has learned, has inherited the estate of Elisabetta Del Monaco. Kate didn't go to the funeral. The sad news reached her in England too late. She commemorated the death of her teacher by listening to Handel's *Lascia ch'io pianga* and then Janet Baker sing *Dido's Lament*. The two arias helped her to plunge deeper down inside the pathos of the moment. To put her head under its water. Music often makes her feel she is in communion with water. She heard there wasn't a kindly approachable face amongst the mourners at the graveside. The faces all tight-lipped and forbidding with a competitive animosity bristling through the ranks. Marco, the man who owns the art materials shop where as a student she bought all her pigments, oils, brushes and canvas, told her about the funeral. It is awful to think there was no one at the graveside in whom Signora Del Monaco had inspired love. It is, she supposes, an indictment of the way she lived her life. She shared so much of her knowledge but so little of her love.

She meets Signora Berti at a sidewalk café in Campo dei Miracoli. The woman is finishing the last mouthful of a sticky cake when Kate arrives. She has thick arms and a manly face from which she marshals any trace of kindness. As Kate sits down at the table she feels the woman unfavourably judge her attire. Her green cardigan has red daubs of paint on the sleeves. It's a small vanity of hers to believe they might make her look more interesting.

"As I said on the phone, I was once a student of Signora Del Monaco."

"One of her posh English girls," says the woman. Kate doesn't understand the woman's hostility, the nature of the competition she has entered into. She herself has gone through life hiding what she feels. It has always seemed an arrogance not to.

"She did attract posh English girls, yes. But I was probably the least posh of her students." It seems to Kate she has spent her entire life either disclaiming social privilege or feeling insecure that she doesn't possess enough. She still though loves speaking Italian. It makes her feel there is much more to her than meets the eye. That she possesses an entire secret other world. It used to feel like acting when she held conversations in Italian. As if whatever she said had no relevance to her real life. She didn't know then that many of her most pivotal and cherished memories were made when she believed she was acting.

"Well, a lot of good it did her. She died almost penniless. What happened to your face?"

Kate is taken aback by the woman's brazen directness. As a rule a pretence is maintained that there is nothing untoward about her palsied face.

"I had a stroke."

It was two years ago she had the stroke which left the left side of her face paralysed, frozen in an expression of horror. Her reflection in the mirror afterwards, especially the drooping twist of the mouth, was the most distressing and incomprehensible thing she had ever had to look at. She no longer recognised herself. She had been robbed forever of her smile. She was unable to make the peace with this new ugly mask of a face. Her voice too changed. Words emerged slurred or with a faint hiss. She had to learn how to talk anew. For six months she hid from the world as much as was possible. She felt herself to be grotesque, as if she had just climbed out of a coffin. Whenever the doorbell rang her panicked instinct was to hide. Her every attachment to the past as if severed from her. She wanted no witnesses to her disfigured face. She had to accept she would never see again the people and places she cherished. Self-pity became her most dangerous enemy. Self-pity produces only black and white film. It removes all colour from the imagination. It has demanded all her fight to bring back her ugly altered face to the beauty of Venice. She still carries the shock of it every day.

"Anyway, I was wondering what you intend to do with her paintings."

"They're in storage, along with her father's paintings. Why do you ask? You think they're valuable?"

"Perhaps not in monetary terms."

"What other kind of terms are there?"

"I'm concerned about them. That they're being looked after properly."

Signora Berti screws up her face. "Is that any of your business? Unless you're here to make me an offer for them."

"I don't have much money I'm afraid."

Signora Berti turns the wedding ring on her finger. Kate reads the gesture as a criticism of the absence of any ring on her own third finger.

"How much would you say they're worth?"

"I've no idea. That's like asking how much her life was worth."

Signora Berti makes another disdainful mask of her face. She wouldn't continually make her face ugly if she knew what it's like to have no choice in the matter, thinks Kate.

"What will happen to her studio?"

"We've sold it. A company that exports Venetian souvenirs has bought it."

Kate sees swarms of plastic gondolas, silly hats and twee glass figurines. She has to hide the anger she feels that the studio and all its history will be erased as if it never existed.

"Do you think I could see the paintings? I could at least tell you which ones were painted by her and which painted by her father."

Signora Berti takes another sip of her cappuccino. "I would presume the father's paintings are more valuable, being older?"

"Maybe. Have you spoken to anyone about them? About the idea of preserving them I mean."

"Like who?"

"I don't know. An art historian, a curator. Someone who works for an art council or a museum here in Venice perhaps. I know there's an academy of arts here. They might be interested in archiving them. They belong to history now."

"There you are wrong. They belong to my husband and me."

"One of her students, you know, painted the Queen of England. At Buckingham Palace."

"Perhaps you ought to ask her to buy them."

"That's not a bad idea actually. I don't mean the Queen. But some of her old students might be willing to help."

"To buy them?"

Money, evidently, is the only language Signora Berti speaks. She tries not to hold her in contempt. She has schooled herself to refrain, whenever possible, from seeing herself as superior to anyone in life. You never know what a person has suffered. "Yes. Perhaps we could meet up again in a couple of days? And this time I'd very much like to see the paintings."

"I'll talk to my husband. And then I'll be in touch."

Kate allows Signora Berti to have the last word.

3

Most of the girls, elderly women now, it's sad to think of them as elderly women, who studied at Signora Del Monaco's atelier still paint and have websites. It's a testament to their teacher, her ability to inspire, that they have all mustered such long-term commitment and fidelity to their art. The competitive spirit in her means she has, online, intermittently charted the progress of some of these women. But she has had no contact with any of them for years. As a rule she has little desire to disturb the past. There arrives a tension at the back of her neck as she contemplates opening these portals into her former life. She would rather be remembered as she was. In the clear gold light of youth. It wearies her the prospect of having to condense decades of her life into a few sentences, to dress up her compromises and defeats as willed choices. But she owes it to her teacher to save her work. She composes the message with pen and paper at a table in the lobby of her *pensione*.

You have probably heard the very sad news of the passing of our beloved teacher. The woman who has inherited all Signora Del Monaco's work is a covetous individual who has no interest in art. I met with her today. I don't trust her to take care of our teacher's artistic legacy. All her paintings after all were painted with love. They deserve to be treated with love. Love and respect. We can't let this woman erase our teacher from history. We owe it to her to keep her alive and preserve a place for her in the future. If we all make a contribution, whatever you can afford, I feel confident I can persuade this woman to sell us the paintings. We can then look after them with the care they deserve.

She has to summon all her resources of courage to enter the internet café. It is the exclusive domain of youth. She sees through the glass that she is old enough to be the grandmother of everyone inside. Her contorted mouth, she feels, makes her look like she might be mentally impaired. She anticipates for a moment becoming an ostracised figure of fun for the young people if they choose to be unkind. A sensation like seasickness rises in her as she opens the door. She is grateful for the kindly smile of the girl at the counter. The young people ensconced in their cubicles take little no notice of her. Inwardly she smiles at the melodrama she has created. Growing old she has discovered is to ever more frequently make mountains of molehills. She types out the message she has composed and sends it as an email to the various former students of Signora Del Monaco she has been able to track down.

She pauses before sending the email to Phoebe. Her mind goes back to the dinner at the rustic osteria near the Accademia when her boyfriend arrived in Venice for the weekend. By then she had lived in Venice long enough to claim a proprietorial intimacy with the city. She and the other students had been a small enclosed, self-referential community. Eight English girls, the youngest eighteen, the eldest twenty-two. The world outside of Venice seemed of no importance in those days. The moon mission, the Manson murders, the Vietnam war were like feature films they hadn't seen. They were much more interested in comparing mediums, trying out new pigments, blocking in their shadow shapes, softening their sharp edges. Nothing mattered to them save what visually bound the moment. And of course no city in the world is kinder on the eye than Venice. When you open your front door of a morning your mood is immediately lifted. She once saw a virgin layer of snow on the steps of the church of Santa Maria della Salute. She several times saw misted lights through banks of fog over the Grand Canal and the ghostly locomotion of a solitary gondola. She often sat watching the deepening gold of the light over the water towards sunset. Moments when Venice made itself into the magical setting of a bedtime story. Moments she will take to her grave.

They were celebrities in Venice. Restaurant and bar owners, exasperated by the short thrift of tourists, loved them because they came back and brought with them an air of privilege, glamour and gratitude. They avoided the crowded narrow streets behind San Marco and were scornful of tourists. When you live in Venice you appropriate it as your own. You create something you call "our Venice". You don't like sharing it, and especially not with tourists. You felt that Venice had always expected you, had been designed and built partly with you in mind. There was always however the underlying suspicion that their immunity from harsh realities would have to be paid for sooner or later. When you're young you're suspicious of the idea that happiness has anything to do with shelter and ease. You think happiness is something bolder, more hardily won, more circumscribed by menace. They were all seduced into this way of thinking eventually. They believed that whatever happened to them in Venice only had relevance within the perimeters of its waterways, within reach of its echoing bells. All of them except Signora Del Monaco. She, alone among them, seemed to believe she was worthy of Venice.

When Jake arrived she had been eager to show off her privileged intimacy with the city. She had been awash and sparkling with new love. In the restaurant Jake was the only boy with four beautiful girls. She quickly saw him in a different light. Saw how fundamentally unreliable he was. It was apparent he couldn't look at the girls without seeing adventure in them. But it was Phoebe who lit him up. Who brought a predatory look up into his eyes.

Two months previously Kate had gone back to England to attend Phoebe's twenty-first birthday party. The marquee was set up in the grounds of Phoebe's family's honey-coloured Palladian stately home. There were swans on the lake and a deer park. She remembers now standing barefoot on the lawn in her party frock watching the light of dawn brush the clouds. It was one of those moments when she was enamoured of the world, overcome by the beauty of her life.

By the time the coffee and limoncello arrived on the table she knew she had lost Jake to Phoebe. Every time he looked at her he had to look at her again a moment later. Her beauty evoked the grandeur of her family home. As if you could see the deer park, the grand staircase and all the many echoing gilded rooms of the house in her smile. The eyes of the gondoliers and waiters of Venice always widened when Phoebe appeared in their sightline. The lines her clothes made against her body hypnotised them.

At the end of the evening Jake made excuses. He said he was tired and returned to his hotel without kissing her. She didn't see him the next day. Phoebe was missing from the studio on the Monday. She had returned to England for a few days. Then Jake telephoned her to tell her he and Phoebe had fallen in love. That he was sorry.

"You paint from nature. You know nature is the boss and its demands have to be obeyed."

She knew he had rehearsed this speech and was even pleased with it. She felt deeply ashamed of herself for ever having been taken in by him but at the same time couldn't help feeling a tide had gone out which would never return.

She and Phoebe co-existed in the studio with difficulty afterwards. She began to realise Phoebe was more important to her than Jake had ever been. There have even been moments when she has wondered if Phoebe wasn't the romantic love of her life. They had sprawled across beds in candlelight together speaking secret combinations of words. They often looked back at themselves in the same mirror. Phoebe was the first adult she ever shared a bed with. The first person who saw her adult naked body. Her laughter brought a warm flush to her body. But she knows Venice is the great romantic love of her life, not Phoebe.

Because Phoebe was the most glamorous and popular girl she found herself sidelined at the studio. Snubbed at coffee breaks, uninvited to dinners. Even when she was prepared to forgive her friend, Phoebe clung to her disdain as if it was she who had been wronged. Polly became Kate's painting partner. The misfit Christian girl who everyone shunned. She caked her face in powder and wore thick black stockings even at the height of summer. She had to be told to stop humming hymns while she worked at her easel.

Polly is the first woman who responds to her email. "So lovely to hear from you, Kate. Shame it had to be in such sad circumstances. I'm sorry to hear about Signora Del Monaco. But truthfully, the only reason I'd buy her paintings would be to burn them! She once told me I didn't have the talent to be an artist. You have no idea how unhappy this made me at the time. Sometimes I think only my faith pulled me through. I'm happy to say I've proved her wrong." Attached is a link featuring twelve book covers illustrated with paintings of Polly's. They are all garishly pink, childishly decorative with not the faintest inkling of artistry.

She has to admit it's Phoebe she most wants to hear from. She imagines them becoming friends again. At the same time she is ashamed of her eagerness to forgive her old adversary. It seems to point to something obsequious in her nature. Socially ambitious. Phoebe didn't marry Jake. Their relationship ended soon after Phoebe left Venice. It was while she was hurting over Phoebe's betrayal that Signora Del Monaco asked her to sit for a portrait. It was unheard of for her to paint her students. While she was posing for her teacher the other girls began to take an interest in her again. They wanted to know what their diffident and stringent teacher talked to her about. She doesn't now remember the finished portrait at all. She imagines it must be among the canvases in storage. But she does remember the evening Signora Del Monaco took a decision to confide in her and become uncharacteristically candid and talkative. Her private life to her students had previously been no less mysterious than the depths of the sea. Sometimes Kate thinks her teacher put a spell of spinsterhood on her that afternoon. She always has to remind herself that her teacher wasn't a spinster, that she was briefly married, even though, as they all agreed, she never somehow possessed the air of a woman with carnal knowledge.

The atelier had two rooms. The front room was where the students worked, the easels wedged closely together. The back room with the north light was Signora Del Monaco's private studio. The walls though were mostly covered with framed paintings by her father. There were many saints, craggy old sages in rags with twisted necks, flailing arms, euphoric or pained expressions. Large oppressively dark paintings overly glazed which had begun to crack and blister.

She can remember how her teacher studied her from the far end of the studio with the assessing eyes of a cat. How she moistened a finger and applied it to the canvas to soften a sharp edge and then wiped her finger on the sleeve of her smock. It was disarming to withstand the surges of heated vitality in her teacher's body as she strode to the easel and applied paint to the canvas.

"As a woman, I think we often feel there's a wall we need to climb to escape. Sometimes I like to imagine the drop down onto the ground on the other side. The brief moment of flight before the jarring thud of the landing. That's an act we perform too rarely. Like getting out of bed at dawn to watch the sunrise. Or walking barefoot and joyously in the rain."

That was the gist of one of the things Signora Del Monaco had said to her while wielding a paintbrush on an outstretched arm in the half-light of the high-ceilinged studio.

Kate was shy and insecure about her intelligence around her teacher. Frozen by the fear of appearing stupid or frivolous. She rarely found a quick bright answer to any question asked. She remembers enquiring of her teacher if she had a favourite among her own paintings.

"The best painting I ever did is lost. Or I've convinced myself it's the best painting I ever did. Perhaps I believe that because it's no longer here to persecute me with its shortcomings. I now see my idea of it. And my idea of it glows with an inspired sense of accomplishment. Rather like how one imagines a painting before beginning it. The moment you begin transferring a painting from your imagination to a canvas is like waking up from a lovely dream. Bit by bit the beauty begins evaporating into thin air."

"Who was this painting of?"

"A Jewish brother and sister. They were the children of the man who owned the shop where my father and I bought all our painting materials. This shop has gone now. I gave my painting to the brother because his sister had recently died of tuberculosis. I painted her from some charcoal sketches I had done when she was alive. I wanted the painting to show him how much I valued his friendship. That was my inspiration. In those days I believed I would go on to paint much better pictures. I believed what my father taught me. That hard work and discipline inevitably lead to a growing mastery of your art. But the most important thing for an artist I've learned is inspiration which I like to think of as the music. As you know a painting begins as geometry. But at some point you have to hear the music of what you're trying to achieve. You have to lock into those rhythms and harmonies. That's when the adventure begins. If you don't find the music hard work and discipline won't bring you to the brink where you need to be. And inspiration is the most elusive of bedfellows. I was thinking last night. A striking memory can compel us to act and thus change the next moment of our life. Inspiration is often to be found in memory. But for me those kinds of searing memories generally arrived when it was too late to act."

When teaching there was the sense Signora del Monaco sometimes had to discipline herself not to withdraw into private thoughts. No such restraint did she show while she painted Kate. Often there had been long silences in which Kate could detect how rigorously her teacher applied her attention to questions passing through her mind. Kate formed the idea her teacher spent a lot of time trying to make sense of how she had ended up so alone and sad. Sitting up on her podium Kate had wanted to ask if she had been in love with the boy in the painting but there was no overcoming the shyness her teacher induced in her. She can recall no one in her adult life with whom she felt more tongue-tied. However, in the intimate darkening light, it was as if Signora Del Monaco had heard her question.

"I've never enjoyed talking to anyone as much as I did with Marcello. That was the name of the brother. He had such a clear gaze. And he always spoke from his own centre. He could make me talk because there was an intelligent intensity in the way he listened. My father once told me that one of the main priorities in life is to oppose stupidity whenever it stands before you. Marcello did that. He made me feel I amounted to more when he was near. I don't think he did know how much he meant to me. But you can't tell people that; you can only show it. And there I failed, I think. Sometimes in life we wait for the rush of hot blood. We expect it to make our decisions for us. But I never felt that rush of hot blood. I'm a conservationist, not an adventurer. I've dedicated my life to continuing a tradition. The tradition of oil painting as practiced by the Old Masters. I do though meet Marcello in dreams now and again. He always appears like the loneliest person in the history of the world. The sight of him makes my heart ache. In one dream I asked him if I could rest my head on his shoulder. I woke up feeling that being naked is the most wondrous and frightening thing in life." (This, Kate remembers, made her blush for Signora Del Monaco. A woman in a position of authority should not be talking of being naked. She was to tell the other girls, in the hearing of Phoebe, about this the next day in the local bar while they were sitting with their cappuccinos. Not the only time in her life she has shamefully betrayed a confidence to garner public prestige.) "He was the first person I ever showed my private sketches to. He was generous in his praise. I'll never forget that. It meant so much to me. But I could never have married him. If I'd married him I wouldn't be talking to you now. I wouldn't have my atelier. I was adamant I would never allow my self-esteem to become dependent on a man or a mirror. It was the distance between us that made us so fascinating and compelling to each other. The distance that had to be preserved. There's this idea that love always seeks to bridge distance. That's not been my experience of love. That seems more like the aim of biology. Sometimes, though we don't love with the body, we can love with the mind. The union created is no less binding. But I am an unnatural woman. I've never been one to openly shake out my feelings, like a newly washed sheet. I've lived like Emily Dickinson. I kept a whole part of myself in reserve, like a beautiful dress saved for a special occasion which never arrived. Sometimes I think his biggest mistake was never to invite me out in his boat. He never made me submit to any mastery of his. That perhaps was his chance. To make a dangerous commitment a woman needs to feel she is in steady secure hands. Even an unnatural woman like me. You see the night time painting of the boat on the Grand Canal on the wall behind me?"

"The figure punting the gondola?"

"Yes. Except it's not a gondola. It's a *sandolo*. A gondola without the beak. Marcello owned one. If you look closely among the shadows, you'll see the faint outline of a female figure. That's me in Marcello's boat. Or my ghost. I painted it during the war. It's the only picture I've ever painted from my imagination. I had become obsessed by my missing painting. Sometimes I have this awful feeling it might have ended up in the warehouse at Auschwitz. I went to their apartment after I heard about the Gestapo raids on Jewish homes. I'm ashamed of that act now. It's true I wanted to know if he and his family were safe. But I also wanted to rescue my painting. You see the Saint Anthony in my father's painting on the wall over there? The model for that painting had moved into the apartment. His name was Fausto. He was a sinister individual. He worked for my husband as a spy. The frame of my painting was in the apartment but it was empty. Marcello must have taken it when he fled.

"But the thing I've never been able to make sense of is that I received a note from Marcello after the war. It was barely legible but it said he had escaped the camp. The postmark was Italian so I presumed he meant the transit camp where the Jews were held before being transported to the death camps in Poland. From that day on I kept expecting him to return. There were many times when I thought I caught a glimpse of him in the streets or on the water but it was always a trick of the eyes or the mind. Even now I expect him to return one day. This though is probably just the fantasy of a lonely ageing woman. That said, in my experience, nothing much changes as we get older. We still spend most of our time living between the dream and the reality. I don't know why he's so much on my mind today. I think it's because of a loneliness I detect in you and want to capture in your portrait.

"Loneliness of course lies in wait for all of us. You can't escape it. We keep the things we most need close to us but the path we're on is rarely the path we choose. I remember I never stopped wanting my name back when I was married. I felt like a shadow of myself with the alien name imposed on me. One time when I was painting Marcello and was struggling with my shapes he took hold of my hand in his, caressed it and then removed my wedding ring. He placed it on the arm of his chair and told me to go back to my painting. Strangely, it felt like a weight had been lifted and from then on I was able to ascribe eloquent meaning to each of my brushstrokes. It became a ritual every day for him to remove my wedding ring. I suppose in some ways it was symbolic of the bond we shared. It was somehow outside of time. Or I'd like to think that's how he might have seen it. We never know how anyone else sees what we see. At least not until we try to paint the same thing. Perhaps that's what attracts me to the techniques of classical realism. The premise that such a thing as objective truth exists, even sometimes in the realm of feeling. Whatever happened to me then I considered of no importance as long as I could paint well. But I couldn't paint well. Though it pains me to say it, I think I'm a better teacher than I am an artist. My natural talent fell short of my ambition. That, I suppose, is the story of every life.

"My father made me marry a man I didn't respect. He was a fascist. He was shot at the end of the war by the partisans. He didn't really deserve to be shot but when fascism came to an end there was so much anger and desire for vengeance in the air. Men with their idealism again. I sometimes think idealism is nothing much more than an excuse to get angry. I myself was threatened by a mob at the end of the war. There were women who wanted to shave off my hair. They said I was no less a fascist than my husband. The ringleader was a girl Fausto, the boy in my father's painting, got pregnant and then abandoned. She saw us together not long after he abandoned her. I had met him by chance on the street. She regaled him for his treachery but slapped me. I've worn the shock of that slap all my life. It's such a horrible feeling to find oneself misrepresented, even in the mind of a stranger. Sometimes I think one of the reasons we make art is an effort to give a true account of ourselves, so there can be no misrepresentation."

The light had almost completely left the studio.

"It's astonishing how eager people are to recognise themselves in slogans. That's what the war taught me. Half-grown mean-spirited men gained illusory stature and bitter women were able to vent their spite – that was what fascism achieved. The fascists made a crime of kindness. Life cannot be experienced deeply without kindness, just as life cannot be experienced deeply without art. Kindness and art have something else in common. They both help us become less afraid of death."

Signora Del Monaco erased all trace of the evening of intimacy between them when she returned to her teaching duties the next day, as if, like she had said about her relationship with Marcello, it took place outside of time.

4

Kate never found out if Marcello ever returned. Nowadays, every time she reads a novel or watches a film in which lovers are parted with no easy way back to each other, she thinks of Marcello and her teacher. It has become her point of reference for every fictional love story. That she herself isn't the protagonist of the story is a detail she doesn't like to dwell on.

Kate had known little about the conflict in Italy when a student in Venice. Her knowledge of the second world war was more or less limited to the Battle of Britain, the Blitz, the miracle at Dunkirk and the concentration camps. Otherwise she saw the war as essentially a struggle between good and evil. And Italy had been on the side of evil. She wondered where this left Signora Del Monaco. Sometimes they joked that she was like a Nazi with her regimented censorious way of running the studio. More often they liked to compare her to the reproving thin sad woman of the mosaic of the Madonna of Torcello. *Our Lady of the way.* She made them draw casts for an entire year before they were allowed to pick up a paint brush. She forbade the painting of male nudes in the figure class. Even male portrait models she frowned upon if they were young. As if she felt herself the custodian of every girl's chastity. It seemed possible, married to a fascist, her teacher hadn't entirely been on the side of the good during the war. That perhaps she even harboured a shameful secret. That might explain the unhappy expression her face assumed in repose.

She discussed with Polly the things Signora Del Monaco told

her. Polly decided that she might have betrayed her husband with the Jewish model. A wife who betrays her husband was a scenario that struck awe in both girls. The strange volatile medium of excitement and disapproval it gave rise to. Perhaps, they argued over a cappuccino by a canal, she had even played a part in the arrest of the Jewish model.

"That might explain why she has so little time for men. I've never known a woman who distances herself from men as much as she appears to," said Polly.

"Unless they're dead, like Titian and Tintoretto."

Ultimately she found Signora Del Monaco went up rather than down in her estimation as a result of the shared confidences. Which bore out something her teacher had said – that we evaluate people not by what they tell us but by what they show us.

5

Kate stares long and hard at her face in the bathroom mirror. How brutally it misrepresents her. She has to fight into submission her instinct to continue hiding from the world. There is a moment when she inwardly collapses again. When she feels no affinity with the face in the glass. When she looks to herself like a stranger whose ugliness might strike fear in children. She summons an image of Signora Del Monaco to give her courage for what she is about to do.

She walks with her painting equipment to Campo dei Miracoli. She is careful, as is her habit, not to catch the eye of anyone. An unkind look can distress her for days. Her heart is thumping when she sets up her easel opposite the church, close to the canal. The facades of buildings are reflected as vividly in the water as they appear before her eyes. Red geraniums animate the mullioned or arched windows. The reflections in the green water she thinks of as memories while she paints them, the ghost of a lost moment which can only be reflected in the waters of the mind.

She becomes a minor celebrity while she stands working at her easel. The only time she is able to forget her altered face is when she paints. Passers-by compliment her painting; one or two take photographs. People are kind and their kindness breaks her free of the shell of her loneliness. On her way back to the hotel she feels she has escaped from the mirror. There is a spring in her step. Every pleasure she wins nowadays is dispersed by a sadness that arrives soon after. Most moments of happiness are made up of trifles and can easily be dispersed by other trifles. But today her good mood has a more robust quality.

Inspired by the recollection of what Signora Del Monaco said about sunrises she leaves her hotel at dawn the next morning and sets up her easel by the Grand Canal. She is close enough to the water to smell the brine and seaweed, to feel its gentle lapping swell as a presence in her own body. The taste of salt is bracing on her lips. A line of gondolas rock back and forth by her side. A shroud of mist is lifting from the cupola of Santa Maria della Salute. It is easier somehow at this time of day to realise the city is sustained on nothing more substantial than wooden piles driven into the silt at the bottom of the sea. The sun rises higher and shines a golden pathway on the water.

Her painting is of no importance to the world. She knows this. And yet while she's at work on it nothing else matters but the next brushstroke. Her true existence is no longer taking place inside her body but on the canvas. This is what she feels. That she has escaped to a more exacting but also more rewarding world. Never does she feel more consumed by anything she does. Sometimes elatedly consumed; other times despairingly consumed.

By the side of the Grand Canal with paintbrush in hand she finds herself wishing Signora Del Monaco could see her now.

6

When Signora Berti calls, Kate has not received a single offer of help from Signora Del Monaco's former students. It's as though they suspect her of being the architect of some kind of scam. It's some relief to return to her adversarial relationship with Phoebe who hasn't replied to her email.

She sits by the Rialto Bridge with a cappuccino. Tethered gondolas shift in the current. She is excited by the prospect of seeing again her teacher's paintings. They represent to her a kind of lost city of Atlantis. An underwater kingdom where she once lived and will now be able to revisit. She finds herself willing the painting of the brother and sister to have been rediscovered. She feels a deep longing to finally see the painting Signora Del Monaco thought her best work. And to know the face of the young man who haunted her teacher.

Once again Signora Berti lets it be known with expressive eloquence that she doesn't approve of Kate's attire. She's a woman who likes to laugh privately to herself. Her own best friend. The damp and smell of bilge water and mould catches in her throat the moment she walks into the echoing barren basement. It's half boathouse, half storeroom. The rusted motorboat doesn't look like it will ever take to the water again. The canvases still in their frames are stacked against the walls. It's immediately shocking how forlorn her teacher's legacy seems. The majority of the canvases are paintings by Signora Del Monaco's father, stacked one behind another. She looks again at the painting of Saint Anthony, still in its original frame, and remembers what

Signora Del Monaco told her about the model. *His name was Fausto. He was a sinister individual. He worked for my husband as a spy.* For a moment, attracted by the historical narrative it contains, she considers including this painting in the offer she plans to make Signora Berti. But she dismisses the idea. She crouches down and begins thumbing through the smaller paintings. The ugliness of the surroundings seems to infect the work. She wants to see in them the freshness of a newly minted world. But they look sadly commonplace, wretchedly outdated. They begin to make her feel she has invented some of the beauty she associates with her time in Venice.

She finds the oil painting of the *sandolo* at night and then the portrait of herself as a twenty-year-old girl. A painting is an intimate meeting across worlds and time. Never has she been made more aware of this power possessed by pigment to retain light and time than when she stares back at the image of her younger self.

She is disappointed there is no sign of the painting of the brother and sister.

"I wasn't able to raise sufficient funds to buy all of Signora Del Monaco's paintings but I can offer you 500,000 lire for these two canvases," she tells Signora Berti, removing the paintings of the *sandolo* and herself from the pile. The woman accepts her offer with a show of disdain.

It pains Kate to turn her back on all her teacher's paintings, left to fester in that mildewed fungal-smelling underworld realm.

Part Two

1

Venice 1938

He follows his target out of Campo dei Frari and along the length of Calle dei Volti. That she is oblivious to his existence is like a blast of uplifting music to which his body fits its rhythm. He is attentive to every detail of her presence. She has a lonely but defensive gait. As if she is protective of a precarious world she has created in her own mind. He has begun to feel his way into her secrecies. But it is frustrating to realise he has no idea what is uppermost in her mind; what abiding memories she owns; what stories she likes to cast herself in. He makes a mental note of what she is wearing. Floral print red and white dress, a tailored black jacket, black stockings, pins in her black hair which is partly up and partly down, flat red shoes, silver hooped earrings, no make-up. She holds onto her bag with a tight grip. A clue there is something fearful about her. She has an air of wanting more from life. *Don't we all, my darling!*

Three nuns leading a line of schoolgirls in black pinafores separate him from her in the narrow street of shops. Otherwise he would sniff at the air to determine if she's wearing perfume. He doubts it. He suspects she is a virgin. She has an air of taking her young body for granted. As if it is yet to surprise her.

He then has to step aside for a delivery man pushing a squeaking trolley loaded with blocks of ice covered in cloth. A carnival plague doctor mask in a shop window catches his eye. It's not the mask itself which interests him – it is of a tawdry and cheap design – but the theatre involved of hiding behind a mask. The less we reveal of ourselves the less we leave ourselves open to criticism. He imagines saying this to the girl he is following. Wonders what she would say in response. Perhaps he would then tell her it is his ambition to be an actor, a film star. That he has no desire to enter the distant future by way of family. He wants to become part of history as himself. He imagines his face on the cover of magazines and knows a moment of exhilaration, as if a trampoline has lifted his body into the air. He has these sudden inrushes of euphoria. Just as he succumbs to moments of disintegration in his mind when he seems to himself nothing but agitated bodiless darkness.

He watches two sailors in caps and full uniform look her up and down. They both swivel round to assess her from behind after she passes them. He has guessed mirrors are more likely to be a source of insecurity to her than pleasure. This interest on the part of other males suddenly makes her more attractive to him. She goes up from a six out of ten to a seven. Value is not determined privately but by the marketplace, he thinks and wonders if this is true. She has entered an art supplies shop. Her father, he knows, is a painter. She is the dutiful daughter, performing chores for him. He doesn't know why he has been ordered to monitor her movements. Initially he assumed she belonged to some anti-fascist cell of students but he is already beginning to doubt this. She has a solitary air, a lonely life. He is yet to see her with a friend. He is yet to hear the sound of her voice.

He peers in the window of the shop for a moment. His eye goes first to the jars of pigments on a shelf behind the counter. The glistening colours seem concentrated into the essence of themselves. Real life, he thinks, hardly ever takes on the virginal purity of those colours. He sometimes thinks he should keep a notebook of his observations. Why let them float off unchronicled? There are no other customers in the shop. Two men behind the counter. Probably a father and a son. The older man is inspecting the weave of a roll of canvas. The son is attending to his target. She hands him a note of paper. It annoys him he can't see what is written on it. For a moment he wonders if she has a diary in her bag. He imagines stealing it. It's the kind of challenge he most enjoys. Gaining advantage over others by stealth and duplicity. The son's dishevelled dark hair needs cutting. This marks him out as a potential anti-fascist. Committed fascists, in his experience, regularly visit a barber. Another maxim for his imaginary notebook. He's not wearing a tie either. Another cause for suspicion.

He walks over to a shrine to the Madonna with a lit votive candle and a vase of yellow flowers. The belief that a woman from a fairy story could be of any practical help to anyone is beyond his comprehension. He fingers the coins in his jacket pocket, heating them up in his palm. And once more gives thought to the uniform he would like to wear. Probably he favours the tasselled beret, the black shirt, the elegantly tailored jacket, the jodhpurs tucked in the heavy boots of the fascist militia. And of course he would like a pistol buttoned high on his waist. He has not wanted to own anything as much as a gun since pleading with his mother to buy him a train set as a child. He has suggested to his boss he be given a uniform for purposes of disguise. Luigi Volpato laughed at him and asked who he thought he was. "The scarlet pimpernel?" His boss he considers no less a buffoon than Mussolini himself. He can do an admirable impersonation of Il Duce. He has deployed it to make more than one girl laugh until tears arrived. He has imagined doing it for Volpato, to witness his indignation, his horror. To make fun of Mussolini in fascist Italy is like making fun of God in a church.

The girl exits the shop. She has no purchase he can see. She turns into a narrow alley of damp walls, peeling political posters, discarded broken masonry. Red dust comes off the bricks when he brushes them with his hand. He then follows her across Campo San Silvestro (he makes a mental note of the name: he is still mapping the world he lives in) and then through a covered passageway to the Grand Canal. After the labyrinths of gloomy claustrophobic alleys the sweep of glittering open water still has the power to suddenly lift his mood as if he is back in the arms of his father and being swung up into the air. He watches her sit down on a wooden landing stage next to the water. She takes off her shoes. He watches her flex her toes. He has to walk past her. It is the closest he has ever got to her. He can see the veins on her hands. He would compliment her on the beauty of her hands, her long tapering fingers, if he met her at a dance. He walks on towards the Rialto Bridge, past a row of moored gondolas. A black and gold fascist party flag flaps overhead. He sits down on a crate under the arch of an arcade. He lights a cigarette, holds the smoke deep in his lungs. After his next drag he studiously regards the smoke rings he blows out.

He has lived in Venice for three years. He came here from Padua to study at the university. The pale soft light of the city, the drifting haze and the glittering glowing light still sometimes catch him off guard, as if it wants him to become a better kind of person. For a moment the scene before his eyes is held in timeless suspension, as if a struck tuning fork is resounding with its one true note.

He can tell she is happy just idling away her time, letting the sun toast her neck and the back of her hands. He himself derives no pleasure in observing the world continue without him. It makes him fidgety. His eyes move distractedly from one thing to another. He has too many ambitions. And as yet he has no laurels to lay before the world. He flunked university. He still bears the professor who told him he was wasting his parents money a grudge. He told him the next time he would see him would be on the screen of a cinema. Film stars can attract two women into their beds. Two beautiful women. He counts this among his ambitions.

Venice, as background, is more like a film set than a real place. The foreground is always like a stage. The theatrical showiness of the city calls for acting. Three times he has auditioned for minor film roles at the Cinecittà studios in Rome. Three times he has travelled back to Venice indignant that he was rejected. The last time he took comfort from a plain young girl called Bruna. When, three months later, she told him she was pregnant, he moved from his room in Cannaregio to an even more squalid room in the Santa Croce district. He is hiding from her father and two brothers. He told his landlady he had joined the *Alpini* regiment and was off to Verona to report for duty.

He takes out a dog-eared detective novel from his jacket pocket and pretends to read. Two men are unloading a barge, carrying off baskets of fruit, vegetables and flowers on their shoulders. Still holding his detective novel he watches the taxi gondola which is ferrying passengers from one side of the Grand Canal to the other. The male passengers are expected to stand. It's like a test of their manhood. They have to assume a nonchalant air, even when the boat is buffeted by the wake of water traffic, as if they were simply standing in line at a bank teller. There is a fat man who catches him looking at him. Half way across, the gondola is rocked by the waves made by a barge and he can sense the fat man's need for some kind of rail to hold onto. He feels the fat man's teetering equilibrium in his own legs. If only the boat would tip him over into the water! He pictures the scene to himself. Today, so far, has been lacking in comedy. And he has realised he always feels himself in command of his destiny when he can laugh at the world.

Elisabetta Del Monaco, he sees, shows no sign of waiting for an assignation. She is simply putting off the next moment of life. Unless idle dreaming can be called a moment, which he doesn't believe.

Once again he thinks back to the final exchange with Luigi Volpato in his office earlier when his boss asked what his father did for a living.

"Why?"

"Just answer the question."

"He reads gas meters."

"I thought so. One last thing, if ever we meet by chance outside, it goes without saying you're to show no sign whatsoever of knowing me. Is that clear?"

Why had Volpato wanted to make him feel like a bird in a cage? His lips become dry and gummy as if he has been licking envelopes as he recalls the humiliation.

He worked in a radio repair shop before becoming a secret police spy. He had been good with customers, easily getting them to drop their guard. Then he had reported all those who admitted to listening to foreign radio stations or displayed any opposition to the government. News reached Volpato of his gift of gaining the confidence of dissidents and he was summoned to his office and offered a job working for OVRA.

A haze is drifting in from the lagoon. He likes the mist and banks of fog that intermittently descend on Venice when the alleys and waterways assume a still more theatrical cloak and dagger atmosphere.

Elisabetta Del Monaco, he sees, is putting back on her shoes.

2

Marcello's one consuming wish is to return to Giulia's room with the cat cradled in his arms. For a moment his fingers prickle with the phantom weight and warmth of the animal in their grasp. Luna has been missing for three days now. Father thinks it's the medicinal stink of the sick room that has driven the creature away. "That and all the tension and worry circulating through the apartment. Cats are sensitive creatures. They pick up on these things." It's true what Father says – the effect of Giulia's deteriorating sickness on the atmosphere at home is like the inescapable force of suction exerted by a large sinking ship on the surrounding waters. Everyone is being pulled down beneath the surface of the world.

He continues punting the family *sandolo* down the Grand Canal towards the Rialto bridge. His fingers sensitive to the sweep of the long oar through the parting water. The push stroke, the return stroke. The push stroke, the return stroke. It's like the rhythm of his being. It makes him aware his body is made of time. His oar stirs up a smell of algae and seaweed and brine every so often. An intimation of the open sea. The boats tethered to the network of poles on either side of the canal shift in the current. The facades of the palaces undulate on the surface of the water. Every detail doubled, every detail mirrored. The world in the water seems to shimmer with ciphers and secrets not evident in the physical world.

The wings of gulls catch glints of sunlight and throw fleeting shadows over his boat as he nears the fish market. The raucous good-humoured cries of the stallholders fill the air. He has searched up and down the aisles of the fish market every day for Luna. He has come to recognise some of the many cats that stalk the stalls with their crates of crushed ice containing glistening shrimp, prawns, crab, cuttlefish, sea bass, *orate,* octopus.

He wanders around the fish market for twenty minutes. Luna's black face with the white thumbprints under her eyes refuses to jump into his sightline despite all the willed urgency of his longing. His entire body is primed for the wondrous reappearance of the family cat. It seems so little to ask for. And at the same time has taken on the magnitude of asking for a miracle. As if the distance between the everyday and the miraculous has been compressed. The increasing presence in the newspapers of pseudo-scientific anti-Semitic rhetoric led Father to suggest some militant fascist neighbour might have kidnapped or harmed the cat because it belongs to a Jewish family. Mother reminded Father of the Venetian superstition that anyone who hurts a cat will die within the year. Then everyone was uncomfortable because she said this in front of Giulia. "In case you're wondering, I've never in my life harmed a cat," said Giulia from her bed.

He returns to his boat. Later he will again comb the neighbouring alleys. As he decides this he sees something that makes his legs sag under him and his heart pound in his chest. For a moment he almost loses his balance at the stern of the boat, almost loses his grip of the oar. Massimo, the best friend of his youth, is punting his boat towards him. Marcello has known Massimo since they were small children. They have a hoard of memories they share in common. They learned to punt a boat together, they learned to swim together, built cities in the sand at the Lido, shared a consuming if short lived enthusiasm for collecting stamps which, in essence, was the discovery of how thrilling is exclusive ownership. Twice Massimo has fought boys who tried to bully Marcello because he was deemed to be girlish or stuck-up. The first time he played football it was with Massimo;

the first time he went to the cinema it was with Massimo; the first time he loved a book and a piece of music it was with Massimo he shared his excitement. In Massimo's company he knew a freedom from inhibition he has known with no one else. They fell out when, eighteen months ago, Massimo kissed a girl he knew Marcello liked. Marcello saw it as an unforgivable act of betrayal. They argued for five minutes, then Marcello stormed off. They have not spoken or even greeted each other since. That the girl in question no longer holds any attraction for Marcello hasn't restored any warmth to his feeling for Massimo. The vendetta has sucked significance and sustenance from entire stretches of his memory. The memories he shared with Massimo had always made him feel better about life, as if the warm hum of vitality they contained belonged to the present and the future as much as to the past. Excitement was always more likely to reach him through Massimo.

Their boats cross no more than six feet apart. There is no acknowledgement on either side. That emotion can change somebody intimately known and loved into a passing shadow reveals to him how much overriding power emotion has to formulate our reality. He has the feeling he once had looking at Etruscan artefacts – that important knowledge has reverted back to unfathomable mystery. Massimo is wearing a uniform. He himself is wearing a shaggy grey pullover. He recognises the insignia as belonging to the 6th Alpini regiment. He guesses he must have been called up, for Massimo had nothing but scorn for soldiery. It's yet another sign that the world is changing in front of his eyes. He feels a moment's sympathy for his former friend. Afterwards, as he is mooring the boat, he is struck by the senseless absurdity of the nature of the feud between them. He would like to tell Massimo that Lucia, the girl, no more attracts him now than the old woman who sells slices of *castagnaccio* at the market on Riva degli Schiavoni. He can picture the smile with which Massimo would greet this remark. It's the smile he most wanted to win for so many years.

Giulia often now leaves her window open, as if to entice Luna back into her life.

"I saw Massimo. In uniform. We ignored each other."

She moves her head on the pillow to better lock eyes with him. "He'd be a better person if his parents didn't have so much money," she says. She has always criticised people with money and yet, when healthy, was always asking Father for money. Her hypocrisy is a family joke, kept secret from her.

"The feud is more my fault than his," he says. "Anyway, his family aren't that rich."

"They have a holiday villa," she says. It pains him to watch her grapple with a force that is stronger than anything she can muster to oppose it. He never imagined that drawing breath could be so difficult in a young body.

Later, he stands on the small balcony smoking his last cigarette of the day. The flowers in Mother's boxes are wilting. He wonders if Giulia will ever see the irises flower again. Every year the blossoming of the violet flowers marks the family's celebration of the arrival of spring. In the drawing room Mother is playing the violin. Massenet's Meditation from Thais. It's like a mourning for all the songs Giulia will leave unsung. He looks out at a montage of rooftops, searching among the shallow silver pools of moonlight on the tiles for any sign of the cat.

3

To pull open the heavy wooden downstairs door strains at the muscles in Elisabetta's slender arms. Marcello stands in front of her, seeming slightly larger than life. It's the first time she has seen him outside the shop. A woman is scrubbing the front step of the house opposite. Above her a line of ugly washed clothes, like pennants of poverty, stretches from one green shuttered window to another. A miserable forecast of the life that awaits every young woman. She studied her face in the hall mirror before coming down to open the door, altered her hair. She supposes there are few women who don't sometimes wish themselves more beautiful. She has no steady estimation of herself, though she's more likely to feel displeased than meet with her own approval. Often she prefers not to think of herself at all. The last time she saw Marcello he came out from behind the counter and stood unnecessarily close to her in the shop and then suddenly touched her arm. The expression on his face a puzzling mystery to her. The touch of his hand heightened her intimacy with her body in a way that was new to her. Later she looked down at where he had touched her, ran a finger over the spot as if trying to find again the heat in his hand.

"Everything your father ordered," says Marcello, holding up two canvas bags, one in either hand. There is a raindrop on his cheek and another one sliding down his forehead. They bring to the fore a vulnerability in him and make him look more attractive. Then a gust of colder air brings more drops of rain and ruffles his black hair.

"Sorry I couldn't collect it at the shop. I've got to prime canvases for Father later. Come in out of the rain. I'll make you a coffee," says Elisabetta. At eighteen, not yet quite ready to think of herself as a woman, she is still practising at appearing more confident in the world. She uses her bedroom mirror to perfect posture and poise. Ashamed of herself when she imagines her father watching. Almost everything she does and thinks in private she takes pains to hide from her father. She has not yet learned to say what she thinks. Her father and his refusal to brook any contradiction has long since trained her to bite her tongue.

She notices Marcello's braces hang loose from the waistband buttons of his trousers. It's not the first time this has been the case and she understands it's a look he cultivates, a clue as to how he wants to see himself and be seen, as if nonchalant, at ease in the world, a little disdainful of convention.

"Our cat has gone missing," Marcello says in the echoing kitchen. "It feels like I've searched every nook and cranny in Venice for her."

"Cats are vain creatures. They like to believe they are independent. She'll come back when she's made her point."

"I wish I could share your confidence."

There are cobwebs high on the ceiling cornices and cracks in the stucco. A map of damp shows through the white paint on part of a wall, creating a kind of mother-of-pearl effect. She hasn't noticed these signs of neglect before. Marcello removes jars of dry pigment, stretcher bars, a roll of canvas, sun-thickened oils, a bottle of varnish and white spirit, sable and hog's hair brushes, counting off each item from the list he holds and placing it on the marble-topped table.

"What's it like to handle all the materials required for painting every day and not paint yourself?"

"Do I wish I painted, you mean? I have no talent."

He leans down to tie up a loose shoelace. It's the first indication he shows he might be nervous.

"You're not from Venice, are you?"

"Ferrara. But I've lived in Venice since I was four."

"What do you make of us Venetians?" Shyness, she realises, is making her ask too many questions. She stands with her back to him while she cleans the coffee pot at the large sink, conscious of the white ribbon in her black hair, her exposed neck and the places where her thin dress clings to her hips.

"I'm not one to generalise but our neighbours love to pry and eavesdrop and gossip. They flock to anyone carrying news of domestic strife. Bulletins are updated in the campo where the women stand in groups around the well tutting and shaking their heads. They themselves of course are lynchpins of virtue. But they scavenge on moral outrage. Nothing excites them more than a scandal, especially a sexual scandal."

The word sexual makes her blush. She sometimes believes that had her father allowed her to go to university she would much less be prey to disarming rushes of blood.

"It's common knowledge and a source of excitement in the *sestiere* that Giulia is going to die. It's also common knowledge that the family cat has disappeared. Our household is viewed as a sinking ship."

"I was going to ask about Giulia."

"I wish I could at least give her back her cat."

She picks up a dish rag, realises what she has done and puts it back down. She doesn't want to be identified with ugly things.

"I once did some sketches of Giulia. Do you want to see them?"

She spoons coffee into the filter of the silver pot, screws it shut and lights the stove. Then she rummages about in a canvas bag hanging from a chair. The book she takes out has scuffed red leather binding. She already regrets making this unprecedented offer. It was the moving image of him returning without the cat to his sister that made her want to give him something.

"Traitor," he says. "That sketchbook is not one of ours."

"No. I bought it in Florence. This is my private sketchbook.

I never show it to anyone. Not even my father has seen it. It's like my diary," she says. Blood rushes to her face as she owns the enormity of what she is about to do. It's like she is about to lift up her dress for his eyes. Her hands tighten around the book. All her sketches suddenly seem like little more than inept doodles. There is a falsetto note in her voice when she tells him her drawings aren't very good. "I still have so much to learn."

The coffee machine begins percolating. She is relieved to leave his side. To no longer have to look at her drawings through his eyes. While she is pouring out the coffee with her back to him she feels like she is balanced on a tightrope in her mind. She hears a page turn without comment. His silence becomes the pounding of her heart in her ears. She walks over to the table with the two small porcelain cups. She sees he is looking hard at the sketches of his sister, one in graphite, one in red ink and one in charcoal.

He thanks her for the coffee, then turns the book back to the first page. There is a pencil sketch of a cat in the act of fleeing in fear, its fur raised, its ears pinned back.

"I love this. The sense of flustered movement," he says.

His praise gives her the sensation of finally being able to swallow something caught in her throat.

"I once saw a cat fleeing from a dog and the image stayed with me. Cats are such proud regal creatures. It was awful to see one lose all its dignity. I felt like I understood the full belittling horror of what it means to be humiliated in that moment."

She watches him knock back his coffee in one go. Then he turns the pages forward to the drawings of his sister again.

"These drawings of my sister are almost too beautiful to look at," he says. "They remind me of how eager she always was for the next moment of her life."

"It must be hard for you."

"There are times we both fall silent or look off into the distance when the impending inevitability of her death is like a live wire we're both touching. Soon the entire history of her mental activity will count for nothing. Everything she's known and felt will vanish. She says she can't bear the thought that she will cease to exist. Then she says how strange it is that she is still prone to boredom. Other times, she's absolutely convinced she will get better and she begins making plans for the future. You'd like to think the death of a person is like the death of a star, that it will enrich the cosmos with precious elements, with added meaning. But it's hard to believe that."

She is flattered that he appears to enjoy talking to her. And especially that he is willing to confide in her. At a time when people are so mistrustful of each other, so wary of exchanging secret thoughts. "It's good of you to be so attentive to her," she says.

"She makes me think of my own life a lot. I realise I'm not living most of the time. I'm just killing time. I spend whole days that are not my life."

"Tuberculosis is infectious, isn't it? Aren't you worried about catching it?" She quickly berates herself for her indelicate prying curiosity and is relieved when he shows no sign of taking offence.

"Terrified. You would think the proximity of death makes life more authentic but I've found the opposite is true. It demands a lot of acting. I've steeled myself to show no thought of contracting her sickness in her company. I'm careful not to offend her. But there's also manly pride involved. Stupid really." He smiles, his long fringe hiding the highlight in his eyes. "Do you remember what you felt when your mother died?"

"She didn't die. She just walked out on us one day, when I was about three years old. My father tells everyone she died because it's less embarrassing for him that way. It's a flattering fiction. Flattering fictions play a big part in how we represent ourselves, don't they? Our maid was a surrogate mother to me. She was called Maria. She died last year. She lived here in the apartment. I don't remember my mother. Sometimes I wonder how different I might be if I had grown up under her influence. My father never talks about her. There's a painting of her he did when she was young. But it's not very expressive. And a few photographs, not many. She always looks as if she longs to be somewhere else. But perhaps it's simply that I know she will leave us and I can't help imposing her desire to be gone on her face. Do you think I should try to find her? I fantasise about doing it sometimes. My father though would be furious. He would see it as an unforgivable act of betrayal."

"Every move I make towards my mother makes my father angry," he says, smiling.

There is a squeaking of the rusted wheels of a hand-held cart beneath the kitchen window and the blurred shape of a bird momentarily flashes past the glass.

"Before you leave I'm going to sew that loose button back onto your shirt," she says, lifting both hands to the crown of her head. She watches him look down at the button in question, the third one down on his white shirt.

"Will I have to take my shirt off? I'm not wearing a vest underneath."

"I won't blush if you don't. Anyway, my father is presently painting a Christ. I see the model's naked torso every day."

"What are your father's paintings like?"

"I suppose they would be described as classical. I don't think though he uses his own eyes enough. He tries to see everything through the eyes of the Old Masters."

"He's a copyist rather than an innovator?"

She is in shock that she has openly criticised her father's painting. These are private taboo thoughts she has released for the first time into the world. For a moment she feels as if she has desecrated a holy relic. "No. That's too harsh. Technically he's incredibly gifted. And he's worked tremendously hard to reach the very high standards he's set himself. He still believes his best work is in front of him and I believe that too. He's only just discovered a new and better recipe for medium. He has tried all sorts of combinations, including honey and vinegar. Recently he got hold of some secret document of Titian's. He's very secretive about it but apparently he has discovered how Titian made up the medium he used. There's a secret ingredient. He believes the nature of the medium is the key to great oil painting. Because it determines the texture and fusion and fluidity of the paint as it's distributed over the canvas."

"There's always a secret ingredient required to lift us above the commonplace. Sometimes I think it's simply kindness."

She looks into his eyes. He smiles.

"I've wanted to be a painter ever since I can remember. A portrait painter. I love people's faces. They endlessly fascinate me. A person's face can make me feel better about everything in a moment."

"I sometimes think a person's voice tells you more about them than their face. It's like the voice contains the principle of music. The ability to summon up invisible worlds. And you can't paint a voice."

"I'd like to think if you paint a face well enough you're able to hear the sitter's voice."

"It's always bothered me that I don't like my father's voice." She can tell he immediately regrets saying this, as if he has betrayed some ugliness about himself. He lights a cigarette. "I like your voice," he says, as if the nicotine has made him bolder.

"Thank you," she says, flushing again. She slides the sugar bowl over the surface of the table. "Actually, I think atmosphere is the most real thing in life. Everyone has a distinctive atmosphere. It's often how we recognise people in dreams. That's what I hope to capture when I finally begin to paint."

The bells of Santa Maria Gloriosa dei Frari begin to chime the hour followed a moment later by those of San Rocco. She notices the sound of the bells makes him sit up straighter in his chair.

"I used to think you were very shy," she says. "But you're not really shy at all, are you?"

"I don't think so. I don't like talking unless I'm genuinely interested in what's being said. Often what people say is just them humming a song to themselves. And waiting for the other person to hum it back."

She laughs.

"I've never seen you laugh before," he says.

She covers her mouth with her hand. "I'm not very good at enjoying myself. I hide at home during *carnevale*. But I like laughing. Don't you?"

"I like making you laugh."

"If you take your shirt off I'll go and find a needle and thread."

When she returns to the kitchen he hasn't taken off his shirt. She sits down next to him and moistens the frayed tip of the cotton with her tongue and delicately threads it through the tiny needle. Out of the corner of her eye she watches him unbutton his shirt, disclosing his thin tanned hairless torso. She detects a frisson of self-consciousness in him as he performs the act with exaggerated attention. She recognises it from the models who strip off for her father. Almost everyone mistrusts the visual effect of their nakedness. As if a cherished illusion or a belittling insecurity is under a microscope. She herself, she knows, would not possess the confidence to subject her naked flesh to scrutiny. She has asked him to do something she would not be prepared to do herself.

He hands her his shirt. She arranges it in her lap and while passing the needle and thread through the white cotton is aware of him closely studying her. The visual intimacy of his shirt strewn over her lap and her hand guiding the needle in and out of the fabric has moved them closer together. Her body slews off her mind for a moment as it registers a whisper of eroticism in the air. It is a sensation which both urges her to contemplate the future and roots her intimately in the present moment as if time is both standing still and racing forward.

"I'd like to paint your face one day," she says, snapping the thread with her teeth. "At the moment my father won't allow me to paint. I'm only allowed to draw. He says my draughtsmanship still needs improving. It was the way he was taught. Years of diligent drawing before he was allowed to hold a paintbrush. He says there has to be poetry in you before you can create beauty. And poetry is only acquired with age because its medium is memory. Your shop has been the most poetic place in the world ever since I was a little girl. It's like it brings magic into the world. I especially love all the colours of the pigments. It's as if they are the beginning of all the beauty it's possible to create in the world. As close to the act of creation as you can get. Lapis lazuli is my favourite."

She hands him back his shirt.

"Thank you," he says.

She notices he has lowered his head and there is a look on his face she does not recognise. And then he suddenly lurches forward and presses his mouth to her mouth. In the ensuing struggle she falls backwards off her chair. The fall knocks the wind out of her. And she is in a state of shock. Sprawled out on the kitchen floor. Her dress has ridden up her parted thighs. She notices and pulls it down.

"I'm sorry," he says, still naked to the waist.

She glares up at him, bewildered by the unguessed at violence of his behaviour, and then watches him walk out of the kitchen holding his shirt and hears the sound of the front door closing behind him. The angry noise is like an event taking place inside her body.

4

"Why have they made us enemies of Italy? I love this country. It's our blood."

There are tears in Father's eyes and his hands are trembling. Marcello has never seen his father cry. A frontier has been breached. The sight of this unguessed at vulnerability in his father makes Marcello feel unsteady on his feet, more so than the cause of his father's tears. Marcello picks up the newspaper with its sinister headline. *Le leggi per la difesa della razza.* (On an inside page is a photograph of five nuns giving the fascist salute.) He notices now what he missed the first time he read the article. Among the privileges now forbidden to Jews, besides joining the armed forces, being listed in the telephone directory, frequenting public libraries and employing Catholics, is marriage to non-Jewish citizens. It occurs to him that Elisabetta is now forbidden to him. He fingers the button she secured on his shirt. The shame of what he did returns to him. His perception of Elisabetta as an individual has narrowed down to little more than a source of humiliation. And because she makes him dislike himself he finds himself disliking her. Why did she make him take off his shirt if she didn't want him to kiss her? There are moments when he tells himself he doesn't even find her overly attractive. There are other moments when he admits to being too young to understand females and their amorous stagecraft. Whenever troubled he enters into lively conversation with a second Marcello to whom he attributes a deeper understanding of life's mysteries. But not even the second, wiser Marcello can solve the enigma of Elisabetta's conduct.

He and his father are in the cluttered stockroom at the back of the shop. Marcello has finished packing an order for a local private school. He lifts up the box, to test its weight. There are only two regular tasks in his life which test the muscles in his arms – lifting boxes of merchandise and punting the family boat. He is not physically strong. Bronchitis several times left him bedridden as a child. His recollection of his mother rubbing the pungent *Limas* ointment onto his chest is among his most tender memories. He sees her walking towards him in smoking shafts of sunlight stealing through the shuttered windows of his bedroom. And every time he was ill his mother bought him a book. He still has those stories inside him, tales of exotic lands and acts of courage. It was he, not Giulia, who most often required a visit from the doctor as a child. There is sometimes now a troubling fume of guilt at the back of his thoughts when he stands by Giulia's sick bed as if he has managed somehow to exchange fates with her.

"They're going to steal our shop from us. That's what all this is leading to. Brazen theft."

Marcello looks into his father's deep set dark eyes and as he does so realises how rarely he looks closely at his father. There are more lines of worry, more signs of collapse on his face than he realised. "As far as I can gather we will be allowed to keep the shop. It's only big Jewish businesses they are confiscating."

"And what gives them the right to do that? No doubt people have worked hard to build up those businesses. What kind of world are we living in?"

"If the worst comes to the worst you'll have to sign over the deeds to someone you can trust who will agree to only play a nominal role in the ownership. A Catholic, I mean. You'll have to examine very closely to what extent you trust your various Catholic friends. You'll be trusting them with our livelihood."

"Put like that, I'm not sure I'd be capable of trusting any of them."

"Flora will be the one most affected. She will have to leave school."

"A fifteen-year-old girl. What threat does she represent to national security?"

"I have to make this delivery. Will you be all right on your own for a while?"

"Of course I'll be all right." He immediately holds himself more erect. "I'm still your father. You go and do some work."

Marcello carries the box on his shoulder. He stands to one side in the narrow street as a man carrying a ladder approaches. He greets one or two of the locals. There is Signora Conti sitting on the balcony of her first-floor apartment crocheting. There is the aproned Signor Ceccharelli varnishing a piece of wood outside his workshop. He can't decide if they look at him differently today. Do they even know he is a Jew? He feels better when he climbs over the railing and drops down into the battered old black *sandolo*. It rocks under his shifting weight as he positions himself upright on the stern and pushes off. For a while he restricts himself to enjoying the physical sensations in every stroke of the oar. It feels good to be navigating a vessel he has full control of. A defiant and liberating riposte to these new racial laws. At least now he is inside the current of a world which makes sense. The water is shivering with light. His exertions feed a feeling of health into his body. The direction of the breeze apparent in the open spaces. He ducks down under a low bridge. In the streets and alleys there are places of poverty and degradation where Venice loses its beauty; this is never true on its waterways. He remembers the days Massimo's father taught him and Massimo how to row and how to use the oar as a rudder. A time when he had no knowledge of belonging to a different race from his friend and all his school classmates. On the water there is no sign the world has changed. Here a gondola, here a barge, here a waterbus easing through the misted glitter of the October sunshine. He moors his boat at the landing stage near Campo San Provolo.

He goes home for lunch. His father is pacing about the drawing room. His thick greying hair is distressed. He is holding a photograph and talking heatedly to Mother who is out on the wrought-iron balcony pegging up washing. Sunlight streams into the room through the open door.

"What's wrong?"

He hands Marcello the photograph. It's the photograph of his father wearing the fascist uniform he bought for himself after joining the party in 1934. The fez, the belted jacket, the jodhpurs and the pristine shine of the high boots. His hands in the picture are proudly planted on his hips, his chin raised. The theatrical uniform brought out a new vanity in his father. Marcello and Giulia made a private joke of it. Every Saturday afternoon he made the whole family, except Mother, dress up in their fascist uniforms. Giulia was the first to rebel. Marcello initially liked the uniform when he was a *moschettiere del Duce*, the black shirt, the grey-green shorts and fez in which he had to present arms with a small wooden rifle and swear an oath to carry out the Duce's orders. But soon he got bored of the parades and hymn singing ceremonies all schoolchildren were forced to participate in every Saturday.

"I've always cherished this photograph. What a blundering fool I've been. You and Giulia were right to mock the pleasure I got from wearing that absurd uniform."

He leaves the room and soon returns holding the black felt fez. He places it on the large red rug and, standing beneath the Murano glass chandelier, stamps on it. Marcello and his mother exchange a conspiratorial smile.

"Get me my copy of *The Merchant of Venice*. No, I'll get it." He returns with the book. Puts on his spectacles. He somehow manages to find the page he wants almost immediately, as if by force of will, and begins to read aloud. "*He hath disgraced me and hindered me, mocked at my gains, scorned my nation, thwarted my bargains, cooled my friends, heated mine enemies – and what's his reason? I am a Jew. Hath not a Jew eyes? Hath not a Jew hands, organs, dimensions, senses, affections, passions. Fed with the same food, hurt with the same weapons, subject to the same diseases, healed by the same means, warmed and cooled by the same winter and summer as a Christian is? If you prick us, do we not bleed? If you tickle us, do we not laugh? If you poison us, do we not die? And if you wrong us, shall we not revenge?* This scene, let us not forget, took place a stone's throw from where we're standing. At this moment I hate all Christians and their damn arrogance. Ten years ago, when the *squadistri* were beating up anyone they didn't like the look of, my friend Aldo said we were witnessing first-hand the moral collapse of a nation and he was right. I chose to bury my head in the sand. And now I feel ashamed."

"And we've reached the point where you could be arrested for quoting Shakespeare," says Marcello.

His father sits down at his desk in the corner of the room and picks up his mother-of-pearl paper knife. It's a regret of his that the apartment isn't large enough to provide him with a private study. The desk has a locked drawer where he keeps his black ledger and every evening adds new figures to the columns of numbers. There is an Italian flag, neatly folded, in another drawer. It is always taken out and displayed on the balcony on national holidays.

Giulia is asleep when he goes into her bedroom with a bowl of hot chocolate and a brioche for her. She woke everyone in the middle of the night with her coughing, as happens almost every night now. The shutters are fastened and the thin slats of sectioned light give the room a ghostly drifting atmosphere. He himself is momentarily a shadowy presence in the three-sided mirror at her dressing table. He opens the window and flings open the shutters. Two pigeons on the tiles of a nearby rooftop take to the air in a clapping flurry of wings. The light of the day enters the room.

Giulia wakes up in stages, straightening her legs beneath the blankets and stretching like a cat. He sees in her eyes the brutal recollection of her illness take place in her mind before her body registers it. Every time she wakes up, he realises, she has to accept her death sentence anew.

She shakes one foot free of the coverlet and looks down at it as if it is a new source of wonder. "In the dream you've just woken me from I was dancing barefoot."

"Sorry."

"Do you remember the sensation of walking barefoot on newly cut grass when tiny blades stick to your feet? How much of my life I've wasted wearing shoes and stockings. I hate shoes and socks and stockings. Why do we wear them? Let's throw all my shoes and stockings away. There's nothing like the sensation of grass or sand or even gritty stone underfoot to remind you how precious and exhilarating life is."

There's often now a kind of falsity in the excited tone of his sister's voice which troubles him. It's as if her mind is rarely on the things she says. He knows it is understandable that there is an urgent resistance in her to relinquishing the body to the spirit. But this knowledge doesn't help him deal with the overriding sensation that more often than not she is deluding herself and expects him to enter fully into the deception.

"All hell has broken out today," he says.

"What's happened?"

He tells her about the new laws.

"Nationalism is the poison everyone has been goaded into getting drunk on in Mussolini's Italy and they don't want to believe Jews are capable of nationalism. We are the homeless ones."

"Certainly feels like that today," he says.

"So it's official I will never get my degree. How is Papa?"

"He's finally realised he doesn't think for himself enough. Which is why I'm so rarely able to have a truthful or meaningful conversation with him."

"You have to tease out his more private side. You're not very good at that. Otherwise you just get the daily news, the weather report, the financial page, a little sport and then, at the dinner table, the editorial."

Before long Flora returns from school. The entire family gathers in Giulia's room.

"In class our teacher gave this long speech about the glorious destiny of Il Duce's Italy but how there are enemies within the ranks of the Italian population and how these enemies have to be weeded out. I don't think she believed a single word of what she was saying. She looked like someone who had been hit over the head. Then she picked up the register and read out my name and told me to leave the classroom. The school janitor was waiting at the door to escort me outside. My classmates didn't even know I'm Jewish."

"How can they not know?" asks Mother. "Don't they see you don't cross yourself or recite the Lord's Prayer every day?"

"I do cross myself and recite the Lord's Prayer. I've done it for years. What's the big deal? I'm not disrespecting my own religion. I don't want to be the odd one out. That's when girls gang up against you and become cruel. In the playground there were four other younger girls. One of them was sobbing. Signora Giannini who teaches Italian came out to talk to us. She was kind. She said this madness won't last long."

"We shouldn't have become so lapse in our worship," says Father. "It's my fault. I can't even remember the last time I recited the Shema."

It has been years since any of the family set foot inside a synagogue. And they practice few of Judaism's prescriptions for daily life.

"It's not your fault," says Giulia. "Why should any of us do what we don't feel?"

"A lot of it was vanity on my part. I didn't want to stand out. I was like Flora. I wanted to belong. I've always been too anxious that people like and respect me. I'm ashamed now I ever wore that damn fascist uniform."

"Have you ever felt yourself different from your friends because you're Jewish?" Flora asks Father.

"I felt different that I was the last boy in my class to grow body hair," says Father. "I felt different when I couldn't work out a maths equation that everyone else seemed to solve with ease. And I felt different from everyone when I had a toothache. Never because I'm Jewish."

"You never told me you were the last boy in your class to grow body hair," says Mother with a smile.

5

The thick primal stink of rabbit-skin glue is almost a torture to inhale. The half dozen canvases she has primed for her father are propped against the walls of the studio. Elisabetta is standing at her easel with a piece of charcoal in her hand. Her father stands by her side. He is wearing a navy-blue smock smeared with crusted pigment. His critical eye is like a magnifying glass through which she sees all the humbling shortcomings in her drawing. She looks at her hand and has rarely felt less affection for it. As if it is an ugly unwieldly tool. She is in the throes of drawing a life-size plaster cast of a Roman head of Hermes. The three high arched windows of the top floor room, almost at a level with the circling seagulls, are partially draped by black cloth adjustable by a pulley system her father has constructed. Charcoal dust hangs in the diffuse north light. An old sofa with the stuffing showing through splits in the cushions sits in a corner. Dozens of her father's paintings, mostly framed, hang on all four walls of the studio and more canvases are stacked on the floor. There are some cityscapes of Venice, a few still lifes, several sketches of Christ but mostly they are life-sized depictions of saints.

"What have I always said? No strategy survives the first contact. But this doesn't mean you abandon your strategy. Strategy is paramount. Attention to detail isn't sufficient in itself." There is always argument in his voice as if forestalling contradiction. "You must hold fast to your strategy. Never lose sight of the big picture. Now would you say Hermes is a handsome chap?" He grins at her.

"I suppose he's handsome in an effete kind of way."

"Exactly. It's not difficult to picture him with limp wrists. Rather like Donatello's David in Florence. So how best to characterise this effeteness, as you put it?"

"The mouth."

"Exactly. It's the mouth, rather than the eyes, which betray a person's secrets."

Elisabetta feels an inrush of vulnerability, as if her mouth has long been revealing her secrets without her knowledge.

"I've always said you have an admirable sensitivity in your handling but you don't give sufficient thought to the overall design. Perhaps that's simply the nature of woman. An excess of sensibility, a dearth of intellect. I've always questioned the rigour of your thought processes. They don't possess enough muscularity. Sometimes the flaws in your drawing are intellectual in nature. The processing of the information of the eye into idea. But perhaps I'm asking the impossible of a female. Perhaps it just isn't your nature to process thought intellectually? Women are much more guided by emotion than men. How different, mentally, do you think men and women are? To me sometimes it seems like the difference between the land and the sea."

"I feel I have both the land and the sea within me," she says. Her attitude towards her father is honed to what he expects and demands. An unquestioning reverence and obedience. He brooks no contradiction. She is frightened of his anger and reluctant to ever disappoint him. It still shocks her that she found the audacity to find fault in her father's talent while speaking with Marcello. As if Marcello acted on her as a truth serum. She knows her father would disapprove of Marcello were she to develop feelings for him. The son of a shopkeeper and Jewish to boot. He wants no trouble from the authorities. He only wants to be left in peace to paint. Essentially, her father is a tyrant. But, on the whole, a good-natured tyrant. She has enormous respect for his knowledge – not just with regards to the art of painting and drawing. He is also learned about the

Bible and Greek mythology, poetry, architecture and astronomy. And he is generous with his knowledge despite all his baseless irritating convictions about the inadequacies of her sex. He is generous with his knowledge but he isn't interested in listening to the thoughts of anyone else. As if he has nothing new to learn. He refuses most of her timid requests for any new item of clothing as unnecessary and criticises her for indulging in frivolous desires. And he has prevented her from studying history of art at the university. Said taking a degree would impede her household and studio duties and he couldn't afford to hire a servant or an assistant. She understands how the exacting control he exerts over every facet of his life might have driven her mother away. There is a painted portrait of her turned to the wall by the disused fireplace. She sometimes looks at it when her father is absent. It is dirty and unfinished. She has an eerie forsaken air in the painting and stares out across a void of loneliness. There is more cadmium yellow in the skin tones than he usually mixes.

After dinner every night her father goes to a local bar where he plays cards and gets tipsy. Alcohol works quickly on him - it drains blood from his already pale face, glazes over his blue eyes and leaves a blueberry stain on his lips. Drunk, he is more excitable, more easily roused to anger. She retreats to her bedroom before he returns home. She doesn't like to admit she is constrained to hide in her own home. This sense of captivity, of circling back and forth behind bars, brings her closer to a wildness within which frightens her. Sometimes she overhears him talking to himself through the wall. Then it is like living in close proximity to a frightening stranger. She has the impression he is often defending himself from imagined criticism.

He returns to the table in the corner of the studio and begins grinding lead white pigment with a pestle. After a while he looks at his watch then shakes his arm. It's what he does to start up his wristwatch again. "Time for coffee," he says.

In their local bar there is a photograph of Mussolini with Hitler on the wall above the espresso machine. The new racial laws have disgusted Elisabetta. She decides the time has come to take a stand.

"Can we go to another bar?"

"Why?"

"They've got a photograph of Hitler in Mario's."

"I don't like Hitler either but it'll attract attention if we stop going to Mario's," says her father. "And Roberta will be upset. You know how fond she is of you. It wasn't her that put the picture up."

Inside the bar, Elisabetta stands with her back to the photograph. Her father concentrates his disgust on the framed map of Venice made with seashells further along the wall. "I wish they'd take that awful thing down. It's offensive to the eye. Can't they see that?"

For a moment she thinks he might wink at her as if he is cryptically referring to the photograph of Hitler and Mussolini. But she can tell by the look of suffering on his face that he is serious. Bad art will always be more offensive to him than social injustice.

"Luigi Volpato was asking about you again. I think it's the third time he's remarked to me how pretty you've become."

"There's something distasteful about him," she says.

"You're not wrong there," he says, lowering his voice. "There is something distasteful about him."

"And he has the face of a carnivorous farm animal."

Her father guffaws. He loves to hear other men criticised. It's like caffeine to him. In every male face he is prone to see a Judas. She loves to make him laugh. It's like receiving a thoughtful gift from him. "Nevertheless, I've invited him to dinner Saturday night. No harm in that. He's the kind of man we need to stay on the right side of. Especially after the arrest of Pino. I never agreed with Pino's ideas but people won't know that. They believed we were much closer than was the case in reality."

Pino, who was her father's only friend, has been exiled to a village in the Abruzzi for what seemed to her an innocuous anti-fascist remark he made in this same bar.

"You could make your crab gnocci or else your carbonara or how about spaghetti with clams? It's been a while."

Signor Volpato, twice her age, has an important job, veiled in secrecy, in the Venice office of OVRA, the fascist secret police. Her father, she knows, is frightened of him, of his power to make things awkward for any individual who displeases him. It worries her that Luigi Volpato is not married.

She tries not to think about Marcello because she is always left feeling she is to blame in some way. She remembers he apologised. But he didn't seem to be sorry. He seemed aggrieved, as if he felt she had tricked him. She is unused to excesses of feeling. She has been left with a roaming unquiet in her body. Probably she shouldn't have sewn that button back onto his shirt. Until then there had not been a single false note in their time together. He had seemed to enjoy talking to her. She wondered if he simply enjoyed talking to everyone and there was little credit she could take personally for the ease and vitality of their discourse. She would like him as a friend. She feels like an oddity that she has no friends. Her father has created a kind of lagoon island on which she often feels stranded.

6

Marcello sits at a table in a bar, his tie pulled loose, lost in his own thoughts. He wonders if there is something unknown to him in his nature that seeks to push people away when they get too close. Because it now seems he wilfully created an impasse with Elisabetta, just as he had done with Massimo. It's a revelation for him to realise how impatient he is to make Elisabetta smile again. He envies whoever is enjoying her company at this moment. He had believed her too intelligent and perceptive not to be aware of what he wanted from her. When she laid his shirt in her lap it was like she was whispering in his ear. He keeps remembering the horrified way she looked at him after he tried to kiss her. He suspects now she is more unconscious of her motives than he thought. Often, he recalls, she wears a puzzled expression on her face as if she has heard her name unexpectedly called out in a crowd. He is still too young to have any well-informed idea of what it is a woman seeks in a man or how to decode her gestures. It's like men and women sing different words to the same song. He suspects he thinks about her in a way she never thinks about him. It pains him that it is so. And now the racial laws, the incitement to shun Jews, will make it still more difficult for him to redeem himself in her eyes.

He doesn't register the beginning of the daily government communique on the radio and so doesn't stand up, as required by law. There are two blackshirts in the bar. He has studiously ignored them. He avoids the eyes of all men in uniform. Their scrutiny can feel like the first scornful shove in a physical assault.

He feels more ill-suited to the times in which he lives than he did a week ago. On his way here he saw a black pigeon floating amongst a shoal of red vine leaves by the marble steps under a bridge. The bird's matted plumage was half submerged in the grey-green water; only its head, bobbing about gently on its limp twisted neck, and its glazed empty eyes disclosed the presence of death. Not indifferent to signs, Marcello wondered what oracle might be speaking through the dead bird.

He comes out of his trance and gets to his feet before the broadcast ends. One of the two blackshirts though is scowling at him.

"You didn't stand to attention, you're not wearing a uniform or a party badge and your hair is too long. And what's the meaning of this?" he says, grabbing at Marcello's loose braces.

For a hot-blooded moment Marcello wishes this confrontation could be resolved by a fair fight. He can't remember ever wanting to hit someone so much. He makes fists of his hands and adrenalin swarms into the muscles in his arms. This rush of rage is immediately followed by an inclination to meekly apologise. How would it ever be possible for anyone to understand him when he is so confusing to himself? He puts his hand to the back of his neck to press at the stiffness there.

"Show me your papers."

"Let's do this outside," says the other fascist whose eyes are kinder.

Outside, by the side of a canal, Marcello hands over his papers.

"He's a Jew." The fascist, a bristling force of self-righteousness, tosses his identity card to the ground with a theatrical show of disgust. As Marcello leans down to pick it up he sees his persecutor is in the throes of kicking him. He shoves at the man's standing leg in an unthinking act of self-preservation and the man falls backwards into the canal. Marcello watches him claw at the surface of the water with a look of terror on his face. It's like he is engaged in a panicked physical fight with the water.

As if the water is an adversary he might overcome with brawn. It becomes clear he doesn't know how to swim. His companion jumps into the canal. Marcello makes the decision quickly. He runs. He turns a corner into a narrow alley. A door is open. He enters a hallway and closes the door behind him. He opens another door and finds himself in a small garden overgrown with creepers. He scales a wall. It feels good to vigorously inhabit his body, push all his weight up into his arms and then drop down the other side with a jarring shock to his ankles. He scales three adjoining walls in this way until he finds himself in an alley he does not recognise. He has lost his bearings, something which often happened during his adolescent years in Venice. He goes back to those years for a moment, when he was carefree and Giulia was healthy and it was largely an irrelevance that he was a Jew.

Giulia is sitting up in bed. A red cardigan over her nightdress. A fierce smothering heat rises from her bed. Every movement she makes highlights her bodily weakness. He tells her what happened to him.

"What fascism does is give unearned authority to ignorant thugs. The kind of people who get more pleasure from burning books than reading them."

"I warned you," she says. "Like Father you preferred to bury your head in the sand. You were both guilty of passive complicity. You and Father think you're good people but are you really? Can someone be called good who never fights any battles in the cause of what they believe? What we shut our eyes to can end up defining us."

Like a cat, she is always poised to scratch. It's a way she has of keeping the world at a distance. He sometimes detects a coveted meanness in her. She is overeager to find fault in others. As if she herself is a shining touchstone of integrity and generosity. He feels she bears him a grievance, as if he, in an outrageous miscarriage of justice, is the privileged sibling. He hates harbouring feelings towards his sick sister that aren't generously clean.

But it's like she wants his share of health as, in other families, one party disputes a will. Often now she serves as a reproach to him. He knows she might die and yet he still finds himself guilty of not being able to love her uncritically. He wonders if he is incapable of love. And if she isn't the same. If they are both incapable of any emotion which isn't ultimately self-serving. If perhaps his entire family isn't the same. There is little evidence in the home of the reality of love. They are a functioning pragmatic unit, deploying pretence like actors in front of a painted backcloth to preserve a mythology of shared love and devotion. It's impossible not to suspect the constant presence of unkind thoughts in the family apartment. The silent messages passing back and forth are fraught with criticism rather than alight with thanksgiving. It is rare for any family member to make another feel good about themselves. He himself is as guilty as anyone. Before her illness it was clear Giulia believed she had outgrown the family. They were impediments to her. She couldn't wait to launch out into the world alone. Her illness has restored her to a servitude she loathes.

He lets the comment about him not being a good person pass, though it will trouble him later. Instead he mentions the sketches Elisabetta made of her.

"Elisabetta?"

"The daughter of the painter Piero Del Monaco."

"Oh her. She means well but to be honest, she got on my nerves. That breathless way she has of talking as if she's run up a flight of stairs to meet you. It seems false to me. She's always struck me as being locked up within herself. Her shyness is fierce, like that of a wild animal."

One symptom of Giulia's illness is to sometimes make her scathingly critical of people she has always professed to like. As if they are undeserving of their good health. He is taken aback not so much by this overspill of bitterness in her but by the nervous excitement Elisabetta's name on his sister's lips brings with it.

"That's true. Her shyness is fierce." His face heats up. He has never confided anything to his sister with regards to girls.

"I've been thinking, revelation often occurs in our body before it reaches our mind. My body has spoken; now I have to use my mind more to combat this sickness. I have to stop behaving as if I'm very sick. I'm submitting to this illness too passively. I think I have to conquer it with my mind. I have to deploy the power of the mind more." Even as she talks of being well she is having to take deep laboured breaths. Marcello chooses not to look at the pulse jumping in her neck. He picks up the copy of *The Brothers Karamazov* from the bedside table. He is never quite sure if she will make it to the end of the stories she reads.

"I was thinking today how much I'd love to go to the cinema. I had such a vivid glimpse of the red curtains opening on the screen and then all the cigarette smoke billowing in the blue beam of the film projector. I wouldn't even mind all the fascists singing their ugly hymns. Lying in bed all the time my mind has become like a film projector. Unexpected images often return vividly to me. Today I remembered two dogs chasing each other with exuberance around an old man who was repairing a fishing net. I could see his hands vividly. And then I remembered what a joy it is to watch animals at play. It makes you realise how very rarely us human beings are able to slake off our inhibitions. Then I remembered the stockings over the fireplace at Befana. How much wonder those wrapped presents excited. Always far more magical wrapped up and waiting to be opened than the reality of what was inside."

"The neighbours haven't let these racial laws affect them. The Rossinis invited me in for a coffee today and the Magnanis have been friendly too."

"Small mercies," she says. He knows throughout her life she has always scorned trivial consolations; every consolation must now strike her as pathetically trivial.

He hadn't dared returning to his boat earlier. After dark, he walks back towards the canal where it is moored. His heart is beating too fast. His footsteps echo ahead of him. The memory of the face of the fascist he pushed into the water prevents him from seeing anything else with clarity. He expects the face to reappear on the other side of every bridge he crosses. Then he has the troubling premonition that, like the family cat Luna, his boat will have disappeared. As if a pattern of impediment has been established and from now on his life will consist of one setback after another. The sweep of thanksgiving when he sees his *sandolo* is still where he moored it takes him by surprise. Were there a beggar in the vicinity he would empty his pockets into the poor soul's palm as a thank you to life.

He feels much better about everything when he is back in his boat. The stars are reflected on the black water and he has the sensation of moving through interstellar space. It is a liberating feeling he wants to share with someone. He knows it's an impossible paradox to want to share the thrill of being alone but realises the desire itself is part of the pleasure.

The dread of bumping into the two fascists again makes his life wretched in the following days. He wears a hat low over his eyes. He rarely takes off his sunglasses. On the good side he didn't recognise either of them as being local to his *sestiere*. But he finds there is barely a moment he can relax into, can take for granted. Every opening of the shop door when his back is turned tightens all his muscles. The apartment doorbell has never sounded so shrill. Every sound is enlarged. He tells his mother about his anguish. A rare occurrence of him confiding in her. Any display of secluded intimacy with his mother seems to threaten the rest of the family. His father especially is hostile to the demonstration of any private relationship existing between his son and wife. His mother is aware of this and keeps these tête-à-têtes to a minimum. Whenever Marcello emerges from a private conversation with his mother his father is bristling and scowling. Both Giulia and Flora resent any further evidence that he is their mother's favourite, as they both believe. It's as if nobody in the family feels sufficiently loved, including himself. As if there isn't enough love to go around.

Today, she makes light of his apprehension, telling him he will now have to grow a beard and dye his hair blonde. However she appears distracted. He can't find her in her eyes. As if she is preoccupied with private perils of her own. One day recently he surprised her by being at home when she returned to the apartment and there was a look of guilt on her face that she quickly hid. Nothing was said because the parish priest then arrived, a gentle, always smiling man who had come to benedict their home, a ritual he performs every year, despite them being Jewish. "We're all of one family."

7

There is the sound of sizzling oil and a strong odour of garlic and basil in the kitchen. A smell to which Elisabetta feels she intimately belongs. She hasn't used her favourite and trusted pan from the line of copper pots and pans hanging from hooks over the sink. Instead she has fried the garlic in a pan she can't ever remember using before. It has an unpleasant smell. She has deliberately set about spoiling the meal she is about to serve up for her father and Luigi Volpato. Her courage fell short of committing any dramatic act of sabotage. She has restricted herself to not salting the water in which the spaghetti is cooking. She has already practiced the pantomime performance of the scatterbrained young girl she will offer up at the table when the omission is noted. She knows she will have to embarrass her father to repel Luigi Volpato. But she is angry with her father for inviting this man to dinner. And it is clear to her that she has to rebuff any attraction the middle-aged Luigi Volpato feels for her. She can't help thinking of Luigi Volpato as everything about her native country she has come to loathe, as if he personally drew up and implemented every fascist law. When he arrived tonight he complained that the constant requirement to climb up and down the steps of bridges to get anywhere in Venice was ruining his posture. It was meant as a humorous remark but she detected truth in it too and understood he is much more vain of his appearance than she would have thought.

While the pasta is cooking she goes out into the hallway with the lipstick belonging to her mother which her father, mysteriously, has never thrown away. It's the only thing in the apartment, so far as she knows, that belonged to her mother. She herself has never before worn lipstick. Her skin prickles at the thought that she is about to touch her lips with a substance last touched by her mother's lips. A troubling continuity is created. But without any eligible detail. In the glass she is as if shrouded in all the mystery of her mother. For a moment she has no idea what to expect of herself. She might be a frightening stranger, capable of unforeseeable acts. To know so little about her mother makes her feel an important part of her is developing in darkness.

Her intention is to use the lipstick to make herself look as unattractive as possible. She will apply it in excessive measure. She will appear with a bloody mouth. She knows a superstitious misgiving about using something belonging to her mother to make herself ugly. A single anxious thought sometimes has the power to flood her entire being with darkness. It worries her how easily she can succumb to depression. As she is standing in front of the mirror, poised to paint her mouth, she notices in the glass the edge of a scrolled document poking out of the inside pocket of Luigi Volpato's coat. Her heart is thumping when she extracts it. She doesn't know why she's doing this. The document is a typed report from someone known only as agent 362. The typewriter has punched holes in the paper for the *O*'s. The presence of Marcello's family's name on the piece of coffee-stained paper makes her skin shiver. "*The name of the woman who regularly visits Paolo Levi is Melissa Zecchi. She too is Jewish. Married to the man who owns the Zecchi art shop in Calle Saoneri. She might be some kind of courier or else they're having an affair. I knew her daughter at university. Giulia. She was never circumspect about criticising Mussolini's government.*"

Elisabetta's hands are shaking when she replaces the document. A gale of urgency sweeps through her. She is buoyed up with a sense of her sudden importance, luminously aglow with the knowledge she now has. Her impulse which she has to quash is to run to Marcello immediately and tell him what she has just read about his mother and sister.

She applies the lipstick with childish imprecision. Her face now grotesque to her in the glass. Then she loses her nerve and dabs away the excess paint with a wet fingertip. To harbour resentment, she realises, is to allow immature and unworthy instincts to take precedence. When she appears in the dining room with the steaming pan and her painted lips she has to steel herself against the quickly erased flash of horror on her father's face.

Luigi Volpato is a good four inches shorter than her tall sinewy father. He is dressed in civilian clothes, a smart black suit and tie. He wears the fascist badge on the lapel of his jacket. (So does her father, a rare occurrence.) His black leather shoes are polished to a dazzling burnish. His complexion is waxen. His dark hair is cut close to his skull and glistens with oil. His tie is black with red stripes, like the Nazi flag.

"I've just been teasing your father. I couldn't help noticing a hat had been placed over the telephone." He speaks louder than necessary. His voice rings with entitlement. He wears small round wire-framed spectacles. Even through glass she finds it hard to meet his dark eyes. There are shards of ice in them.

She knows her father will be furious with himself and then with her for not removing the hat. He is mistrustful of most inventions made after the time of Titian and Tintoretto. She has several times, in a respectful diplomatic manner, told him it is a pointless caution, but he is unwilling as a rule to concede a superior wisdom to her.

"I explained to him that no one can listen in on conversations unless the receiver is active which isn't the case if it's on its cradle. But of course it made me ask myself what kind of conversations you and your father have that you don't want anyone to eavesdrop on them."

"I never talk about politics with my daughter. In fact, I very rarely talk politics with anyone. There are many days when I don't even glance at a newspaper."

"I'm not sure that's something you should be boasting about. It's our duty to keep abreast of current events. Thank you," he says, turning to Elisabetta who is serving up the pasta.

No one mentions the absence of salt in the pasta. She has never in her life cooked such a bland meal.

"I can sense you're a rather strict father," says Volpato, twisting strands of spaghetti around his fork. "My father was very strict with me. There was a time I resented his iron-fisted rule but I've come to appreciate the values he drilled into me. He has given me a healthy respect for authority and discipline. What are your views on authority and discipline, Elisabetta? For example, what do you think about state institutions and the role of governing authorities in our lives?"

"I suppose they are a necessary evil," she says. "I don't though believe a government should tell us what art to like, what books to read, how many children to have and what to think."

"You think this government is too intrusive?"

She registers the amusement in his eyes as a further irritant. Her father discreetly pours himself another glass of wine. She can sense him willing her to submit, to play the obedient daughter. He likes most of all to see in her the shy self-effacing child she once was.

"I would have thought that's obvious. And I don't think people should be persecuted because of their religious beliefs, especially if in every other way they are loyal and cherished members of the community," she says, screwing up her serviette.

"You mean the Jews? You have Jewish friends?"

"That isn't the point. It's disgraceful you've singled them out and made them appear different to the rest of us."

"You make it sound like it was me personally. I'm merely a policeman. I uphold the law; I don't make it." Luigi Volpato smiles across at her. Then he caresses his moustache. He often tenderly strokes his moustache of which he is evidently very proud. His moustache, she has understood, is the outward show of his self-satisfaction.

"The shop where I buy all my painting materials is owned by a Jewish family," says her father, in a conciliating tone.

Volpato's face reveals no hint he knows of the people her father has mentioned. She understands in this moment how skilled he is at hiding the truth. That his job makes him an accomplished liar, a deceitful individual, miserly with confidentiality.

"Nobody wants to persecute the Jews," he says. "The law-abiding Jews I mean. These new measures are probably just a way of appeasing Hitler. I'm afraid we've reached a point in international diplomatic relations where alliances have to be cemented."

"I see eye to eye with Hitler with regards to his taste in art," says Father, evidently pleased to find a truthful way of aligning himself with Luigi Volpato. Her father's hand gestures are broad and heedless; Volpato's by comparison are miserly and fussy. "I too loathe all forms of modern art and see them as degenerate."

"I know little about art. For example, who is the better artist, Titian or Tintoretto?"

"Titian is unquestionable the more accomplished, the more aesthetically pleasing in terms of his handling of paint but Tintoretto was more innovative in terms of his perspectives. He makes the viewer enter his paintings from a unique and challenging point of view."

"Interesting. What about you, Elisabetta, do you have any hobbies?"

"Art isn't a hobby," she says, defending her father against what she feels was a deliberate slight. "Playing cards is a hobby. Collecting stamps is a hobby."

"No, of course not. That's not what I meant. Art is a noble endeavour. But in these times perhaps sensibility is becoming a superfluous luxury. After all, our racial destiny is presently at a vital junction. The sky could turn black with enemy planes from one day to the next. We all have to be prepared to make sacrifices for the greater good of the fatherland and for future benefits."

For a moment she succumbs to an urgent desire to show him how much he bores her. She squeezes together her hands in her lap. She wonders if some people become nothing but caricature. If there exist people who have nothing that is uniquely theirs and lively to share.

"Like women donating their wedding rings to help finance the spraying of poison gas over Abyssinia?" To say anything aloud Elisabetta often has to force her way through a reef of shyness. And when she talks about politics what she says sounds in her mind like the words of a child – but this doesn't mean she doesn't believe they aren't true.

"Your kind of people also contributed to the war effort. Artists, I mean. Pirandello famously donated his Nobel prize medal to be melted down. But I had no idea you gave so much thought to politics."

"I do when politics moves into the realm of ethics."

His top lip beneath the moustache is glistening with oil. "Politics," he says, "always possess ethical tentacles though, do they not?"

"Often they are simply a vehicle by means of which ambitious men gain power."

"Like me, you mean?" He smiles broadly. Picks up his serviette and presses it to his mouth as if to wipe away the smile.

"Only you would know that."

"I had no idea your daughter was so opinionated and feisty," he says, swilling about the little red wine left in his glass. "In my experience most people are generally inattentive and often indifferent to everything outside of their own small concerns."

"I think she's just showing off a bit. She wants to impress you. I have to admit I'm perfectly happy as long as I can go to my studio every day and paint," says her father. He helps himself to another glass of wine.

She doesn't like the liberties Volpato's cold assessing gaze takes with her. As the evening progresses, he looks down the front of her dress more and more brazenly. His eyes are like a finger pressing against her chest.

When Volpato leaves, her father unknots his tie and throws it to the floor. There are purple stains on his lips.

"What got into you? You do know he could have you arrested for some of the things you said tonight?"

"I didn't like him. He brought out the worst in me. I couldn't help myself."

"Well, that's something you need to learn. Because by not helping yourself you don't help me either. And what's with the lipstick? Is that your mother's lipstick?"

Though self-conscious about his growing paunch, the legacy of all the red wine he drinks, her father is a handsome man. His face is long and lean with an elegantly chiselled bone structure. His silvered hair is thick and he has long tapering slender fingers. It pains her when he makes himself ugly like this.

She nods. She knows he wants to tell her she looks like a tart. But that would be a statement too loaded with unruly emotion. Her father's habitual outward show of dignity and poise is too cherished and hard-won an achievement for him to sacrifice it to the whims of a moment. Habit is stronger in him than any passion. Even his anger is controlled by internal gears. But beneath the dignified carriage she knows his inner life is subject to a highly pressurised volatility.

"You made a special effort to attract Volpato?"

How good he is at misunderstanding her! She imagines laughing about this exchange with a close friend. *He thought I wore lipstick to attract Luigi Volpato!* But she doesn't have any close friends. And there is no precedent in her relationship with her father for confidences of an emotional nature.

"No," she says. "The last thing I want to do is attract *him*."

"Well, if you ask me, he is quite taken by you. Despite your contentious behaviour."

She has to fight down revulsion when she picks up Luigi Volpato's stained serviette. She notices his fingerprints are imprinted on his clouded wine glass.

8

Marcello's first thought when he opens his eyes and sees his sister standing by his bed in the half light of early morning is that she has died and this is her ghost visiting him. The abrupt violence with which he sits up startles Giulia and she steps back with an expression of alarm on her face. She is wearing a hat and a fur collared coat with raised lapels and a red scarf. He is struck by how sunken her cheeks are, how brightly her eyes burn.

"What are you doing? Why are you wearing a coat and hat? Have you been out? It's four thirty in the morning," he says, picking up his watch which sits on his bedside table beside the model ship with the orange sails he built as a child.

"Let's go out in the boat. It's magical outside. I need some magic."

He has become unaccustomed to seeing her on her feet and fully dressed. He notices how stooped her shoulders have become. How she pivots forward. How there seems to be a wheeze of pain in every breath she takes.

They tiptoe past their parents' bedroom door. He is wearing a coat over his pyjamas. It's like a return to childhood, this performance of a clandestine illicit act and he senses Giulia too feels this and enjoys it.

He has to help her down the two flights of stairs. The familiar malodorous chill of dampness seems more acute to him today. He is sensitive to every danger on her behalf. Painfully alerted to her uneven breathing and gasps of struggle. Their progress is slow.

"I remember when I used to take these steps two at a time," she says.

A magical floating and twisting mist, sea-flavoured, has descended on Venice. He feels light on his feet. He has only half emerged from a dream. It's as if gravity still hasn't quite exerted its laws on his body. He reminds Giulia of when they visited the Sistine Chapel and how looking up with such concentration at the frescoes the ground had seemed to shift underfoot.

"It feels like that now."

"Now you see why I had to come out," she says. He does understand. The physical world seems to float a little off the ground. Everything is incorporeal and transparent. The mist like an eraser rubbing out everything superfluous, restoring the world to its pristine origins, to a new beginning. There is a hushed quality to the air as if silence has been called for because something important is about to happen. Marcello can see no further than his next footstep. They walk over a bridge, a stone hump with low balustrades. Waves slopping up over the marble steps have a dreamlike quality. They are in the vicinity of a nearby bakery and its wood stoves and the sweet smell of freshly baked bread carries the surprise of a virgin moment.

He helps her down into the *sandolo*. Watches her settle with difficulty on the thwart of the rocking flat-bottomed boat. It feels to him more and more like they have entered some kind of parallel universe where the ordinary objects and the noises of the familiar world possess a new purpose. Life seems governed by spirit. Her sunken shape in the boat wreathed in mist resembles a bodiless apparition. He punts off into the thick fog. Not being able to see more than a few feet into the distance he realises how intimately he knows these canals. He wonders if he could navigate them blindfold. He can barely make out the outline of the approaching low bridge but he knows instinctively when to duck down. He gives a good push on the oar to make a right turn. It feels good to be able to count on his own strength, his own agility. He feels at one with his boat, as if part of its fittings, its cadences and creaks and rhythm. On the Grand Canal detail of the palaces on either side float in and out of visibility as if made of the mist. Moisture dampens his hair and soaks into his clothes. He worries again for Giulia's wellbeing.

"Are you okay?" he calls out.

"Life is no more than a dream, don't you think?"

"Seems that way at the moment."

"And perhaps when we die we wake from the dream."

The water becomes choppier when they reach the lagoon. He tightens his grip of the oar. More force is demanded of his body to keep to his own rhythm. The orbs of blurred golden light from the waterfront lamps burn small perforations in the sea-fog. He experiences a moment of held breath. A moment when he realises only his heartbeat prevents him from being nothing, from being nowhere. It is easy for him to imagine Giulia disappearing into this mist, never to reappear. The mist makes the idea of death beautiful, he thinks, and perhaps this is why she wanted to come outside. As if this is a kind of rehearsal for what awaits her.

The fog hides the islands across the lagoon, including the Lido where the Jewish cemetery is located. He catches himself looking in that direction and then hopes Giulia hasn't read his mind. He runs his tongue over the salt on his lips. He moors the boat at the Riva degli Schiavoni, the waterfront promenade behind San Marco. It is too early for the merchants to be setting out their stalls. The gondolas rocking back and forth on their moorings look like ghost ships. There is a kind of choreography to their lilting and swaying in formation.

He walks with Giulia on his arm towards Piazza San Marco. The grand vista of the square and basilica is lost in the mist. The two Moors on the clock tower can only be imagined. Then approaching footsteps shatter the dream. The metallic presumption of army boots. The appearance of the two uniformed fascists quickens Marcello's heartbeat. He can tell Giulia has registered his agitation and he feels ashamed of his fear. But it would be an apt punishment for this reckless act were he to now encounter the fascist he pushed into the canal.

It has been years since Mussolini banned the handshake, because it was unhygienic and belonged to an effete bourgeois culture, and instead made it law to greet people with the Roman salute. Often when Marcello leaves home the muscles in his stomach clench with the dread that he will be called upon to make the fascist salute. He has a developed a kind of phobia around it. All around him men click their heels and raise their right hand all the time, some with fervour, others with reluctance or wry amusement. He has practiced performing it with a measure of inoffensive irony. But he can never get it right. He hopes these two young men won't humiliate him in front of his sister.

There is a little relief when he sees neither of these men are his nemesis. One of the fascist militia smiles into Marcello's eyes and makes the what-the-hell gesture with his cupped hand. Marcello's solace is immense. He would like to embrace the young man and show him how much his small kind gesture means to him.

A gust of sea spray sweeps up into his face and sends a shiver through him. Then Giulia begins coughing and gasping for breath. Her body convulsing. Her familiar face is distorted into that of a nightmarish stranger. Her face sunk back to the bones of her skull. Her eyes stare into his wild with fear. She makes a motion of clawing at her coat lapels. It's like she's drowning in an invisible element and there's no way for him to reach her. He considers running to fetch help. She pleads with her eyes for him to stay. He sees she has coughed up blood. The red bead glistens through the mist like oiled pigment at her feet. He stands uselessly watching her try to catch her breath. Then the insurrection of her body abates and she recovers control of her breathing and he wants to offer up a prayer of thanksgiving.

The journey home seems to take forever.

Mother and Father are standing at the open front door of the apartment in their dressing gowns. Father is fighting down an explosive rage. Marcello can sense his father has to exert hard-pressed powers of self-control not to strike him. But it's as if he has hit him all the same. It is a moment in which he receives knowledge of what his parents secretly think about him. That they harbour misgivings about his maturity as an adult. The motion of the boat is still in his legs as he stands bowing his head in front of his father.

"It wasn't Marcello's fault. It was all my idea," says Giulia, fighting back the wheezing in her chest. He has understood today that Giulia's life won't peacefully shut down like a watch in need of winding; that when the moment of death arrives there will be violence and horror. That this moment lays in wait and he doesn't know if he has the strength to endure it.

Upstairs a troubling warmth emits from the open door of his parents' darkened bedroom. Their night time intimacy exposed. The sight of their unmade bed shocks him, the intimacy of it, the shamelessness of it. He has never before seen his parents' marriage bed anything but decorously covered. It is like catching sight of them both naked. And the familiar cloying scent of Mother's face powder is especially pungent. It's a smell he associates with childhood and the secret oppressive life of adults. It now makes him wish he and Giulia were still children with only the sing-song language of childhood at their disposal and he didn't have the thud of this ominous drumbeat at the back of his thoughts.

9

During the night a relentless wind whistled and wailed in the fireplaces and made the rusty hinged shutters of her bedroom groan. It unnerved her, as if all meaning in the world was being turned into gibberish. The rain is still lashing against the kitchen window when she makes her father breakfast. Coffee and a piece of toasted bread with cherry jam. She is relieved her father shows no signs of recalling last night's conflict. He doesn't mention Luigi Volpato. He is good at turning a blind eye to everything he finds embarrassing, like the fact that she washes his underclothes. It seems to her he rarely, if ever, gives any thought to the past. Only the canvas he is presently working on is of consuming importance. She often marvels at his ability to erase everything ugly in life. As if it is no more than a clumsy brushstroke he can wipe clean with turpentine.

She fetches him his galoshes. She notices he has covered the telephone with a hat again.

Many of the canals have flooded their banks. The clouded water sometimes slops around her calves. There is the smell of overflowing unflushed drains. In Campo dei Frari she watches a pair of young lovers kick up water at each other. They give off a contagious radiance. She thinks how beautiful young love is. Kissing in the rain. She would like to paint it. It becomes a challenge she greatly looks forward to tackling.

She purchases the five different shades of shot silk for her father which he will use for the robes of his Biblical figures. Now she has to tell Marcello what she has discovered. It seems less urgent today. The piece of paper she read like something she dreamed. Probably because she doesn't want to confront Marcello. The thought of him intimidates her. She can't help feeling it will look to him like she is creating an excuse for seeing him. As if she has come to approve of the liberty he tried to take with her. And she can't tell him his mother might be having an affair. Once again she wishes she had a female friend with whom to confide and help untangle the knots in her feelings. Might it not be possible to experience his attempt to kiss her as a compliment instead of a violation? She has played over and over again the moment when he lunged at her. Sometimes she makes allowances for him and finds herself wholly at fault. Other times she is still angry with him for misreading her so badly. The incident has brought up her entire life for critical review. She often feels the wick in her doesn't burn through the wax. The flame expires before illumination arrives. She wonders if the absence of a mother has damaged her ability to behave in the world as a confident sophisticated woman. A mother would surely have made it easier for her to find her stride by creating a warmer and more human atmosphere around her. She had difficulties making friends at school; for a long time she was frightened of entering shops alone. Her father didn't help, quick as he was to show irritation every time she failed at a task he set her. As a girl she often suffered his outbursts of temper when he would rebuke her for inadvertently breaking some rule he had laid down and she would know an overpowering sense of shame. He didn't seem to know how easily he could hurt her to the core. She wasn't allowed to cry in front of him either and very rarely did. It was an unwritten law. All her misgivings about herself might be offset by the encouraging complicit laughter of a mother. She knows how to create a likeness on paper of what's before her eyes but is confident of little else in her life. There is a controllable self-sufficiency in this discipline which she likes. She is dependent on no one else for reward. But perhaps, as is the case with her father, it's becoming a kind of insulation. To prevent life from touching her. Knowledge and its application in daily life, she knows, is important. But perhaps what's more important for the wellbeing of the spirit is relating to other people, caring, listening, loving. In this realm she is a fearful novice.

She has been circling the art supply shop owned by Marcello's family for fifteen minutes. While she is wading through the flood water, walking through the light rain with its marine smell, the cobbles underfoot slick, the smells of the algae and seaweed and brine in the canals more acute, she notices how quick any crowd is to part and provide a free passage to any man in the fascist militia uniform. An obsequious world meets them, grants them privilege, enables them to put themselves at the head of every queue. Men are increasingly speaking with loud berating unfriendliness. The thought of Marcello's languid way of expressing himself contrasts him in his favour with these men but also hints at some missing resolve in him. As if he might not have the conviction to lift any woman off her feet.

She passes a building from inside which a radio or a gramophone is playing Verdi. She tries to remember the name of the opera. It eludes her. But the music gives her the courage to enter the shop. Marcello isn't there. She buys a bag of lead white pigment she doesn't need and leaves feeling irritated with him and with herself.

10

"For a moment she stood watching a boy and a girl kiss in the rain. Whether with envy or disapproval I couldn't say because she had her back to me." He smiles and wipes some imaginary dust from the sleeve of his jacket. "Then she bought some silk fabric in Calle Prima de la Donzella." He doesn't tell his boss he studied her legs through the window of the shop when she climbed a ladder to inspect the bolts on the top shelves, hoping to get a glimpse of her knickers. Why is a sneaked glimpse of a woman's underwear so immeasurably more exciting than would be the sight of the same woman half naked in swimwear on the Lido? He wrote this observation down in his new notebook. He bought it in the shop where Elisabetta buys art materials for her father. The younger man served him. There was no fascist party pin on his lapel. And he refused to be drawn into conversation. "Then she baffled me. For half an hour she walked in circles. Initially, I thought she was going to the art supplies shop. But then she seemed to change her mind. Then she seemed to change her mind again. She doesn't strike me as a very purposeful kind of person. Not at all. If she was ever engaged in any kind of subversive activity I'd say she's got cold feet. Often she has a startled look on her face as if she's returned to her body after being up in the clouds. Eventually she did go to the art shop."

"And that's it? No meetings?"

"There was one meeting. Of great intensity." He studies Volpato's face for signs of discomfort. He has made it a challenge to get under the man's skin at least once every meeting.

"She went into the Frari. Picture the scene. The stink of incense and expiring candle wicks. The widening echo of footsteps. The bridal path down the aisle. The cold breath of ancient stone."

He is gratified to see Luigi Volpato is tapping his pencil on the desk with more agitation than usual.

"And then the secret meeting took place. She stood in front of Titian's painting of the woman in red for ten minutes."

"You should be on the stage, Gentile."

"I know, Signor Volpato. But life likes to waste our talents. Sometimes it seems to me that's life's raison d'être."

"Nothing else?"

"Then she returned to her father's studio. Do you want me to write a report?"

"No. You're to tell me in person everything she does," says Luigi Volpato. "And I want you to offer your services as a model to her father. He's a painter."

He makes clear his distaste for this chore with a theatrical grimace.

"I'm not very good at holding a pose. I like to move around."

"I've noticed. You're always fidgeting."

"What is it you suspect this girl of anyway?"

"That's for me to know and for you to find out."

"And what about Signora Zecchi and Paolo Levi?"

"I've got another agent watching Signora Zecchi. And it won't be long before we arrest Paolo Levi."

Agent 362 cracks his knuckles and gets to his feet.

"One last thing. Do you find her attractive?"

"Signora Zecchi?"

"No. Elisabetta Del Monaco."

He senses he has to be careful how he answers this. He puts his hand inside the open collar of his white shirt. "Rarely do great beauty and great virtue dwell together," he eventually announces, quoting Petrarch and picturing himself on stage. Although Elisabetta Del Monaco is everything the fascists object to in women: she is slim hipped, she possesses a disconsolate air, she never wears thick stockings and shows no ambition where procreation is concerned, he has understood that Luigi Volpato is having him follow her for lewd personal reasons. The old pervert has got his eye on her.

After leaving the office he spends an hour in a bar near the university, eavesdropping on conversations. Mostly it is vacuous gossip. The students he listens to might as well be reciting nursery rhymes. It appals him how determined they all are to have their say. The vitality they squander on inanities. Two boys and a girl in a corner interest him for a while. Only driblets of their heated conversation reach his ears. He hears the word freedom repeated often. The importance of independence of thought and action. But he soon understands the two males are simply vying for the attention of the girl. They are talking about philosophy but not far beneath the surface a mating contest is taking place. He has always disliked the spectacle of boys using arts to impress girls. The required vanity of the performance. He studiously avoids any similar inclination in himself or else theatrically plays it up. He has acquired many behavioural rules of this sort. A kind of censorship he imposes on himself. Men use talk to show their feathers. Women use talk to inhabit their bodies. He writes down this observation in his new notebook.

What he would most like is to infiltrate a group of subversives. He would find excitement in this. The challenge of adapting himself to their expectations of him. Of tricking them into trusting him. The risk of being discovered. The attraction of becoming the mutant bee in the hive. He has always enjoyed putting those around him on a false footing. It has been how he has convinced himself of his cleverness. In truth he has no interest in collective endeavours or binding himself to formal agreements. It's one of the secrets he keeps from his boss, Luigi Volpato.

He looks at his watch. He has to give an Italian lesson to the German man who lives with his young family in the apartment next to his own. A Jewish man with a battered hat. His wife though is attractive. He is always attentive to her three year old son. Because he knows she is vain of her child and there's no better way of attracting a woman than exploiting her vanities. He also works two nights a week in the ticket booth of a cinema. It brings in little money but he gets to see films for free. This week *Sotto la Croce del Sud*, a hackneyed piece of fascist propaganda set in the recently occupied Abyssinia about the dangers of being seduced by the exotic and *Incantesimo* from which he drew the conviction he himself could have played the Cary Grant role with more aplomb and gusto. It will be a struggle again to find the 300 lire he owes in rent this month. He has to find a way of making more money.

He buys a sandwich and eats as he walks, barely aware of what he is chewing. A priest in his greasy black vestments walks hurriedly past him. A man with the ability to forgive sins. "Deliver us from temptation," he says in passing, perhaps not loud enough for the priest to hear. He is watchful of the continuous, repetitive, dutiful activity around him. It is strange to realise that the life of every person is mapped out, a bounded horizon of coordinates traversed over and over again, as familiar to them as the shape of their hands. And that they all believe their lives are the centre of the universe. It appals him how ordinary every moment is for most people. That's not how he wants to live his life. He walks until he loses his bearings. His mind is never idle. He wants to commit to memory a map of Venice in its entirety. Every bridge crosses into a new territory, a new square on the board. Today he walks through the Castello district. Soon he finds himself in a warren of high walled alleys. Refuse dampened and crushed into a slippery paste underfoot. Overhead the crisscross of wretched laundry. The smell of drains, of damp stone and decay almost at times overwhelming. There's an atmosphere here that calls to mind the chipped and stained china of his childhood home, the draperies yellowed with age, the splintered straw-bottomed chairs, the gloomy rosaries and etchings of saints. Soon he has entered a realm of cats. They perch on the high walls and look down at him with hostility. Gulls screech overhead. He walks the length of one long narrow deserted alley with rotting masonry only to arrive at a dead end. It's like he has entered a realm where everyone has died. He has to retrace his steps. It takes him half an hour before he is able to get his bearings again. Venice, he realises, will not submit to coherent map making. This area though, he decides, is where he would hide out in if this ever became necessary.

11

To the bystanders, death grants Marcello and his family a kind of regal distinction. For the time being they cease to be social outcasts; they arouse fellowship and sympathy. It's an impression that seeps its way through Marcello's benumbed sensibility. The launch purrs slowly across the lagoon in the wake of the gondola that contains Giulia's coffin. He remembers standing between her lifeless body and the open window of her room and the guilt he felt when he turned to look out of the window. As if he was already looking to the future, caught in the act of turning his back to the past, the only place Giulia now exists.

A *carabinieri* boat motors past, its wake rocking the gondola. Marcello looks at the men in their cocked plumed hats and theatrical cloaks with the deep aversion he feels now for all men in uniform. His father is sitting beside him, his head bowed, his sobbing a constant background noise. He has barely spoken since falling onto Giulia's breathless body. He is making it plain he is enduring the unendurable. It's as if he has confiscated everyone else's grief. Marcello still hasn't shed a single tear. The stamp of death on his sister's face will not cease to strike him as some kind of catastrophic error.

Giulia was alone in the middle of the night when the haemorrhaging occurred, when the arterial blood gushed through her fingers. Marcello ran into the room, turned on the light in time to see in searing detail the beseeching terror in her eyes and the carnage of blood on the coverlet.

Earlier she had asked him to find for her books about

Chekhov and Katherine Mansfield, both of whom died of tuberculosis. He had been looking forward to the challenge. Had already made an itinerary of the bookshops he would visit. He had anticipated the pride and pleasure he would know returning to the apartment with at least one of the books she wanted. He agonises now over how glibly, how hurriedly he terminated their conversation. He suspects Giulia wanted to carry on talking when he made excuses and went to bed. As if she had something to tell him that he will never know now. He can't rid himself of the feeling he ultimately failed her. At times guilt seems a more active component of his grief than sadness.

When they arrive at the Lido and Marcello gets to his feet in the rocking boat he gazes down at the ghostly blur of his face reflected in the shadowed water. He looks like an outcast, a beggar. It's a face he feels no sense of ownership for. A horse and cart is stationed outside the gate of the cemetery. The smell of the horse earthy and warm, redolent with lively life. Marcello strokes its flank. There is comfort in the contact. Just as, when a child, the family dog was able to give him more comfort than his parents.

He walks behind his parents with Flora. He is struck by the familiarity of their outlines but the unfamiliarity of the way they move. He feels a rush of tenderness for both of them. Then the cemetery momentarily takes him outside of himself. The undisturbed scents of earth and tree bark and flowers. The leaf strewn path between the old engraved stones. All those names. He feels the dead crowd close. He catches sight of Hebrew text of which he has little knowledge. For a moment he thinks of the lost homeland. It is the first time in his life he has thought of it with longing. It is safety he is longing for.

By the side of the open grave he sees Alessandro, Giulia's best friend at university who has been in love with her for years. The sunlight, inappropriately, conjures up memories of wellbeing and adventure. Then he notices Massimo. For a heartbeat he is like a magical apparition. Something wished for but never expected. The death of his sister has made him ashamed of the malice he has bottled up against both Massimo and Elisabetta. He is made to feel he has been a little man, a man unworthy of respect. It's as if from now on Giulia's role in his life will be to recruit him for a higher purpose. Massimo offers his hand and tears come to Marcello's eyes.

"I'm sorry for being such a jackass."

"Water under the bridge. I'm sorry about Giulia. It's not fair."

"I've missed you," he says. To speak from the heart, as he so rarely does, heightens the intimacy with which he inhabits his body.

There is no sign of Elisabetta. Not that he expected her to show. He pictures her for a moment as she might have come, dressed in black, her head bowed. Does she even know? The new Racial Laws forbid them to place a notice of Giulia's death in the newspaper. But the shop has been closed for three days with a notice explaining why. He has thought of her as the only person who might bring him some comfort.

He looks down at the unfastened white cuffs of his shirt protruding from the sleeves of his black jacket. Giulia had recommended this look to him. Said it made him look like a romantic poet. "Girls will find that attractive." He expected his father, a stickler for correct appearances, to insist on him wearing cufflinks but he hasn't noticed his small tribute to his sister.

His father rocks and sways and groans by his side. Mother holds Flora's hand and keeps adjusting the hang of her jacket. She is staring into a void. Standing by the graveside he realises how much of his time he has spent living in imagined futures. Every future in his head now quickly tapers to a vanishing point. He dreads the journey back across the lagoon. The recommencement of this new world of racial hatred without Giulia. He cannot imagine the world without her. For the first time in his life the thought of suicide passes through his mind. It brings both a shard of light and a chill of shadow.

Marcello thinks back to the eclipse of the sun on the first

day of 1936. He and Giulia had stood on the balcony looking up at the sky. When the sun vanished it was like losing all his sophistication for a moment. He experienced himself as an ancient cave dweller. Vulnerable to superstition, a stranger to all textbook knowledge. He sees Giulia vividly on the balcony. He has brought her back to life for a moment. This is how she will now return to him, suddenly sliding beneath his skin. Every time he momentarily brings her back to life he almost immediately sees again the immense charged stillness of her dead body in the bed, her mouth wide open. Then he has to experience the pain of losing her again. This keeps happening to him. Giulia dies over and over again. And every time it is a different Giulia he has to grieve.

12

Her father is delicately softening the edges of his wet brush-strokes with his fingertips. The model, dressed as Saint Anthony in a brown cassock, gets to his feet and performs an elaborate choreography of stretching movements. He has an air of amusing himself. Then he walks over to his heap of clothes. He catches Elisabetta's eye before stripping off the robe and standing before her stark naked. He wriggles his hips with a grin. For a moment his anatomy is charged with carnality. She senses he derives a pleasure from exposing himself to her, as if it activates a secret conspiracy between him and her at the expense of her oblivious father. Her father's face is pressed up close to his large canvas. She has never deemed this young man a suitable model for a saint. There is something scheming and duplicitous about the cast of his handsome features. He would be better as a sinner. She turns away before he bends down to put on his trousers.

"Thank you, Pino. Same time tomorrow."

"Goodbye, Maestro. Goodbye, signorina."

Pino winks at her before leaving the studio. She waits for her father to begin cleaning his brushes. The smell of turpentine sharp in the dusty nimbus of north light. She takes a deep breath. Shadows seem to move behind her. There is strategy in her choosing of this moment to broach the charged subject with her father. She has waited until he has a satisfying day's work behind him.

"Marcello Zecchi has asked me to go to dinner with him."

She has tried to pitch her voice in a casual register but it is shaky with high emotion. He narrows his eyes. The red pigment on the sable brush he points at her matches the colour of his heated cheeks. "I absolutely forbid it," he says.

"His sister has just died."

"I know and I'm sorry. But he's not suitable. That's all there is to it."

"Suitable for what?"

"You know what I mean. Don't make me spell it out."

"I'm not asking to marry him."

"I don't care what you're asking. The answer is no."

"His father has always been very good to you."

"Are you questioning my authority?"

Flecks of red appear in his cheeks again. His lips are pinched. But he also looks a bit frightened. And older than she is accustomed to seeing him. She *is* questioning his authority. They both know it. She feels constrained to oppose him because the prospect of saying no to Marcello takes her to a wretched barren place within. She could sense how much courage it took him to ask her to go out to dinner with her. She was disappointed he didn't ask her to do something simpler. Something she would not need her father's permission to do. She knew his request would meet with opposition from her father and a conflict would ensue. But she could not tell Marcello this. She didn't want to admit to Marcello how little freedom of movement her father grants her. The instinct to shield her father from criticism is part of the core of her identity.

Her father's two ambitions are to be a great painter and, outside of his cloistered world, to be an unobtrusive man. He believes in his genius. Is sure all forms of modernism in art are nothing more than a passing fad and when technical bravura is again the touchstone for evaluating the painted image his works will be granted the recognition they warrant. Otherwise, he asks only to be left alone. He reserves all his tyranny for her. She likes to think it's because he doesn't want to lose her. But the subservience he shows to Luigi Volpato has revealed to her he might be prepared to sacrifice her too if his freedom is threatened.

"You've always been hard and cruel with me," she says. The harshest words she has ever spoken to anyone in her life. Her father is dumbfounded, a fixed unseeing stare in his eyes. "Fine. I'll go and tell him you don't approve of him."

When she leaves the studio she knows he will be unable to work. He will put himself on trial. And eventually he will find himself innocent of all charges. She suspects a good deal of thinking has this exclusively self-exonerating end for most people. But he will exhaust his energies for the day in the process. She on the other hand is already feeling guilty. Is tempted to return to the studio and apologise. Yes, she resents the constraint he enforces on her of behaving subordinately, decorously around him. She thinks the strain of withholding in his presence everything independent in her is drying up her resources of vitality, deadening her feeling. But she always feels wretched when she incurs his disappointment. It is shocking to realise she can love and hate at the same time.

As she walks through the light cold rain she keeps changing her mind about what she will tell Marcello. She even considers disobeying her father and accepting his invitation to dinner. And she realises she can't say for sure her father wouldn't disown her as a consequence.

In the shop she is immediately struck by the saddened bewilderment in the eyes of Marcello's father. She can feel arise from him all his heartbroken love for his daughter. Her feeling towards her own father softens. At the same time she has to harden herself to disappoint Marcello. It is the masks we're made or choose to wear that often make us ugly, both to ourselves and others. She is also more painfully aware than usual that he is Jewish and doesn't want him to feel this in any way affects any decision she makes about him. She is unsteady on her feet when she reaches the counter. It amazes her how matter-of-factly she is able to impart the information that she won't be able to have dinner with him.

"We could do something together in the day though. Perhaps

we could go to the Accademia. Or else you could take me out in your boat? If it ever stops raining."

She notices he is looking down at her hips and realises she is unconsciously and repeatedly smoothing her coat against her thigh. She can feel the heat of her blood in her fingers.

When she leaves the shop she wants to cry. She finds it hard to withstand prying eyes. She has disappointed both Marcello and her father. The frustration of not being understood brings with it the feeling that nothing else matters. One of those locked cages in the mind from which escape can take hours. She now has to face the consequences of creating the confrontation with her father. She dreads the moment when they will have to face each other again. She doesn't want to go home. She wants to put off the next moment in her life for as long as possible. Then she realises she has forgotten to tell Marcello his mother is being followed by the secret police.

13

He follows her to the canal flanking Calle dei Miracoli. Never has he seen her appear so distressed. Twice he watches her walk into people. As if the physical world is an apparition to her.

He is proud of how finely tuned is his peripheral vision. He has eyes in the back of his head. There is enough activity – men unloading baskets of fruit and flowers from a barge, women shopping with their string bags – for him to conceal his presence. Now that she knows his face, if not his real name, he ought to be more circumspect. But he finds he no longer cares if she sees him. He stands for a while outside a grocer's watching the shopkeeper cut thin slices of mortadella through the glass, allowing her to put some more distance between them. He is still aglow with the memory of flaunting to her his naked body. The recollection of the little jiggle of his hips he performed for her makes him smile.

He hears the repeated chime of a blacksmith's hammer on an anvil. For a moment he thinks it's the sound of his mind working. He pictures the flying sparks. He already knows where she is going.

It is requiring more and more of his thespian skills to conceal the loathing he feels for Luigi Volpato. The humiliation and boredom of sitting motionless, dressed in a monk's robe, in the dusty studio while the fastidious painter stares squinting at him has increased his determination to one day take his revenge on his boss. The dust motes in the shafts of light seem to slow down time. The minutes crawl by behind the draped windows. The maddening sense of frittering away valuable time. The knowledge he was made for better things. Pretending to be a saint. Pretending his name is Pino. Pretending they are still living in the age of Titian and Tintoretto. It's all too ridiculous. Today, he brought up the famous attack Marinetti made on Venice in San Marco. He recited what he could remember of it, deliberately misquoting some of the original text.

"We want to demolish museums and libraries, fight morality, feminism; we want to heal this putrefying city. We want to prepare the birth of an industrial and military Venice. Let us fill in its reeking canals with the shards of its leprous palaces. Let's burn the gondolas – those rocking chairs for cretins."

The painter blew his gasket. The fiery bluster of contempt he expressed for Marinetti made him unable to paint for fifteen minutes. He found it difficult to suppress his laughter. His daughter didn't know where to look for embarrassment at her father's loss of control.

He is now certain there are no political motives for this assignment Volpato has given him. Volpato simply has designs on the painter's daughter, a girl almost half his age. He wants to know about possible rivals. To irritate his boss he has greatly exaggerated the intimacy existing between her and Marcello. Today he goes one step further.

"He gave her a kiss on the mouth before they parted company. She was beaming with happiness when she walked away. She doesn't appear to mind that he's a Jew. In fact, I'd say it's part of the attraction he has for her. Forbidden fruit, like Juliet with Romeo."

How he enjoyed the bristling rush of irritation this invented vignette caused Volpato. He began fiddling with things on his desk. He wagers Volpato's next move will be to want him to get some dirt on Marcello Zecchi. To want him locked safely away in the Regina Coeli prison in Rome or exiled to some remote Calabrian mountain village.

14

Marcello is punting against the tide from the stern while Massimo punts from the prow. He is out of practice at this sharing of duties. There are few boats on the water at this late hour. They ease a course through the fidgeting elongated lights on the black water. The shuttered palaces on either side shimmer on the surface of the water as if about to dissolve at any moment.

"Every day I take all this for granted." He has to raise his voice and he talks to the silhouette of his friend's back.

"But not tonight?" Massimo shouts back.

"The same things can look so different on any given day. It's like the mind has lots of windows and each one gives a different perspective of the same view."

"I guess these disgusting laws must make you feel like the kid with dog shit on his shoes," says Massimo. That he doesn't lower his voice when he says this makes Marcello appreciate his friend all the more. The return of Massimo's company has reminded him of how good they are at building each other up, fortifying each other, glamorising each other.

"That's exactly how it feels."

"I ought to be making the most of what I see too. I got my call-up papers today. I have to report to the barracks in Verona on Monday."

It sends a chill of foreboding through him that Massimo will no longer be around. As if a quota of his physical strength has suddenly left his body.

"At least in this respect you can count yourself lucky you're

94

Jewish," says Massimo, this time lowering his voice. "No uniform, no mindless drilling, no military parades or hymn singing for you. Doesn't that make you feel blessed?"

"Except before long Jewish men will be conspicuous as the only males not wearing a uniform. Everyone will be inwardly pointing a finger at us."

They are quiet for a while. As they pass by the lights of a hotel he notices a woman on a balcony. He wonders what she's thinking as she looks down at him. She won't of course know he is a Jew. He supposes he might look a romantic figure and for a moment experiences himself in this transfiguring guise. It's a welcome escape from himself. He is still smarting from Elisabetta's refusal to have dinner with him. Even though he knows he asked of her something she would have little choice but to refuse. As if he sought another excuse to feel sorry for himself. After all, she has offered to see him in the daytime. But he wants a bigger, more daring concession from her.

He calls out to Massimo, "Is there a girl in your life?"

It's a delicate subject, recalling the motive for their feud, and Marcello feels his face heat up.

"One or two. What about you?"

"I've been branded a leper. I'm the kid with dog shit on his shoes, remember?"

"You'll have to find yourself a woman with a big heart and gentle unselfish hands."

"I suppose if any girl does find me attractive I'll know it's because of who I am."

"And not because of how much money you've got in the bank or how lucrative your profession is."

"We're not allowed to have money in the bank or a lucrative profession."

"Exactly. You'll have to come up with poetry. I read somewhere that the only memories which endure in our mind are those with poetry in them."

Marcello looks up at the moon and then down at the lit-up palaces in the dark water.

"Sometimes I think it's some essence of the sad beauty of memory itself that Venice reflects back at us. It still comes as a shock that Giulia isn't in her room when I return home."

Marcello can feel his friend's sympathy reach out to him in the darkness.

They bring the *sandolo* to a halt in front of the church of Santa Maria della Salute, its white marble façade as dazzling under the lamps as freshly fallen snow, its dome smoky in the misted air. Massimo makes the sign of the cross in front of the church.

"I've never seen you do that before."

"The Salute was built to protect us from the plague and I've got the feeling a new plague is about to arrive."

They share a straw-wrapped bottle of red wine and smoke cigarettes. The smell of brine is sharper and cleaner. A friendly presence deep in his lungs. His eyes are attracted to the few bobbing lights of fishing boats out on the lagoon. Now and again he looks up at the flickering map of stars overhead.

"My father is thinking about sending me and Flora to London. He has a cousin living there. The closer Mussolini sidles up to Hitler the more sleep my father loses. He worries he might lose the shop. Takings are dropping every month. It's like no one anymore is interested in the act of creation. Everyone seems suddenly more attracted to the act of destruction."

"If you go to London we might find ourselves fighting for different sides in any upcoming war. Insane, isn't it?"

"Sometimes it's hard to believe what we experience first-hand is the real world and all the things going on beyond our reach are just shadows. At the moment it feels like the opposite. As if the world of consequences is somewhere else, but steadily getter closer. Perhaps that's why most of the time I feel like a piece of driftwood at sea. Why can't one decide oneself what one is going to do with one's life? Why is it we allow a handful of arrogant power-hungry men to make most of our decisions for us?"

"I know. Sometimes I feel guilty for not having committed more of my energy to opposing fascism. But it always felt like trying to stop a battalion of tanks by standing in front of them."

It is painful to say goodbye to Massimo, much more emotional than he anticipated. As if this leave-taking might be forever. He suspects it's Giulia's death that now makes his expectations morbid. He hides his overspill of tender feeling from Massimo. As if it's unmanly. They exchange a firm handshake before parting.

After he moors the boat he walks over Ponte dele Tette, so named because prostitutes were ordered to bare their breasts on the bridge when, in Renaissance times, a wave of male homosexuality swept through the city. It might be Renaissance times now. The history of the city seeps out at night. But it is a sinister kind of history. The streets are deserted. He might be the last person left in the world. The acoustics are otherworldly and razor sharp at this time of night. A footfall a hundred metres away sounds like the next moment of your life. The slopping of the water against stone sounds like something that is happening inside you. And there's the sense of being shadowed everywhere you go. Watched by ghosts.

15

The ordinary objects of the house can depress him now. The umbrellas no one ever uses, the ornaments no one ever notices, the books no one ever opens, the gramophone records no one ever plays. That they have all survived Giulia is a squalid fact. He picks up a scent of her in unguarded moments which is like losing his place in the book of his life. He has to return several pages back to get his bearings. In her room remain all her clothes and possessions which no one can bring themselves to throw away.

He has finished packing. In the kitchen he takes no notice of the labels on the foodstuffs he consumes with his family each day. Not realising how exotic and charged with pathos and longing the familiar logos and illustrations will soon become in his imagination. He is casting one last look around, breathing everything deeply in. He presses down his hands on the table, as if to leave his prints there. For a moment he catches a smell of his childhood. He cannot bed down the thought that everything he now looks at will soon become fragmented and ghosted into recollections. No room of his home, repositories of an ever-changing medley of formative memories, quite looks familiar today. Since being told he is to leave Italy he has felt he is a witness to his own actions, as if an act of separation has taken place inside him.

Flora enters the kitchen. They go out onto the balcony together, overlooking the canal. He looks down at the line of pot plants, pinches a leaf of the basil and brings his fingers to his nose.

"You've finished packing?"

"I never truly believed it would come to this," she says. "I thought Papa would change his mind. I still don't want to go."

"It can't be any worse than you imagine it."

"How do you know?"

He looks at his watch and makes a discovery. To be aware of time is to be anxious.

"Don't you think Mama and Papa are creating a mountain of a molehill?"

"Maybe."

"They argue in bed every night."

The arguments reach him in the darkness, accompanied by the grim ticking of the grandfather clock outside his bedroom.

"I hate it," says Flora. "They never argue. I don't want to go to England. I've barely in my life ever given England a moment's thought. It doesn't feel right I'm now going to live there. And I hate the language. It's like trying to talk with a pebble in your mouth. And how do we even know how the English treat Jews? Perhaps they're no better than Germans."

He has argued this decision of his father's out several times with both parents. The trump card his father delivers every time is Hitler. Hitler has become a kind of supernatural being, his malevolence omnipotent. It seems crazy that one unknown man in a faraway country has accrued so much far-reaching intimidating power.

"Time to go."

He watches his mother close the apartment door behind her. He finds it hard to look at her, to acknowledge her presence, as if he is practising experiencing her as an absence. The interior of his home disappears into what immediately seems an irretrievable past. The building is a maze of corridors and staircases. Dark even during the day. The damp peeling whitewashed stucco of the walls. The exposed electrical wires. It's like being down in the depths of a ship.

He stands for a moment looking at the flaking pink and grey

stucco of the building's façade. Then he walks down the cobbled alley with his suitcase, following his mother and sister. He sees a man arguing with a woman. His face brutal, venomous and ugly with rage. Then he notices the artless and trusting face of a little boy who shyly catches his eye. He doesn't, he realises, feel much older than this little boy. Boyhood still often seems the time he was most real to himself and most wise, as if every habit acquired since is merely fancy dress.

When they arrive at the shop Father is showing a customer sheets of vellum. He handles everything he sells with respectful tenderness. Marcello stands by the shelves of coloured pigments in glass jars, the little bottles of coloured inks, the trays of pencils and brushes. He looks at a jar of lapis lazuli and remembers Elisabetta telling him it is her favourite pigment. He never got to take her out in his boat. She came into the shop to say goodbye after he telephoned her to tell her he was leaving Venice and it was all very polite and formal. He didn't find the right words. She wore a buttercup yellow dress cut low in the neck with a red belt around her slim waist. He had never seen her look so attractive. Every time he caught a glimpse of her tongue he felt how frustrating it was to be in such close proximity to the most secret things about her and yet denied intimate knowledge of them.

When the last customer has left, his father brings an ivory box from the safe. Without asking permission he unpacks Marcello's suitcase and places it at the bottom. Marcello, open-mouthed, shakes his head for his mother's benefit.

"These are some of your grandmother's jewels. In case of emergency. Do you think they will be safe there?" he asks his wife. "Why didn't we sew them into Flora's clothes? Why didn't I think of that?" He slaps his forehead.

"They'll be safe there," says his wife.

Father repacks the clothes ineptly and has to sit on the leather trunk to get it to close. Marcello doesn't like seeing him in such an undignified pose. It seems to put him in more danger. Outside, he pulls down the iron shutter and locks it. Never has

Marcello seen him look so old. Or so false to his true feeling as he smiles across at Flora. There is no trace today of the irritation and anger that has recently dominated his father's moods. Today, he looks as he does when visiting Giulia's grave.

Marcello punts with his family seated in the middle of the boat. His father tries to impose a familiarity on the proceedings by talking of banalities. He always needs the distraction of talk when emotion runs high. Marcello has the sensation he is moving the boat through a succession of slowly dissolving memories. It is belittling to realise the surroundings won't be in any way altered by his absence. He takes a deep draught of the familiar smell of the salt water. He doesn't want to think this might be the last time he eases his boat down the Grand Canal. But the thought is a presence in his body, a jittery lightness in his limbs as if he is already becoming a ghost to his surroundings. Venice meets his eye with the look of love. Or so he feels. Its spectral world of reflections shimmering in the ethereal light is a reminder of the fragile nature of every earned security. He feels he is seeing everything as if for the first time. Or the last time. He is amazed the people he sees will go on living their lives in Venice without him. That everyone else is performing the acts of an ordinary day while for him the hour is so momentous. He licks his lips, relishing the taste of Venice in his mouth one last time.

Everything assumes a more pressing finality at the landing stage at Santa Lucia. The steps up to the station concourse which once upon a time filled him with excitement now fill him with foreboding. It doesn't quite make sense to him how the same place can create such conflicting moods on different days. He feels physically sick.

On the platform he grows irritated by his father's fussing. It will haunt him that the last look he gave to his father was pulsating with disdain. It is his mother's eyes he seeks through the twisting pennants of steam and smoke when the train pulls out of the station. As he leaves them he is made to think of all the things he doesn't know about his mother and father. They become mysterious strangers to him, formed by a history he has scant knowledge of. The games they played as children, the fears they knew as young adults, the gestures they made and words they spoke and places they cherished as lovers. He realises he has never looked into the heart of either of his parents.

He touches the button Elisabetta sewed onto his shirt. It has become a kind of talisman to him. It makes him feel she has given him a few moments of life. The long bridge over the lagoon brings with it the realisation of having lived on an island almost his entire life. The pull of his home, of everything he knows, tugs at him like a contrary current sometimes tugs at his boat out on the lagoon. He can't help feeling it would have been braver to stay put. He feels he is being made to run away, desert his post, commit a cowardly act. For a while now he has been angrier with his father than with Mussolini or Hitler.

As Venice slips further and further away, he finds himself remembering the puppet shows he put on with Giulia. The highest reward in those days was to make his mother proud of him. There was a pirate puppet, his favourite, and a mermaid puppet, Giulia's favourite. He was able to impart to that puppet an engaging evolving life of its own. He made it speak. One of those magical gifts of childhood. It became his best friend for an entire year of his life. For a moment he can feel the precise weight and texture of the toy in his hand. As a child he felt the pirate transmitted to him the possibilities of glamour and excitement which awaited him. It foretold his love of stepping onto a boat. And Giulia, like a mermaid, has disappeared beneath the surface of life. He regrets now not taking a last look at those puppets. He became more secretive when the puppets lost their glamour. He remembers cutting out pictures from magazines and gluing them in a scrapbook no one was allowed to see. As if that book charted the pathways of his secret life. What happened to that book? He imagines it might tell him things about himself he has forgotten.

Half an hour into the journey he realises Flora is almost a stranger to him. How little attention he has granted her. He takes out the map of Paris and unfolds it on his lap. There is a purring of excitement in him at the sight of the famous landmarks. He tries to include Flora in his fascination. He shows her the three exotic French banknotes he has in his wallet.

"So we can reward ourselves with a nice lunch," he says. He realises he still treats her like she is a child. And that it annoys her. There is an awkward silence for a while.

"Do you take notice of your dreams?"

"Sometimes," he says. "Why?"

"You know how you wake from some dreams feeling they will bring you luck? I've been having a lot of the opposite kind of dreams. Can I tell you something?" she asks him, looking out of the window. "I often didn't like Giulia. I never felt any love for her. Her voice annoyed me. That high-pitched pretence of generosity it had. She could be mean and scheming and selfish. She was always meddling with greedy calculation. I feel horrible for feeling these things."

He looks across at the man and woman sitting opposite in the carriage. The man is reading a newspaper. The woman has closed her eyes, her dry-skinned hands folded in her lap. He moves closer to Flora on the seat. "I've been thinking about Giulia a lot today. It's good you're honest. You should always be true to your feelings, even when they create difficulties. Father once said something similar about her. Now he's pretending she was some kind of perfect being. I don't think it's healthy to force yourself into feeling what you believe you ought to feel. Giulia was insecure behind that policing self-righteousness she could manifest. For some reason she had little confidence in herself. That's why she was always competing for attention. That's why she often couldn't see the truth about herself. But she wasn't a bad person."

"I know she wasn't a bad person. But I don't like not being able to like her. It makes me feel like I should have been the one who died."

"Don't say that. I admire how honest you are. I would guess the public façade of most families is a construction of sentimental half-truths. Sometimes I think to learn an adult perspective on life is simply to become good at telling lies, mostly of a flattering nature and mostly to oneself. And to take a great interest in weather."

He is gratified to see he has got her to smile. He has little confidence in himself as a reassuring presence.

"Do you think it matters how much love we carry in our hearts for someone after they have died?"

"I don't know. I suppose if anything matters in the end that does. We all want to be loved."

"Do you feel loved?"

"You're asking some difficult questions today."

They smile at each other. Every time he looks out of the window it's like reading one sentence in a different story. After two hours it is night outside. Lights like lanterns string threads through the rural darkness. It feels appropriate that he is separated from the things that surround him. Trees rush by as if magnified by the light of the window. There are the vacant streets of small towns.

There is a commotion when they stop at the border. Doors are flung open and men call back and forth in gravelly voices. Through the window and the ghost of his face reflected there he watches the platform sway about in the light of a lantern held by a railway worker. The compartment becomes like an extension of the dark unknown world outside. Marcello's passport is studied by an official wearing a holstered gun with frowning suspicion. For a moment he is made to feel he is illegitimate or that he is hiding something contraband.

Doors slam shut, the hollering of railway workers rings out, a long whistle resonates and then there is a hiss and the grinding of iron on iron. He cannot sleep after the policemen have left and the train shunts into motion again. Cannot take any pleasure in the momentous achievement that for the first time in his life he has entered a new country. He slides the carriage door open as quietly as he can and goes out into the corridor. He is thrown off balance by the swaying and jerking momentum of the train. A force more powerful than he is testing his strength to withstand it. The sharp smell of urine plunges him further down into his physicality when someone opens the door of the toilet.

He is back out in the corridor when darkness begins to lift off the land. He has the feeling of standing between two parallel worlds. Every detail that attracts his attention in the passing landscape evokes momentarily an alternate life which is quickly snatched away when the train moves on. He can't help thinking of the isolated farmhouses he sees as hiding places. When he eventually sees the sun rising in a new country he for the first time escapes his anxiety and settles wondrously into the moment.

There is a sense of disbelief and accomplishment when he steps out of the station and absorbs his first impressions of Paris. The foreignness of the atmosphere makes him feel weightless. All the newspapers and magazines in French in a kiosk as exotic as a wild animal in a zoo. He would like to share his excitement with Elisabetta. He needs to stop seeing Flora as an inadequate companion. They have a coffee and a brioche in a café opposite the Gare de Lyon. He opens up the map of Paris on the table. It seems to want him to form a new idea of himself. An adventurer, a pioneer. He tells Flora they will walk to Gare du Nord and shows her the route they will take. It's a long way. He is nervous of the metro. As if it might involve procedures he is unacquainted with and result in some loss of his dignity. He hates anything which risks reducing him to the uncertainties and dependencies of childhood. He is only twenty-one.

"I've never been on an underground train before," she complains.

"It'll do us good to walk and we'll see more of Paris this way."

He knows she becomes irritated with him during the endless walk across Paris and its wide chaotic dirty boulevards.

In Boulogne, the vast distance he has covered is a moving current in his blood, an inarticulate wonder in his mind. He feels dizzy with lightness as if he has shed weighty parts of himself. It is the closest he has ever felt to being someone else, someone not himself. They have time to kill before the boat arrives. They walk along the quayside, past the brightly painted hotels with fluttering flags and the cafés. The shriek of gulls is a circling presence in the glittering air. He watches the white ship steam in towards the idle cranes and the two black and white wooden piers.

"That must be our boat," he says.

"Marcello…"

She never calls him by his name. It sounds alien, exotic. It's the first time he has been made to think about his name. As if only now does it belong to him.

16

London

Marcello is manning a barrow in London's East End markets. He is selling cheap women's underwear manufactured by his father's cousin, Tony. There are three sizes, three colours and no refunds. His English is rudimentary but he has learned the phrases he needs to conduct sales. The decoding of strange words charges the most ordinary moments of the day with endeavour and mystery. It is sometimes like an adventure to seek a foothold in the world his interlocutors create with language. He has accustomed himself to the risqué jokes people make. Usually he doesn't understand the joke itself. He finds it difficult to find the breaks between the slurred quickfire words. The lewd twinkle in the eyes of the joker, especially if a woman, can heat his blood. The older women generally test the elastic. The younger women, as a rule, are more shy. As if to touch the knickers is to be seen wearing them.

As a newly arrived foreigner England holds mysteries as confusing to him as the rites of High Mass in a Catholic church. The complex nature of the monetary system perplexes him. Pounds, shillings and pence. He doesn't understand why there are three denominations. It seems unnecessarily complicated. The British, he learns, are less straightforward in many regards than Italians. The daily language is crammed with catchphrases of humble politeness which often contradict the behaviour of the speaker.

Polite words, he learns, are often used to express rudeness. He is more aware in London of life as a contest in which everyone is fighting to prevail. He thinks of Elisabetta to make the vast city less hostile. Sometimes the smell of turpentine and linseed is wafted over to him from the furniture stall nearby and he is lifted back to the shop in Venice for an aching moment. He returns home of an evening with the stink of rotting vegetables and cooking fat in his nostrils. In London he is made to feel he no longer belongs to an educated class, as if he has undergone another relegation in status.

He and Flora are living with his father's cousin and his wife in Whitechapel. They share an unheated attic room with a skylight. He is woken every morning by the scratching and squabbling of pigeons on the roof tiles. The room swarms with bugs and smells of the sulphur Tony's wife uses to kill them. The walls are painted a creamy white with traces of the brush hairs visible. The walk to the market where he works takes him past a brothel, three pubs, a workhouse, a fish and chip shop, a bathhouse, lines of grubby laundry and a synagogue. The pavement is sticky with spilled beer. This, he has learned, was Jack the Ripper territory. Tony takes pleasure in frightening Flora with details of the murders. Marcello has to later assure her that the murders occurred fifty years ago and that even if Jack the Ripper is still alive he would be, at the very least, over seventy years of age.

Tony Dixon rents a workshop where he employs three women to make his cheap brand of women's underwear. It was the mass production of rayon, half the price of silks and satin, which changed Tony's fortunes. It's a story he likes to tell. He takes credit for identifying the desire of working girls for more exotic underclothes than were previously available to them.

"A stylish pair of knickers makes a girl feel more attractive. Isn't that true, Flora?"

Flora, who Tony has forced to show him all her Italian underwear, blushes.

"Before I came along women were still forced to wear

passion-killers. You don't know what passion-killers are, do you Marcello? Explain to him what passion-killers are, dear."

His wife does as she's told. Tony though soon takes over the narrative. Marcello listens closely. There is an exciting sense of accomplishment to be gained from extending his vocabulary. Any subject of conversation, no matter how tedious, is of interest when you're learning a new language. It pitches concentration in the everyday world on a higher key. He rediscovers how much vivacity there is in the act of learning.

He doesn't like the way his father's cousin treats his wife. Everything is always her fault. If Tony can't find his slippers or the newspaper she is to blame. If a light bulb dies or there isn't enough hot water she is to blame. He is meticulously critical of her ironing, always finding fault with the creases. Quick to subject the food she serves up to criticism. Marcello suspects he has hit her more than once. It's evident in the way she timidly cowers before him. She too is Jewish, of east European heritage and speaks with an accent that he mocks. Tony is the son of his father's sister. He was born in England. It worries Marcello that the same blood runs in this man's veins as in his own. As if he might too have a buried propensity to bully those weaker than himself. It's depressing to realise we are a conglomeration of traits loaned out in different packages from generation to generation.

Tony jokes he would enjoy a one-on-one boxing match with Hitler. He jumps out of his cherished armchair and shadow boxes on the rug. After a few minutes he stands with his hands on his hips looking down at his imaginary floored opponent and counts to ten.

The surface Marcello's life has formed would have been unimaginable a year ago. The moonlight of Venice could not seem further away. It feels belittling how conclusively he has traded one way of life for another. As if he has been born merely to make up the numbers. It's often in the first drag of a cigarette that he retrieves himself, emerges as himself again from a period of alienation. Anything that re-establishes a connection between his present self and the past he cherishes. His parents send him and Flora postcards. There is little space for them to write on because *vinceremo* ('we will win') is printed on the back of the cards and it is forbidden to write over the fascist slogan. When he writes to his parents he sees all the reflected vibrating lights on the Grand Canal. He can feel on the heels and soles of his feet for a moment the responsive kinship he shared with his boat. The muscles in his arms remember the working of the *sandolo*'s oar. He hears the slow plash of the oar in the water. Venice, especially when he lies in the dark, becomes like a piece of music he has transcribed and can play to himself.

In a basket outside a book shop in the Charing Cross Road he discovers one of the books Giulia asked him to find for her – the Journal of Katherine Mansfield. For a moment it's as if Giulia has been returned to life and he will hurry home to present her with the gift he has found for her. He buys it and reads it avidly. It is lively with lived life and helps to provide him with a key to understanding many of the ciphers of the English language. Katherine Mansfield reminds him of Giulia. Perhaps because her life too will be tragically shortened before she reaches the height of her powers. She helps him to see again Giulia's living hands. How they did up the buttons of her coat, how they glided over the keys of the piano, how they took out pins from her hair.

He never quite feels comfortable handling women's underwear all day. He writes this in a letter to Massimo and then agonises over whether or not to tell Elisabetta what he does for a living. On the one hand it might be a humiliating picture of himself he is giving her; on the other, he imagines it will make her laugh. And there's an erotic undertone in the image which he likes. As if it might lead her to form a picture of him and her own underwear in the same frame. When writing to her he is forever censoring himself. It frustrates him that he cannot talk to her in person with the freedom he talks to her in his mind. He thinks how much more exciting life might be if we didn't feel constrained to keep so much of ourselves secret. He writes of the discoveries he has made about himself through learning a new language. Speaking English makes him feel more withheld within himself. *I've become a bare branched tree. No trace of the leaves and flowers I produce in Italian*, he writes. He wants to give her the impression his experiences have made him more sophisticated. He tells her about the novelty of the food he eats. Cornflakes, porridge, baked beans, tapioca, marmite, tinned salmon and spam. And how much he misses pasta and strong Italian coffee and even polenta. When he holds the finished letter he has written her his self-esteem seems no less flimsy than the sheet of thin paper with his handwriting on it. The moment he slips the envelope with its exotic stamp through the mouth of the red post box he feels vulnerable and light on his feet. The hope of a reply keeps him in a state of impatient expectation. He begins every new day with a disappointment when there is no letter from her on the brown wire mat. He spends the rest of the day wishing away the hours, eager for tomorrow when the postman will arrive again. He is still yet to see what her handwriting looks like.

On his days off he often catches a bus with Flora and together they explore London. It is a novelty to sit on the upstairs deck of a red bus. He enjoys walking in Regent's Park. It is an escape from the hurry and noise of London. He hires a boat and rows Flora out onto the lake. With water beneath him, it's the closest he has felt to Venice since arriving in London.

"*Cosa pensi…*"

"Speak in English," he tells her.

"What you think Mum glend Dad do at this moment?"

"Perhaps they're asking what we are doing at this moment," he says. He is pleased with his growing mastery of the English language though he doesn't like the sound of his accent. There is no music in it.

"When I speak English," she says in Italian, "I don't feel like I have a personality. Do you think I have a personality?"

"Of course you do."

"Describe it."

"I don't know. You're reserved, secretive."

"You see. I'm boring. I used to be jealous of all the attention Giulia attracted. I still think it should have been me who died."

He stops rowing for a moment. Looks across at her, deep into her dark eyes. "You have to stop thinking that."

"I hope there is a war. It'd bring some excitement. I hate my life here. Do you know what sums it up for me? Marmite. How do people eat that disgusting stuff? It's like eating axel grease."

"I quite like it. On toast."

They are both disappointed to learn most of the animals at the zoo have been moved elsewhere. There are only a few seals, some parrots, a cage of forlorn monkeys. They share a bag of peanuts with some of the animals. Most of the paintings in the art galleries have been relocated too.

Flora surprises him when she asks him to accompany her to a synagogue. There are many in the area where they live. She reads books about their religion. She has covered the small mirror in their room with a black shawl. "It's for Giulia," she tells him. "I know shiva is supposed to be respected the seven days after a death but we never did it for Giulia at the time so I want to do it now."

He is glad Flora seems to have made the peace with her memory of Giulia. He is also glad she has formed a close bond with the family dog. The small black mongrel sleeps at the foot of her bed and she takes it out for walks. The animal livens her up as little else does.

All the talk is of war. BBC bulletins are greatly anticipated. The nightly gathering around the wireless. Following instructions in a manual he and Tony create a gas-proof room of the kitchen. Marcello goes with Flora to the local town hall to collect their gas masks. They each carry home the cardboard box with the string handle. The sight and touch of the rubber mask fills him with horror, the nightmarish experience it augurs. That there is a need in the world for such a sinister ugly thing strikes him as a damning indictment of the human race. When he tries it on he is reminded of Giulia and her struggles to catch her breath. With the mask clamped to his face, his head fills with the sound of his own blood. Flora, on the other hand, seems to enjoy the experience.

The presence of sandbags becomes more noticeable every day, stacked up high against the entrances to public buildings. Anti-aircraft gun emplacements begin appearing in the parks and by the river. The number of men and women in uniform increases too. After the non-aggression pact between Germany and Russia is announced queues form outside grocery shops. It is rumoured people are hoarding food, especially tea and sugar and tins of soup. There are more arguments in the streets. Barrage balloons float over the cityscape and at night look like silhouettes of prehistoric beasts in the sky.

Then arrives the day the evacuation of children from cities is ordered and the blackout is enforced. The streets are busy and tense with children being marshalled to stations. Marcello has never seen so many people carrying suitcases. It's like the entire population of the city is on the move. He helps Tony seal the windows. Everyone agrees it's a government measure which signifies war is inevitable and imminent. At night the streets outside are eerily silent.

The day Great Britain declares war on Germany is an ordinary day, bright with sunshine, and yet unlike any other day of his life. There is an immediate felt shift in the nature of reality as if everything loses some of its solidity. He knows a foreboding deep in his being and his thoughts are as though bordered with a black outline. He stands at his barrow as the news is conveyed from one person to another in the market. German bombs are expected at any moment. The first effect of the news is to make people friendlier, more openly talkative. Less than an hour after the declaration is announced the air raid alarm sounds. It is shocking how much strength it sucks from his body. Fear becomes like part of the weather, palpable on the air. It's the expectation of poisonous gas that terrifies everyone. Already people around him are putting on gas marks. As he is about to make his way to the nearest building with a basement he sees a man stealing tins of golden syrup from the abandoned barrow of his neighbour Tom.

"Stop that!" he says. Dismayed by how feeble his command sounds to his own ears.

The man, furtive and shifty, stares at him for a moment. He is short and stocky with flushed cheeks. "Who are you to tell me what to do? You're a bloody foreigner anyway. Fuck off back to your own country."

For a moment Marcello believes he is about to have his first fist fight since school days. It's a fight he quickly calculates in which he will probably come off worse. But with a leisurely gait the man takes to his heels with his booty. And he is enormously relieved. His body still thumping with adrenalin.

In the following days the streets are crowded with servicemen with their kit bags. The queues outside every food shop grow longer. Pedestrians walk with a more hurried step. There is a woman shopping at the market who wears her gas mask. Everyone looks up at the sky more often. The sky has become what everyone most fears now. Suspense every time the looped air raid siren sounds takes the form of a dry gummy taste in the mouth, a prickling of the tender regions of skin as of the chafing of itchy clothes. There are several air raid alarms in the following days. Every time he feels a sharp jerk in his body like the pull of invisible strings. In the evenings everyone in the three-storey building traipses down into the damp basement. Here he is forced to become physically intimate with strangers. A thigh pressed against his thigh; an arm squeezed against his arm. The physicality of life has become more emphasised since the declaration of war. He has trained his face to assume a nonchalant expression, as if fear is unmanly. He pictures his face as still and quietly thoughtful. He has learned hiding fear is like a childhood game. The more wholeheartedly you pretend the more you believe in the pretence. But down in the basement, a sleeping serpent of dread coiled up in his stomach, he understands what it means to be helplessly susceptible to the vagaries of chance. His life feels like a baby in his arms he has to protect from all the dangers of the world. The low growl of the bombers is always a whisper away from materialising from a fear to a fact. He feels he has to be stronger than he feels for Flora's benefit. Except Flora has repeated her idea that war excites her. That she is bored with her life in London.

When they return to the living room Tony picks up his newspaper again. "It says here it might be kinder to destroy all family pets," he says. He looks pointedly across at Flora on the sofa who is stroking the dog curled up on her lap. "Poor old Rags, eh? Looks like he's going to be the first casualty of this war. I'll have to buy myself one of those bolt pistols I've seen advertised."

"You're no better than a Nazi," says Flora. She gets to her feet with the dog in her arms and leaves the room.

"Hey, I was joking, Flora," he calls out, grinning at Marcello.

17

Some of the boys who work at the market have been conscripted and complain bitterly. There is little patriotic spirit in evidence. Many of the older men have joined the ARP. Marcello has not been called up. He doesn't know why. He assumes it's because he is still officially listed as an alien. He feels though he ought to be doing something. Ought to be wearing a uniform of some description. He wants to make a show of his disgust for Hitler and the Nazis and for Mussolini and the fascists.

The post of the local ARP group is in a disused brewery not far from his home. A sickly smell of stale beer clings to its floors. Marcello has never once got drunk in his life. Three men are playing darts when he arrives. He has never played darts in his life. He has to fight down the sensation that he is still at heart a child. Unequipped to being of much use to anyone. A sensation not helped by a man called Alf who is rudely dismissive of him.

"Another bloody foreigner. How do we know you're not a spy? Tell me that."

"He's the lad that sells women's drawers at the market."

There follows a series of jokes he doesn't understand. His ignorance makes him feel still more hotly and conspicuously out of his element. He wishes he never came. He considers how he might make a dignified exit. Then a young black man walks over to his side.

"Take no notice of him. He gave me the same warm welcome. Alf gets all his ideas from the *Daily Express*."

Marcello notices there are tiny green flecks in his brown eyes.

Obi, he learns, is from Nigeria. He's studying law in London. He's the first black person Marcello has ever spoken to. There's a shine, a humorous light in Obi's eyes which immediately makes Marcello want to become his friend. He admires his self-possession, the easy confident way he brushes aside Alf's hostility as if the man's ideas are of no more consequence than a mosquito. There is nothing boastful about Obi. All the boys who work at the market do little else but posture and preen – how many girls they've had, how many fights they've won, how drunk they got. Their manner always boisterous, their voices always raised, needy with the determination to proclaim themselves unignorably alive. It's largely because of Obi that he returns to the disused brewery the next evening and begins his training as an air raid warden.

Marcello gradually learns by mimicry to fit in. He identifies everything that makes him stand out as different and sets about hiding it from public view. He is given a tin helmet. This helps him feel he belongs, that he is assimilated into the group. There are no military procedures, no saluting, no uniform. One of the first things he has to do for his training is acquaint himself with the odour of the poisonous gases the Germans might use. His instructor heats up little glass vials over a bunsen burner until they break. The first contains mustard gas which smells enough like garlic to transport him for a bittersweet moment into the kitchen of his home in Venice; then there is a gas called phosgene, a deadly choking gas, which with its stink of rotting vegetables reminds him of the market; then finally the geranium smell of lewisite. He is taught which ointments to apply to the burns and sores and irritants of the eyes each gas will inflict. He is told how to enter a damaged building and what duties he will be expected to perform. He is told he must remain calm and inspire confidence when directing the public to shelters during a raid. He learns how to put out an incendiary bomb. He learns how to operate a stirrup hand pump. He is told he is expected to assist with casualties and damage when bombs drop. He is given the operations and training manual; he has to learn every topographical and utilitarian detail of the sector. He likes the stance of defiance he finds among these men. He likes it they scorn and mock Hitler and the Nazis. It restores some of his faith in humanity. It's the attitude his own countrymen should have adopted and had they done so he would still be with his mother and father and have the opportunity of making Elisabetta smile at least once a week.

For a while he is nervous with Obi when they are alone together. He is conscious of trying too hard to make himself sympathetic. He realises he is making an effort to let Obi know the colour of his skin is an irrelevance to him. Which, ironically, he realises, means it isn't. He finds it easier to understand Obi than most Londoners. His enunciation is clearer. Alf Barton continues his baiting behaviour. He jumps on every mistake Marcello makes with the language. He watches for any sign of unmanliness in Marcello and berates him for it. When he talks he uses his rolled-up copy of the *Daily Express* as a kind of baton. He is unkind to the two female members of the group as well. "A woman's place is in the home." He recites this platitude as doggedly as he stands to attention whenever the national anthem is played on the radio.

One night Marcello accompanies Obi in the ARP's old laundry van. They are both sucking on a peardrop. Obi is learning to drive through their designated sector in the dark without headlights. The kerbs and tree trunks have a painted white stripe which imparts a faint glow.

"I had to drive wearing a gas mask one time. Another part of the training. The mask steamed up with condensation and I couldn't see anything."

Marcello is impressed that Obi can see into and negotiate the billowing wall of darkness.

"I'd like to learn to drive," he says.

"You should. Especially at a time like this it feels good to be in control of something. I'll teach you. It's easy."

Driving through the almost deserted streets Marcello experiences a sense of aristocratic privilege. London in the blackout is like the beginning of a fictional world. At one point, over in the West End, searchlights swivel up into the darkness, lighting the undersides of the clouds and the barrage balloons and their network of cables. It's a moment of beauty which makes him remember how many such moments Venice grants almost every day. Obi, meanwhile, has taken it upon himself to discuss politics.

"As I see it, there are too many people in the world who believe in slavery as a model of social order. Even many people who are effectively slaves themselves believe in it. Like Alf. That's the sad part. People need better educating. We can't go on living in a world where fictions of racial imparity determine social policy. Hopefully, if nothing else, this will be a war which will put an end to these elite self-serving caste systems."

"I hope so. The Nazis are terrifying. I remember when Hitler came to Venice. There were Nazi flags hanging from all the palaces along the Grand Canal. The Nazis managed to make even Venice look ugly."

"You must miss Venice. Is it as beautiful as they say?"

"Often it's like my body is here and my mind is there."

"I can understand that. I miss my mother and my sisters. We lose things when we leave our native country. A sense of connection. Without that life can be like dancing without knowing the steps. We're a pair of castaways here."

"My older sister died just before I came to London."

Obi takes his hand off the steering wheel and touches Marcello's arm for an instant. It's the first time he has brought up Giulia's death to arouse sympathy, as a kind of accomplishment to make himself more interesting. He derives pleasure from Obi's empathy but he also feels a troubling urge to apologise to Giulia.

"I hope to go to Venice one day."

"You must. You can stay with my family and I'll take you out in our boat."

The war though has made Venice as remote as the dark side of the moon.

He is glad to see Obi is for the most part a popular figure in the neighbourhood. His ready smile and kindliness is appreciated. It's like people believe his exoticism is some kind of totem of good augury, as if he has magic protective powers. Sometimes, at night when on patrol and they have to ring the bell of a building where a light can be seen, he shines his torch up at his smiling black face with the pearly white teeth when the door is opened.

"Everyone loves you. Everyone except Alf anyway. Alf was born in the wrong country. He'd be much happier as a Nazi."

"They wouldn't be so accommodating if I wanted to marry their daughter."

"I found out what that feels like when the racial laws came into force in Italy."

"Was there a girl? A girl you can't quite wash off your skin?"

Obi's smile often has an enlivening effect on Marcello, like the clap of hands.

The path to Elisabetta is as if sheeted in ice on which he has difficulty keeping his footing. He would like to tell Obi this but his command of the language isn't up to it. Probably a good thing as even in Italian it sounds like a pompous remark.

"Not really," he says. "What about you?"

"Too busy with my studies."

Marcello invites Obi home to tea. Obi is a towering presence, over six feet tall. Tony is uncomfortable around him, perhaps even frightened, a nervous grin pasted to his face. He sees Flora blushes every time Obi singles her out for attention. It's obvious Flora likes him. For a moment he becomes his father. Overly protective, censorious. He knows his father would disapprove of Obi as a suitor for Flora. And it would largely be on the grounds of race. In which case Mussolini and Hitler serve him right. It becomes important to him to show he is different to his father. Even if Flora is only seventeen. *If they like each other so be it, I will not stand in the way …*

18

"You're a natural at handling a woman's knickers. Do you think I'd look nice in these?" She holds up a pair of cream coloured camiknickers and pouts at Marcello and then laughs. "You must spend all day imagining the women wearing the underclothes they look at. Unless they're old and wrinkled like her over there. There's no point in being shy, you know. Not with the way things are going. You've got the wrists of a ten year old boy." She takes his hand and circles his wrist with her thumb and forefinger. "Where are you from anyway? With that accent of yours."

"Italy. Venice."

"The most romantic city in the world. Say something romantic to me in Italian."

He looks deep into her eyes for a moment. She's the first young girl who has shown any interest in him since he arrived in London. Objectively, she's not very attractive. She's short and has wide hips and thick arms. What's compelling about her, he realises, is the force of attraction she evidently feels for him. It's a bristling magnetic energy which has the power to sweep aside misgivings. But it makes it hard for him to see her as more than the promise of a moment's pleasure.

"Cat got your tongue?"

"What does that mean?"

"You need someone to give you English lessons."

"Are you offering?"

"I might be. What will you give in return? I'm learning first aid at the moment. You could pretend to be my patient and I'd

121

apply the necessary ointments and bandages. Think about it. See you around."

She walks off leaving him with a broad grin on his face. Tom, his neighbour at the market, ambles over to him.

"I'd be careful with that one. You know who she is?"

Marcello shakes his head.

"That's Beth. Alf Barton's daughter."

This news makes her more attractive to Marcello. Alf's determination to make his life a misery is a cruelty that bewilders Marcello. He has tried to win over the older man with politeness and the occasional kindness. He has shown him respect and bitten his tongue at every insult. But Alf appears insensitive to everything about him except for the fact that he wasn't born in England which for him is reason enough to hold him in contempt. To be disliked for being Italian when Italy has renounced him as an Italian is another on the list of life's grotesque ironies.

He keeps an eye open for Beth. It introduces a note of alerted expectation into the drudgery of life at the market barrow, like a song he sings to himself. He tells himself it's wrong to use his daughter to pay Alf back. But he keeps thinking of how available she made herself appear, how pressingly and generously she brought her sexuality up onto the surface of her body as if it was a gift she was willing to give him. It's a source of shame and waste to him that he is twenty-one and has still never known the sensation of the weight of a woman's breasts in his cupped hands.

The next time she appears in the market he invites her out for a walk. They meet outside St Paul's after dinner. Alf, he knows, is on duty roof watching in Canon Street.

He is carrying a small torch to light their path through the blackout. The thin shaft of light into which they walk heightens the intimacy of the moment. Before they have walked a hundred yards though the battery stutters and dies.

"You won't find a new battery for that. I tried to find a battery for my dad's torch the other day. Sold out everywhere. Like candles."

"I work with your dad. He doesn't like me."

"I wouldn't worry about it. He doesn't like anyone. Except the King and Winston Churchill. I don't think he even likes the King very much. He makes fun of his stutter. He thinks he stutters because he's effeminate."

They now keep bumping into each other in the billowing darkness. He is sure she uses the darkness as an excuse to put her hands on him. And each time she touches him the exciting heat of her body insinuates itself into his body.

"Are you going to tell him about me?"

"I might do. If I want to annoy him."

"I can't imagine that's very difficult. Annoyance seems like his favourite emotion."

"Stop being rude about my dad."

"What's he like at home?"

"He likes laying down the law and he especially likes punishing me and my mum. It makes him feel important, like he's the head of a government. He always wanted to work in a bank. He hates working at the docks."

At the riverside he can barely make out the outline of Tower Bridge. The smell of the river's effluent is rich in his nostrils. It provides the motivation to kiss her. Initially a clumsy act on his part because, in the thick darkness, he finds himself pressing his lips to her ear instead of her mouth. However, she seems to like this and when his mouth finds her lips he has more confidence in what he is doing. Her body gives off a private smell.

The next evening at the disused brewery Alf is carrying a water bucket when their eyes meet.

"If you go near my daughter again I'll kill you with my bare hands."

19

Belgium has surrendered to the Germans. France has virtually fallen. The miracle at Dunkirk takes place. Winston Churchill gives his "We will never surrender" speech.

As they stand around the wireless Marcello can't help marvelling at the magic of the invisible radio waves which bring information from other parts of the world into their home. He wonders what other miracles might be discovered in the future. Except he has a foreboding that his future has been foreshortened by the news he is listening to.

Then Mussolini finally decides to join the war. The day after Italy declares war on Great Britain, Marcello is arrested. Two police officers arrive at the apartment at eleven in the evening. He is made to feel all the more vulnerable because he is barefoot and wearing striped pyjamas when they enter his and Flora's room. The dog jumps down from Flora's bed and wags it tail while sniffing the boots of the two officers. His air-raid warden's helmet counts for nothing. The two officers are not unkind. One of them stays in the room while he dresses. He tries not to let the fear on Flora's face infect him.

The short trip in the police car through the blacked-out streets of Whitechapel is another experience which makes him feel like he is in someone else's story, not his own. He plays with his hands in his lap. The limit of his autonomy. He is fingerprinted and escorted into a small white cell. Before an hour has passed the harsh light seems to burn through his skin, as if it is slowly dissolving his physicality. It is so quiet he feels he has been abandoned, as if the world has no further use of him. The experience of solitary confinement moves him ever closer to some dangerous edge in his mind. He fears he is losing the distinctions of a polite sophisticated young man. That he might become a feral creature if he has to stay in this cell much longer.

The next day Eugenio joins him in the cell. Eugenio is a middle-aged man with thinning brown hair and a neat moustache who owns an Italian restaurant in Soho. He talks constantly of his two adolescent girls. There is a rarely absent startled look in his brown eyes. He looks through Marcello when he talks. Marcello's inclination, a facet of his upbringing, is to put his own personality at the service of the older man's authority. Except he continually finds himself questioning Eugenio's wisdom, the hesitant construction of his speech. Thinking of his father, he wonders if all men are only ever one setback away from being returned to the insecurities of boyhood.

After three days spent alone with him, Marcello comes to feel he knows Eugenio as well as he has ever known anyone. He learns his physical gestures, his smells, his vanities and his fears. And yet he can see no purpose or sense in this intimacy, this consuming occupancy of Eugenio in his mind. Circumstance has entrusted them to each other. War, it seems, means chance and not choice has become the governing force of life. As if life now might consist of fragmented inconsequential narratives, the replacing of friends and family with strangers as confidantes, the disappearance of old reaffirming habits and the arrival of alien discordant new ones. It's like every new day he has to learn to become himself anew. He no longer has a ready reply to the questions he poses himself. It feels all wrong for him to be here, like a mistake he ought to be able to rub out with his thumb. And yet he feels the experience entering deep into him, becoming an irrevocable part of him.

He tells Eugenio this.

"Before you're much older every change you detect in yourself will be a change for the worse. How old are you anyway?"

"Twenty-one."

"I tried to plan everything in my life. To make sure I was never taken by surprise. Life has made a fool of me." Eugenio constantly reaches down to his shoes as if to tighten the laces, forgetting the laces have been taken away.

Marcello thinks constantly of the little value he has given to his life. Of how much time he has wasted, of how many opportunities he has failed to grasp. He tells himself things could be worse. He imagines himself as an old man when perhaps he might look back on his present unhappiness with affection, with a longing to return here even.

They are brought a meal twice a day. A meal he has to force himself to eat.

"One thing I've learned about the British, they might have colonised half the world but they don't know the first thing about cuisine," says Eugenio, making another disgusted face at the contents of his plate.

The unidentifiable jellied meat sits heavily in his stomach. He is unable to rid his mouth of the sickening taste of the boiled vegetables. The next day he barely eats any of the gruel. His stomach tightens around its emptiness at night.

He wishes he had a book to read. Another voice to communicate with, another world in which to dwell. Books can open up the heart and quicken forth its gifts of imagination. There might be in the story a girl holding up her skirt and high stepping over the foaming waves or a velvety black cat tiptoeing along a broken wall – images that would enable him to escape these four imprisoning walls. The boredom becomes painful, produces inside him a scream which craves to be let loose into the world. The sharpness of his thoughts keeps him awake. He feels his intelligence and his spirit have never been so intensely engaged and at the same time so powerless.

More than once the air raid alarm sounds but no one comes to escort him and Eugenio to a shelter. He looks up at the high barred window wondering what is happening out in the world.

There is some relief when they are told they are to be moved. He and Eugenio are driven in the back of a police van to a disused warehouse. Here there are hundreds of other men of Italian heritage. There are stories of Italian shops being smashed up and street fights. There isn't much love in the warehouse for the British. There is a heated argument about what language they should speak. A man wearing a black felt hat and leather gloves turns to Marcello and tells him he can't speak a word of Italian. Marcello feels like life is shouting at him, a constant raucous barking in his head from which there is no escaping. He has to sleep on the floor. There is no bedding. His hands, begrimed, cracked with sores, look less and less like his own hands. He wonders if his face is suffering the same fate.

At night, amidst the groaning and wheezing of all the men around him, he shuts his eyes tight and pictures himself in his *sandolo* on Venice's waterways. He sees sunlight passing through prisms of colour. A catch of wind quickens the play of lights on the water. Every night he takes a different route, recalling in as much detail as he can every oar stroke of his progress. The first night he travels the length of the Grand Canal. He recalls the subtleties in the cadence of his boat of the changing tides. Sights and smells taken for granted leap up into renewed significance. The Rialto fish market and the hovering squawking gulls; the shimmering reflected lights on the underside of the Rialto Bridge; the palaces disappearing down beneath the surface of the water; the clear chime of church bell answering church bell across the water; the setting sun, burning on the level of the water, blazing crimson.

Subsequent nights he conjures in his imagination the smaller canals. He sees detail mirrored in the water which has always seemed unworthy of his attention. The silvery traces on the walls, like mother-of-pearl, left by salt and damp. Seaweed washed up on the steps and fretted by the sluggish rise and fall of the water. The smell of algae returns briefly to his nostrils. The taste of salt on his wrists. He punts his boat from one landing stage to another mesmerising himself with the outgoing ripples he makes with his oar. Out on remote parts of the lagoon he is able to imagine the first settlers, tired, hungry and frightened exiles escaping marauding barbarians. Venice began its existence as a refuge, a remote haven for the uprooted and persecuted, a community of homes of wood, wattle and reed on mudflats, on salt marsh and swamp. It is no less a remote haven, a refuge in his mind. He feels in every fibre of his being that Venice is still where he belongs, where he should be in these times of war.

His wish is granted the next day. As if his will still has some power to shape events in his life. There is great excitement when it is announced that all but a few individuals classified as a high security risk are to be given a choice – either they can be repatriated along with their families or else they will be deported to Canada as prisoners of war. Everyone heatedly discusses the options, reanimated by the restitution of choice. He doesn't have to give any thought to his decision though he does imagine himself in Canada for a moment. It's like imagining himself on the moon. It pains him that he will have to leave Flora alone. It seems he is fated to continually betray his younger sister. Flora, for unknown bureaucratic reasons, is exempt from this new law regarding Italian nationals. Eugenio decides to go with his family to Canada.

He is sent home and given two hours to pack. His possessions heaped together seem a paltry sad achievement. He has so little to show for his life. He wants to say goodbye to Obi but there is not enough time. He inscribes his copy of *Great Expectations* with a dedication to him. "I hope to always be your friend." He hands it to Flora to give to him.

"Make sure you tell him that I didn't have time to see him," he tells her. She blushes when he says Obi's name. Then he is standing on the doorstep, taking leave of another sister who he feels he might never see again. When he boards the train for Glasgow he does not know the ship carrying Eugenio, his family and several hundred other Italian and German nationals to Canada, the

Arandora Star, will be sunk by a German submarine and there will be few survivors. He will discover this when he is back in Venice and Mussolini's propaganda will claim it was the British that sunk their own ship.

20

Venice 1940

When she catches sight of Marcello there is a double take in her vision as if he is someone famous she can't quite believe has transitioned from the world of fantasy into her sightline. There is a change in him. She notices it immediately. As if midnight has entered his eyes. She is overly conscious of the soles of her feet as she walks towards the counter as if balancing on a wall.

"You're back," she says.

He smiles, his hair unruly over his eyes. "You're looking well," he says.

She looks down at her pistachio green dress. "How was it in London?"

"Didn't you get my letters?"

"You were selling women's underclothes."

"Why didn't you write back?"

"I tried to. Everything I wrote seemed so dull. And then no longer true the next morning. Like I was misrepresenting myself. Don't forget I've been trained to aspire to accuracy."

"So either you need to find more confidence in yourself or else you're vain about how interesting you are behind an inability to express it."

Her hands look for something to crumple up. That he can't see it's the former that is true annoys her. Conversations with Marcello never take the shape she intends for them. It's like he nudges her off the paths she has beaten for herself. There was a night she spent three hours trying to write him a letter. Not that she would ever tell him this. It became for her a trial of second guessing the meaning he might read into her words. She decided to send him a watercolour sketch of the Grand Canal instead but never got round to painting it.

Her father has invited Luigi Volpato to dinner another three times. His power has increased since Italy joined the war. Her father is obsessively nervous that he will be called to the war in some guise and will have to break his cherished routine of painting six hours every day. She has the suspicion he deliberately strains to make himself appear older in public to deflect imagined criticism of not wearing a uniform. He has bought himself an elegant walking stick which he uses when they go to the bar for a coffee break. She has a foreboding it will only be a matter of time before Volpato asks her father for her hand. And that her father will agree to it.

"I spent several days in prison in London," says Marcello. There is a measure of pride in his expression, as if he now believes himself to possess a wisdom that runs deeper than anything available to her. She looks at him closely while listening to him explain how he would now be dead had he made the wrong choice and opted for Canada instead of returning to Italy. She sees kindness and imagination in his eyes, but also a sulky critical propensity which only increases her instinct to defend herself. If only there were a more direct force in him, a force capable of ripping through her defences with the violence of the pounding of the surf on the Lido on a stormy night. She can detect no trace of this kindling force in him.

The pink, white and yellow ochre marble palaces on either side of the canal and the watery light send that sweep of surprise through him which occurs when we see something beautiful for the first time. He takes a deep breath, wanting the beauty of the surroundings to sing through him for a moment. He marvels how so familiar a sight can appear so radiantly virginal. It fills his body as a spectacle. Cleanses his mind. Makes him yearn to create something worthy of his life.

When he arrived back in Venice it was as if he had lost all track of time. Sometimes it felt like he had only been away for a few days, other times that it was a homecoming after years of exile. He was taken aback by how much his father has aged. His hair has thinned and receded. The grooves bracketing his mouth deepened. Even the tone of his voice has changed. There is no longer ever a note of mischievous wit in it. Every night Father climbs onto a chair to fix the black material to the tiny nails he has hammered into the window frames. He looks heartbreakingly frail when he balances unsteadily on the chair. The framed photographs of Giulia are still arranged on the mantelpiece and the piano in the sitting room.

Takings in the shop have dramatically fallen. The things customers want, like paper, like pencils, like oils and varnishes and spirits are harder to obtain. There is talk of having to sell the shop. Marcello has discovered his mother's guilty secret. Without telling Father, she has been working for a Jewish aid organisation called Delasum. Because she can speak German she is sent letters from the many Jewish refugees entering Italy from Germany and eastern Europe to translate. These letters upset her. Sometimes she reads them to Marcello. Stories of heartbreak and deprivation which sometimes come vividly to life in the detail. Mother has a notebook in which she writes down the sums of money collected from fellow Venetian Jews and sent to these refugees.

"Every act of kindness in the world is now a political act of resistance," she said.

He punts his boat towards Santa Maria della Salute. Sees in his mind's eye Massimo making the sign of the cross. The deep and invisible current he rides like an extension of the momentum of his own blood. Then he is out onto the choppy tide of the lagoon. He sometimes finds himself wishing he was under observation when he is aware of being a focal point in a moment of beauty. He fantasises for a moment that Elisabetta or Obi is able to see him and the romantic figure he cuts standing at the stern of his boat. It's an image that evokes, he believes, all the loneliness of his life.

He looks over at the new air raid shelters built on Riva degli Schiavoni – long concrete mounds like ant hills. Already the war has brought forth ugliness. There are more flags on display everywhere. Twice he has seen graffiti scrawled on walls referring to Jews as spies. Both times the force of the hurt he suffered burned deep into his being. Men in uniform, men carrying weapons walk the streets with an air of believing they are taller than they are. Marcello in his civilian clothes is looked at as though he is untrustworthy, a traitor to the cause. He sometimes has the impression they would like to humiliate and hurt him. He is made to feel he needs to be more outwardly masculine.

The boat rocks on the high tide in the glittering hot July sunshine. The demand made of the muscles in his legs increases. His whole body is engaged. He is a little out of practice and once or twice struggles to keep his balance. The sea around the boat becomes clearer. The underwater kingdom a mesmerising spectacle.

The return to the cloistered cemetery makes his experience in London seem like a dream that has seeped into his waking life. He walks through this world of birdsong, loosened earth and flowering roses. He enjoys the sound of the gravel beneath his feet. It makes him feel more vivid to himself, more consequential. The absence of men in uniform allows him to think and feel with more freedom. In the city everyone seems to want more than ever to crowd together. He would like to spend all his time entirely alone for the foreseeable future. He envies the birds with their nests high in the trees. He finds a stone that feels snug in his palm and places it on Giulia's grave.

Sitting cross-legged among the gravestones he snaps off a handful of grass to feel the sap on his fingers. He watches a white butterfly perform a dance of exaltation in the air. It brings wonder to the moment. And an incitement to feel glad to be alive. Then he experiences for a moment a spectre of the loneliness Giulia must have felt when she was alone in bed at night towards the end. He thinks of the mystery of all the things she kept to herself. Mostly he imagines these would have been things about herself that embarrassed her. He too has secrets which, if known, would make people think less of him. He wonders what secrets Elisabetta might harbour of a shameful nature. It is always the thought of her he turns to when he wants to escape the oppression of the moment. He noticed that her eyes lingered on him longer, more attentively when they met. Her manner though was offhand as if possesses no sexuality for her. The paradox baffles him. Sometimes he wonders what he might do differently. Other times he thinks maybe it's just the fantasy of her he wants.

He soon feels guilty thinking of Elisabetta by the side of Giulia's grave. "The Germans are getting ever closer," he tells his dead sister, sitting on the grass and twirling his hat in his hand. There is a map of Europe on the front page of the newspapers every day with the territories occupied by the Nazis in black and the rest in white. He thinks back to the iron table outside the café in Paris. German soldiers might be sitting at that table now. Nazi tanks are rolling down roads throughout Europe. There are some Venetians who are impatient for the Germans to land in England. They believe coffee will become freely available again when Hitler shares some of England's colonies with Mussolini.

There is an air raid warning that night. There have been many apparently. Always false alarms and always at inconvenient times when people are dressed for bed. Such is the case tonight. He goes down into the basement with his mother and father. The neighbours, mostly in dressing gowns, are friendly. There is an air of solidarity. A woman passes around a bowl of cherries. No prejudice or animosity towards them, though when one woman says to his mother, "If only all Jews were like you and your family" he feels his hackles rise. Earlier in the week there was an article in *Il Gazzetino* about the perfidy of the Jews. It never stops bewildering him that he is seen by his fellow countrymen as someone of exotic and distasteful origins. Perhaps for the first time in his life he understands why for the majority of the human race respectability is an ideal of more import than love or kindness.

Everyone listens out for the sound of bombs. But the only sound from beyond the walls is the gentle slopping of the tide. When no torches are lit and it is dark he finds he's able to give names to some of the voices he hears except the personality of the speaker seems to undergo an alteration without the visibility of the face. He wonders about his own voice. What it says about him. He speaks aloud into the darkness, trying to catch some mystery about himself in the sound of his voice.

A few nights later the sound of distant bombs can be heard. The heavy industry in Marghera is the target. He stands on the balcony watching the waltzing prongs of searchlights light the undersides of clouds.

22

A madman is shouting in the middle of Piazza San Marco. There's something about the force of his wildness that makes the civil behaviour of every onlooker appear a sham. Among the crowd he sees the father of the girl he got pregnant. The stocky little man in overalls shrouded in plaster dust is walking towards him. Their eyes lock across the piazza. In a flash he understands the murderous violence of this man's loathing of him. Between them a little boy is chasing the pigeons. Then there's a resounding metallic clang which frightens all the birds into the air. He uses the momentary confusion to take to his heels.

He climbs the stairs to the office. He finishes his ice cream on the top stair. He is looking forward to Volpato's reaction to the information he has.

"The Jewish boy is back."

He keeps his hands in his pockets. Every opportunity to affirm his independence he embraces.

"Is he now?"

"She wasted no time in going to see him."

He knows Volpato is using government funds to finance his romantic pursuit of Elisabetta Del Monaco and he has discreetly made it known to Volpato that he knows. His prevailing aim at present is to avoid conscription into any fighting force. For this he will need Volpato to employ him in an official capacity. Thus he performs every task Volpato asks of him, including the hated one of posing draped in pieces of silk as a Biblical saint for three hours every day in Del Monaco's studio. The painter is always barking instructions at him. "Chin up!" "Head a little to the right!" "You're slouching again!" He takes liberties with his body too, moving his hand, lifting his chin.

"Any interesting discussions with the daughter today?"

"There was something. Only I don't think I should tell you."

Volpato taps his pencil on his desk. He has come to learn to measure the extent of his agitation by the speed of the rhythm of his pencil tapping. "Do I need to remind you you're being paid to tell me what you hear?"

"It's only because I don't want to hurt your feelings."

"You let me worry about my feelings."

"Okay, the artist did say he thinks you're a man of limited intelligence, incapable of thinking for yourself, the kind of man fascism finds it so easy to manipulate for its own ends."

Volpato stiffens and flushes behind his desk.

"I might have to teach Del Monaco a lesson."

"I think you should."

23

He sits in the cinema with his mother and father watching footage of the devastation wreaked on London's East End by the Luftwaffe bombing raids. Once or twice he thinks he recognises the locations filmed from the air.

"That's less than a mile from where we lived," he whispers to his father in the hazy flickering blue light of the cinema. He regrets his words immediately because he knows his father will now become still more anxious about Flora's safety. He tries to imagine what his duty as a warden would have entailed amongst all those fires and explosions and collapsing buildings. For a moment he is sitting beside Obi in the laundry van. He realises Obi will have gone through physically everything he imagines.

Outside the cinema two blackshirts stop Marcello and his mother and father. They are reprimanded for not singing the fascist hymn 'Giovinezza' at the end of the film. Father meekly apologises. One of the fascists is pushily unpleasant. The more his father tries to be conciliatory the more venomously obnoxious the man makes himself. "I don't like your face," he tells his father. Marcello sees how much humiliating pain this insult gives his father. How belittling it is for him to be help-lessly insulted in front of his wife and son. His father has always prided himself on his courteous manners. It's a quality he shows every day in the shop and is at the heart of how he wants to be seen by the world. He expects the world to respond with the same courtesy. The unkindness of the man, his determination to make his father feel contemptible and insignificant stays with

Marcello, sullies his mood for the next twenty-four hours. He writes a letter to Obi telling him how his patriotic tie to Italy is tested every day. How sometimes he wishes he was English. He wonders how much of what he says will be censored. It's asking for trouble to write that he wishes he was English, even in jest. He tears up the letter.

Massimo, he learns, is in Greece with the Ninth Army, Third Corps, Venice Division.

It appears things aren't going well there for the Italians. The inferior Greek forces, according to the forbidden voice on Radio London (*London calling, the voice of London*) are beating the Italians back. He is cheered by this news. But it is troubling to cheer on the success of a foreign army against the forces of his own country. And it is especially troubling to cheer on the soldiers who are trying to kill Massimo.

In bed any unexpected sharp noise from outside unsettles him. It forces him to inhabit the darkness out there. It seems to bring closer what is to come.

24

The light in the studio darkens again. She has been watching closely how her father uses wax to thicken the paint for the high impasto effects he creates. And the exact measure of mastic varnish he applies to the pigments on his palette. This afternoon he is painting Pino as Saint Anthony. This morning he painted an old man as Saint Mark. He is prickly about this decision to embark on another series of martyred saints, as if it lays bare his ambition to get one of his paintings inside a Venetian church. To her it is an admirable ambition and would give her immense pride if successful. So it confuses her that he treats her as if she is critical of his motives. It feels like he is questioning her loyalty as a daughter.

She is working alongside him on a life-size charcoal drawing of Pino. The only male she has ever seen naked. That she knows what his naked body looks like under his clothes creates a spurious intimacy between them which makes her uncomfortable. He enjoys making her feel uncomfortable. It's like the pastime he has created to alleviate his boredom. Earlier he joked that he was too young to be a saint. "Too young and too full of earthly desires," he said looking pointedly into her eyes.

Her father announces it is time for a coffee break. But then tells them he won't be joining them today.

"I need to soften these edges. You can bring me back an espresso."

"I don't want a coffee today," she says. Her reluctance to be alone with the model makes her feel childishly sulky.

"You go and keep Pino company."

"I won't bite," says the model, showing his teeth.

They both put on gumboots because many of Venice's canals have flooded. Outside in the driving rain he takes her hand and begins running with her. Initially she is frostily indignant but then finds she enjoys splashing through the water. They enter the café with the photo of Mussolini and Hitler above the coffee machine. The overspill of canal water washes through the café and slops around her ankles as she stands at the counter and orders an espresso. Pino orders a *caffè corretto doppio*. None of the five round tables are occupied. The billiard room at the back is empty. The wireless is playing scratchy dance music.

"Thank heavens they still have real coffee here," says Pino. The double shot of alcohol has produced a dark glitter in his eyes. "I hope you've stockpiled it at home. Even if it is a crime against the state. Everyone at heart is more concerned they get their morning dose of coffee than sympathetic of whatever sufferings war causes people in distant places. That's the sorry truth of human nature. The pity we feel for ourselves is always much more consuming than any pity we feel for others. I have a weak heart, you know. In case you're wondering why I'm not in a uniform. I fall in love too easily. Truth is, I despise uniforms. Sameness is the mother of disgust, variety the cure." He speaks airily as though everything he says is no more binding than a piece of fluff extricated from his clothes. "Your father is a bit of a tyrant, isn't he? Why doesn't he allow you to paint? It's obvious you want to."

"It's not that he's a tyrant. He's replicating on me the training he himself underwent. I have to perfect my draughtsmanship before I can take up a paintbrush."

"Families have probably been governed by fascism in the guise of fathers and husbands for centuries. Your father is much more of a fascist than he thinks he is."

She is making ripples in the water around her ankles by moving her foot back and forth. "What about you? Are you a fascist?"

"I can be. Mostly though I think of myself as a kind of wild flower that can only flourish in remote untended places. But if you ask me fascism serves people right. You can see at a cinema how much people love to be passively lied to and dominated. Shouldn't we be whispering though?" He nods over towards the man who served them and is now sitting at a table reading a newspaper. "I don't want to be responsible for getting you arrested. I'd say people who are fanatical about politics don't like themselves much. It's a way of deliberately making yourself unpleasant and daring anyone to oppose you. There must be an attraction in that if you don't like yourself." He flicks a coin in the air, catches it and flips it onto the back of his hand.

"You don't like modelling, do you? Why do you do it?"

"If your father wants to paint saints why doesn't he get an old man to sit for him?"

"Saint Anthony was only thirty-five when he died. He's the patron saint for the recovery of lost things."

"Up on that podium I feel like a dummy in a fancy-dress store. But I need the money. No one yet has appreciated my true worth. Don't you feel that about yourself? One day I intend to be worthy of newsprint. I want my photograph to appear in magazines. That's why I'm writing a screenplay for a film which I also intend starring in. Ordinary life is just a succession of trivialities. I want a better story than the one life's giving me at the moment."

"What's it about, your screenplay?"

"You don't believe me. I can tell. What if I said it's about love. How love is often like politics. Another way to appropriate power and gratify vanity. I've given a lot of thought to the likes of Lord Byron and Casanova. I'm fascinated why Venice attracts men who keep a sexual scorecard. And why women are so easy to seduce. You just have to flatter them. Of course it helps if you're good-looking."

She manages a strained smile. "Are you speaking from experience?"

"Of course. Experience is always the best teacher. Which is why you should be painting."

He moistens his fingertip and gently wipes her nose. She flinches and steps back, sloshing up water.

"Anyone would think you'd never been touched before. You had charcoal on your nose. I think you've got a better likeness of me than your father. I recognise myself in your drawing. I don't recognise myself at all in his painting. It's like he only sees what he wants to see."

"Are you trying to flatter me?"

He performs a theatrical bow.

"How come you don't have any friends?" he asks.

"How do you know I don't have any friends?"

"It's obvious. Anyone can see you're lonely. I don't have friends either. The trouble with friends is that you can always find something unlikeable in every single one of them. I sometimes think the less personality you have the better. Like animals. You can like animals whole heartedly in a way that isn't possible with people. I love the laziness of animals. They don't bustle around relentlessly trying to assert their importance the way humans do."

The things he says never match the look in his eyes. It's like he's always on the verge of becoming someone else. "Are these lines from your screenplay?"

"They might be."

As they are wading back to the studio through the floodwater she sees a girl striding purposefully towards them, her narrowed eyes fixed on Pino. Her wet hair makes her look wild.

"Shit," he says. "Here comes trouble."

"Bastard! I'm carrying your child, Fausto." She unbuttons her coat to show off her swollen belly. Then she looks Elisabetta up and down with a curled lip. Something she sees incites her to violence. She slaps Elisabetta's face. "You'd be an appalling father anyway," she says and walks off.

"Why did she hit *me*?"

"We must look like lovers."

"And why did she call you Fausto? I've never believed your name is Pino. It's like you have to remember my father is referring to you when he calls you Pino."

"Pino, Fausto, Fernando, Benito. What does it matter? Why limit oneself to one name when there are so many people one can be? You're trembling."

"Don't touch me."

Only when she is climbing the stairs up to the studio does she realise she has forgotten her father's coffee.

25

There is a celebration in the apartment at the news that Germany has invaded Russia. Even Father's spirits lift. Surely the might of Russia will defeat Hitler and fascism. They eat cabbage soup for the third time that week and recall the hubris of Napoleon. After supper Mother plays Vivaldi's *Spring* on the violin. Marcello sees the ghost of Giulia dance in circles on the dining room's parquet floor.

In the following week Marcello receives an order to join a Jewish work party. A new government policy to make use of Jewish males in the war effort. For a week he is employed near the old Jewish ghetto. A canal there has been drained so the wood piles and foundations can be repaired. He is first required to scoop up the accumulation of silt and sludge on the canal bed with his bare hands. Then, on a wooden walkway, he has to chip away at and remove old rotting bricks and dirt. The foreman is contemptuous of the lack of manly vigour in his labour. Several times a day he shouts at Marcello to use more physical force. Marcello still has trouble at times understanding Venetian dialect. Every district seems to have not only its own distinctive identity but its own language. He is pressed up close to the precarious foundations on which Venice has been built. His own foundations seem no less precarious.

When the work on the canal is complete he is sent to work on a farm in the Po Valley. Winter has arrived. He is woken at four-thirty every morning. He feels himself a small insignificant feature of the misted frosted flat landscape when he steps out of the house into the courtyard. He grows to like this feeling. He has a sense of the life force flowing intimately through him. And the feeling the world has given him a hiding place. Sometimes he wants nothing more from life now. The foreman is not an unkind man. Marcello assists in the milking of the cows by the light of an oil lantern. Immersed in the smell of cud, cowpat, damp fur, moist earth and warm milk. The rest of the day he spends out in the wheat fields and vineyards or else chopping wood in the courtyard. He feels the pangs of his labour in his muscles every evening. A sensation he grows to enjoy as if his aching body is proof of his usefulness.

He wonders how Father is coping in the shop without him. His father has become anxiously obsessed with finances. The obsession is making all his edges sharper. Making him less likeable as a human being. To economise he has stopped going to the barber every morning. He now shaves himself and bitterly complains. Marcello has tried reminding him how much they have to be grateful for. Their home hasn't been gutted by incendiaries, they aren't forced to wear a piece of cloth identifying them as members of an inferior race or deported to barren far ends of the world. Whenever Marcello tried to talk to him he was made to feel how much he misses his two girls. He has become a lonelier, more vulnerable man since Giulia and Flora disappeared from his life. He told Marcello he couldn't possibly understand what a deep-seated source of shame it is for a man to feel he might not be able to support his family. Marcello both regrets and resents that he can bring his father no comfort.

He reads books in the evening by the light of an oil lamp, one after another. He relishes the escape they provide from the times in which he lives. He often dreams of the cows at night. He is surprised how much affection they inspire in him. It's as if he has a surplus of love within and no one to give it to.

When he catches influenza the farmer's wife is kind to him and he spends four days in bed. He finishes the last of the books he has brought with him.

He is hurt when the foreman humorously tells him he is not cut out for farming. It comes as a shock. He thought he was giving a good account of himself. He is sent back home in a depressed state. Then he learns Massimo has been killed. He finds himself crying into his pillow like a little boy.

Her father has been in an abstracted irritable mood all morning. He has been unkind to the model posing as Saint Mark. Saint Mark sitting at a desk with a studious frown and a quill. Her father has twice reproached the elderly bearded model with unnecessary severity for not staying in pose. Her sympathy as her charcoal scratches marks on the paper goes out to the old man in his threadbare clothes. She tries to catch his eye so she can offer him an apologetic smile.

When the man has left the studio and her father is cleaning his brushes there is a charged silence. She can sense her father is bracing himself to say something difficult. What it might be she can't imagine. She has been hoping he is on the verge of finally allowing her to paint.

"Listen," he finally says. He doesn't look up. He is wrapping a small piece of newspaper around the bristles of a sable brush. A routine he meticulously goes through every evening. It is she who cuts out the little squares of newspaper for the purpose. "I've had to agree to Luigi's request for your hand."

She stares at him open mouthed.

"He's not so bad. I've come to respect him. And he'll treat you well. He's going to make up one of his rooms into a studio for you. I told him it must be a room with north light. And you now have my permission to begin painting. He's also agreed that you can come here in the mornings to help me out."

She is still speechless. It's as if her knowledge of language has been erased. As if she only has facial expression to convey her feeling.

"The marriage will take place next month. I'm of the belief that with a little generosity and effort on your part you will come to like him. He's not such a bad man."

She walks out of the studio. She has to leave because never has she felt such a compelling desire to cause her father pain. She doesn't feel she will ever be able to say a kind word to him ever again. She has walked all the way to the Grand Canal before she takes stock of her surroundings. "What threat has Volpato made to my father?" She can't help voicing the question aloud. She realises a gondolier is looking at her as if she is a mad woman.

27

He is punting his boat towards the Rialto bridge. The sight of Elisabetta sitting on a wooden landing stage is like a granted wish. Her proximity enlivens his mind but weakens his body. He feels some of the strength leave his arms and legs. He suddenly has to concentrate on handling his boat. The tide pulls at his jittery hand on the oar. It will be the first time she has seen him in his *sandolo*. Except she doesn't look up. She is staring down into the water, as if reading a story there. He has spent some of his free time this week looking at paintings so as to understand her passion better. He went to San Zaccaria to see the Bellini altarpiece; to the Scuola of San Rocco to see Tintoretto's *Crucifixion* and the Frari to see Titian's *Assumption*. The paintings excited him more than ever before because he experienced them as something beautiful shared with her. He now eases the boat over to the pier. A row of moored gondolas creak as they are buffeted gently by the tide.

"I'm engaged to be married," she says, looking up at him. She shows him the ring on her wedding finger.

He pretends the news is of mild amusement to him. A reflex reaction which afterwards strikes him as preposterous. The truth is, he feels his nakedness is momentarily on display. He has to cover it up. He once tried to kiss her. He would like to kiss her again. Why deny it? He dreamed one night they were walking by the river in London. They were dressed in elegant evening clothes and holding hands. The sun was rising over the water and he had never felt so happy in his life. He has to remind himself it isn't a memory she shares with him. It makes no sense to him that she knows nothing about this exalted moment they spent together. He would like to ask her if she has ever dreamed of him. To dream of a person is to see them afresh, to give them agency. He looks down at the push of her small breasts against the black fabric of her jumper. It's a bewitching sight and he marvels at how much pleasure and sadness the eye can effortlessly impart to the body.

"You don't appear very happy about it," he says.

"I'm not. The man is almost twice my age. And I find him repulsive. I think he's somehow managed to blackmail my father. My father is terrified of him."

A police boat, pennants fluttering, motors past towards the Rialto bridge. Its wake rocks his boat and slaps against the wooden pylons.

"I feel like I ought to rescue you."

"If only you could," she says, but absently, with no trace of ardour, which wounds him. His stance in the boat becomes more defensive.

"I guess being a girl isn't much better than being a Jew in the world we live in," he says.

He studies her silence with curiosity. It is, he realises, something he often does with her. It's like she disappears into a kind of changing room. And then reappears unchanged.

"I haven't spoken to my father since he told me. We conduct all our daily chores together in chilly silence. I hate how much pain I'm causing him but at the same time I'd like to cause him more pain."

"Fathers are dictators in essence, aren't they? It's impossible not to be irritated by all their rules at times."

"I can always see how much it pains him to ever feel he doesn't know best. My father needs his vanity. Without it he's as vulnerable as a child. A lot of these fascists are the same. The uniforms they wear are like a carapace of vanity underneath which they are insecure children. I think a lot of the evil in the world is caused by vanity. It makes people short-sighted and thus prevents them from seeing the bigger picture of themselves."

She gets to her feet. Brushes herself down. His braces, as usual, are hanging loose from the waistband of his trousers. She reaches out and takes one between finger and thumb and gently tugs at it. He is disarmed. As if it's an encrypted message he doesn't have the cipher to decode. He tries to think of something to say which might further eroticise the moment. But nothing springs to mind. Moonlight might have made dangerous words possible. But he is awash in sunlight. London hasn't emboldened or sophisticated him as much as he might have hoped. Anyway, every time he has tried to flirt with her in the past she has nervously laughed him off. Talk for her doesn't seem to be a means of pushing out from shore, of discovery. It's as if her intentions pre-exist in all her speech, as if it's confirmation she seeks, not surprise. For a moment he contemplates pulling her into his boat. It is dispiriting to realise he doesn't possess the manly confidence to perform such an assertive gesture.

When he punts away he is still wondering why she took hold of his braces. He touches them himself. As if to re-establish the contact with her fingers. He feels he has given a shoddy account of himself, misrepresented himself and his true feeling. It's another of those moments in life he would like to replay. With her a third voice always seems to participate in their conversations. It's like the voice of the times in which they live. The mistrust with which everyone now defends themselves from strangers. The reluctance to ever speak from a true place within themselves. To speak aloud what the heart and mind instruct. He thinks he will always associate this spot on the canal with the moment he has just lived, the moment when the young woman he might have loved disappeared as a possibility. Perhaps, he tries to convince himself, the failure was there from the very beginning and there was nothing he could have done differently. He is unable though to believe this.

28

She is sitting in Harry's Bar – or 'Bar da Arrigo' as it is now called because all English words are forbidden by law. She saw the notice on the door – 'No dogs or Jews' – and felt ashamed of herself for stepping over the threshold. For an hour now she has had a new name. Elisabetta Volpato. She has been married in a municipal office by a fascist, to a fascist. Marriage in her mind is still a distant prospect of maturity and solidity. She is far from feeling ready for its demands. She is barely less flimsy and flighty mentally than a child. She watches with repulsion her husband's adam's apple shift as he swallows another mouthful of prosecco. He is wearing a new suit and tie of which he is clearly very proud. The thought that he bought it with her in mind, with the desire to please her, perhaps ought to inspire in her a note of tenderness for him. But she feels only repulsion. A raw crawling sting on her flesh that makes her wish her body didn't belong to her. Her father sits opposite. In two hours she and her new husband will take a motor launch to the Lido. Never before has she felt so estranged from her life. A puppet for men to play with. And the only outlet her anger has is to treat her father with scorn for his act of betrayal. She never now says a word to him unless spoken to. Hostility infuses her smallest gestures. He has pretended not to notice anything is amiss between them. A stance which makes him appear deluded. A lonely man wrapped up in a world of his own. For a wedding present he gave her a complete set of sable paintbrushes, two jars of his mastic varnish, large bags of lead white, ultramarine blue, yellow ochre, vermillion and black

153

pigments, a roll of canvas, a wooden palette, a mortar, a pigment grinding tray, a palette knife, sheets of papyrus and a new hard-bound sketchbook. Everything she needs to paint. It's the most magical gift she has ever received and it caused her pain that pride choked her from expressing any appreciation. The only compensation now is that she will now be able to venture forth, artistically at least, into a world of colour.

She keeps looking down at her new husband's hands. She can't take her eyes off them. The stubby fingers with manicured nails. The raised knotted veins. The more she looks at them the uglier and more alien they become. These hands that now have a licence to roam at will over her most intimate places. One thing she is clear about. She will tell him she will not get pregnant. She will put her foot down. The prospect of this conversation frightens her almost as much as the act which will follow it. She is naïve about the mechanics of sex. The subject has always made her father squirm with embarrassment.

She taps her fingers against her suitcase which sits by her side. Tucked away at the back of her wardrobe for so long, this suitcase was once charged with the promise of adventure and discovery. She imagined herself packing it for visits to the art galleries of Paris and Madrid. Now it's an emblem of defeat, of humiliation and violation. She doesn't understand why this unknown man wants to share his life with her. She has made it abundantly clear he repels her. That she will not flatter him or even take an interest in him. And he is a man who needs to be constantly flattered. Is it, she has wondered, because he recognises some deeper truth about himself in her disdain for him? She listens now to what he is saying to her father.

"There are times I've been proud of my achievements; there are other times when I have to confess I've been short-sighted."

She is shocked when he takes off his spectacles to clean them. He becomes unrecognisable. His eyes change size and shape and the distances between his features seem to alter. He looks like a different man, less educated, more untrustworthy. Indignation blazes through her that he has no more earned the right to touch her underneath her clothes than one of the waiters. She cannot believe later tonight she will have to take off her clothes in this unknown man's presence. And worse.

29

Giulia's clothes belong to history now. And yet they are a conductor into a timeless realm in the power they have to momentarily make the past contemporary with the present. He holds a pair of her shoes and sees her smile before she dissolves again. Then a memory of her lifting her face to the sun in his boat washes through him with the moving fresh power of new experience as he handles a shaggy green cardigan of hers. It is bewildering how simultaneously close and far away she is at the same moment. He and his mother share memories as they sort through the clothes. It is his mother's idea to give Giulia's clothes new life by donating them to Jewish refugees. He would like to know the women who will give Giulia's clothes a future.

The letters of the Jewish refugees his mother translates, sometimes from German, sometimes from Yiddish, often contain cryptic allusions. Measures taken to elude the censor. He and his mother sometimes sit together trying to break codes. It's the closest he gets to feeling like he's doing war work. Some of the letters are unstamped, delivered by hand, and their content is not disguised. It's clear Jews are being deported from Nazi occupied countries. In sealed overcrowded cattle trucks. It becomes a new nightmare to imagine himself with his mother and father in a sealed cattle truck.

He thinks of all the music his mother carries inside her. The intimate knowledge she has of this music and the ability to recreate it, to keep it alive. And once more he wants to shout out his outrage at this popular notion that Jews are worthless parasites.

He is sitting on Giulia's bed, the bed in which she took her last breath, when he says, "Giulia once told me she had dreams in which she was about to depart on a long journey and was always prey to an underlying panic that there was something she had forgotten. I sometimes feel like that now. If you could spend another fifteen minutes with her do you know what you might say to her?"

Mother is folding up a flowered blouse he doesn't ever remember Giulia wearing. "Just the obvious things. How proud I was of her. How much I loved her. I don't think love is in the telling though; it's in the showing."

"Except in showing, unlike telling, you don't have the hard evidence the loved person has understood."

"It sounds like you feel there was something you left unsaid to her?"

"With family we too often express our irritation and too rarely our appreciation. And yet we relentlessly go out of our way to be polite to strangers."

"That's true. It's hard to enter a world you've never been to before. Giulia's death has become such a world. We're all finding it difficult to get our bearings there. She knew though how much you appreciated her."

"Sometimes I think I like feeling sad. Life seems more beautiful when you feel sad. That's often a power music uses, isn't it?"

"I don't want you to be sad."

"I like best being out on the lagoon where I can feel I'm a tiny figure of little consequence to anyone. I can feel the lightness of the weight my life has in the world. That's when I hear what music there is inside me."

He has never spoken to his mother like this, from the private part of himself, and she looks a bit alarmed as if it is physical solace he is seeking. The truth is he derives little comfort from physical contact with his mother nowadays. It's always a clumsily uncomfortable moment when they embrace which creates distance rather than closeness and leaves them both, he suspects, feeling wanting in natural feeling.

"Probably it's vanity on my part to worry I left something unsaid that she needed to hear," he says, lightening his tone. "Just me wanting to feel better about myself. I looked up that Bible quote about vanity last night. The winds blowing to the south and then to the north and there being no remembrance of former things nor later things yet to come. I couldn't though work out if it's reassuring or not to reduce everything to vanity. If it's any kind of relief to believe nothing matters in the end."

"Do you ever wonder about Luna? It's strange to think she's still out there somewhere. Our beloved cat."

"I think it was the racial laws that drove her away. She was a snob. She no longer wanted to live with a family of Jews when we lost our status as respectable citizens." He smiles at his mother. For some reason he is suddenly able to see her as if after a long absence as if she and not the cat had disappeared from his life. "That dress really suits you," he says.

She beams with delight. It's a lime green dress with collars. He knows he ought to pay her compliments more often. It is so easy for him to give her a moment's pleasure.

There's some kind of tiny moth in the apartment. He has never been able to catch clear sight of it. It suddenly flutters into his field of vision, circles him and then vanishes again. He doesn't really believe it has anything to do with the spirit of Giulia. But he worries when a whole day passes without him catching sight of it.

The family radio has been confiscated. Another petty law to make Jews feel unwanted. He argued with his father about handing it in.

"Who will know we have a radio? Just keep the volume low. Why do you always bow down to them?"

"If you have a problem with my authority find yourself somewhere else to live."

For two days he and his father barely speak. He can't look at him without inwardly criticising him. His daily rituals – the cold shower every morning, the hair oil, the vigorous brushing of his clothes, the shining of his shoes – fill him with irritation. He wants to tell Elisabetta about this silent feud with his father, how it mirrors her situation, as if it's evidence fate is pushing them together. A flimsy notion, he acknowledges.

Without access to Radio London it's difficult to understand what is happening in the war. The newspapers and newsreels are melodramatically partisan. At the cinema he sees footage of Italian soldiers in deep snow in Russia. He finds himself searching for Massimo's features among the faces. And then remembers Massimo is dead. One thing is clear, the Germans initial impressive surge into Russia has been halted. It's a small mercy. In Africa too the battle lines shift back and forth.

He has noticed people no longer now sit on their doorsteps of an evening, gossiping, laughing and making expressive gestures with their hands. Life in the city has become more private, the population more distrustful. Even though Venetians are apt to feel themselves detached from the world outside. As if the storms of events elsewhere will never arrive in Venice. As was so often the case in history. Marcello though can't quite assimilate this confidence. He lies awake in bed. A dark presence stalks the back of his mind. If the infinite is inside us it often takes the guise of terror. So he thinks.

30

"Signora Volpato."

She turns just as a bell tolls and a flurry of birds takes to the air. He sees on her face how hateful to her is her new name. He smiles, showing her the recently acquired gap in his front teeth. He is unsure how ugly it makes him look. But it's a law he has imposed on himself never to appear doubtful or apologetic. So he flaunts his missing tooth.

"I thought you despised uniforms," she says, frowning at his new fascist militia uniform. She is wearing a summer dress and a red cardigan. She holds a string bag with a package inside.

"Suits me though, you have to admit." He performs a twirl for her. "And it exempts me from getting sent to Russia. The last place I want to be. And I've got a gun. In this new world we're living in the possession of a gun has become more important than the possession of a brain."

He is gratified to see this remark earns him a smile. He notices they are being watched by the old woman in black who sells postcards arranged on a table in the middle of the square. He performs a twirl for her too.

"How's the screenplay coming along?"

"The screenplay, the screenplay. If only. I made that up. But you knew that, didn't you? I'm so transparent in my deceits. I have to tell lies sometimes to test just how fixed reality is. I've found a lie is more likely to get you a step ahead than the truth. I say different things to different people. Why appear to be the same person all the time? Children are always pretending to be someone else. It's one of those examples of children being wiser and more inventive than adults."

"And how's your child? Was it a boy or a girl?"

"What a hard time you're giving me today. You see this new scar above my eye? And this missing front tooth. Her father did that to me. He might have jeopardised my career in the movies. I'll only be able to play villains now." He drops his shoulder and raises his forearm as if peering out from an imaginary cloak. He has got her to smile again. "Do you recognise my pose? I'll give you a clue. Scuola di San Rocco."

"I've no idea what you're talking about."

"I thought you were supposed to be an artist. It's a wood carving called The Spy. Can't remember the name of the artist. You should go and take a look at it. Shall I tell you a secret? I myself worked for a while as a spy. It was my job to expose what people tried to hide. Like you with your portrait drawings. Your husband made me pose for your father. He was my boss. Just as he's your boss now. He wanted me to spy on you. He was worried about that Jewish boy. I became quite jealous of him. What's happened to him?"

"Marcello? Why were you jealous of Marcello?"

He sees she is flustered. Ideas are colliding in her head. It always buoys him up when he's able to put people at a disadvantage.

"Well, I hate to admit it but jealousy is probably the key to my character. I used to tell Volpato you talked about the Jewish boy whenever you got the chance. I even told him you kissed him on the mouth. At one point he was on the verge of arresting him on a phoney charge of sedition."

She plucks at the sleeve of her dress. He watches her inhale as if she is about to vent some anger.

"Why? Why did you tell him I kissed Marcello?"

"I enjoyed seeing him squirm. I feel sorry for you, being married to that old codger. It can't have been your choice. You have better taste. It's a sign of the times that mediocrities like him can rise to positions of influence and power. To be honest though, I always believed he liked men rather than women. Sometimes I would catch his watchdog eyes looking at my crotch. Of course only you would know how much truth there is in my instinct about him. But you're not looking like you're with child."

"You were agent 362."

Now she's got him at a disadvantage. A seabird squawks overhead. He looks up to see it land heavily on a rooftop on the far side of the canal.

"What a blabbermouth your husband must be."

"You used to follow Marcello's mother."

"A harmless woman. That was typical of the nonsense your husband had me doing."

"I don't think I want to talk to you anymore."

He thinks of doing a forward roll on the pavement, just to make her smile. It would be easy as a kind of momentum of madness has built up in him, a childlike excitability impatient with formal protocol, but he doesn't do a forward roll because it suddenly seems demeaning to him this impulse of men always to want to earn laughter and approval from women.

He watches her walk off towards the bridge. He deems it, on the whole, an unsatisfactory encounter as if he came out second best. It is his nature to always search for something repelling in the people he meets. An excuse to remain detached. He struggles to find anything worthy of scorn in Elisabetta Del Monaco which annoys him still more. He looks around for someone disagreeable and when he spots a middle-aged man in a smart suit with an air of complacency he marches up to him and aggressively asks to see his papers. It's a constant source of pleasure to him that he can bustle into anyone's privacy and make them answer to him.

31

He helps the two Jewish refugee children into his boat. It is to be a treat for them his mother has organised. The responsibility he feels for their safety and their palpable apprehension makes him sharply attentive to his every act, as if he is protecting a scoop of water in the cupped palms of hands. He has not been able to get a word out of either of them since he picked them up in a campo where they stood apart watching other children play leapfrog. He makes them sit facing him on the wooden strut in the middle of the boat so he can look at their faces while he punts. The little boy is about six; the little girl about seven or eight. They are both dressed in what once upon a time were elegant clothes. But the fabrics are stained and torn and encrusted now. The boy wears a cap which suits him and there are scabs on his knees. He holds a toy bear, even grubbier than he is. He rarely raises his eyes. The girl protectively holds her brother's hand. She has a watermarked red ribbon in her thick long dark hair and a sulky mouth and is so beautiful to look at he feels a constant longing to make her smile, to inspire in her liking.

He ducks down low as he punts under a small bridge. Even so the underside of the arch brushes his hair. "I'm sorry I've made you face backwards but this way I can see your faces and your faces make me feel better about life even though I wish you weren't so sad and frightened. Shall we see if I can help you make a memory today you'll always remember? A good memory. You both make me look forward so much to having children one day. Here comes another bridge. Even you might need to duck under this one." He points and makes a ducking motion. The girl swivels round and then bows her head. It pleases him to have created this momentary understanding between them as if he has now won a more enduring existence inside her.

For a while he concentrates on enjoying the sensation of stepping into every new stroke. The low tide exposes summer's green moss on the canal's brick walls. He glides the boat past a barge on which a man is selling vegetables and flowers. He is already fifty metres further up the canal when the thought of giving the girl a flower occurs to him. It's the story of his life that inspiration always arrives a moment too late. They enter the Grand Canal and its wide expanse of activity and dazzling light. Not for the first time the familiar sense of stillness, of timeless suspension behind all the movement reminds him of the interior of a church. He thinks he detects a note of excitement in the girl.

"I wish I could see what you look like when you laugh. I hope twenty years from now you might look back on this moment and remember it with affection. Remember me with affection. But I've already said that. I'm repeating myself. Don't you wish life didn't make us repeat ourselves so often?"

She wants to hide her face from him. He can feel it and it makes him sad. She has been taught to be afraid of everyone. But when she thinks he isn't looking she sneaks shy glances at his face and the way he works the oar. The light shines off her black hair.

"You're wise not to want anything to do with human beings. Wise like all wild creatures. That's the house where Lord Byron lived. He was an English poet. You'll learn about him when you're older. You might even fall in love with an idea of him. My sister did. My sister's name was Giulia. My name is Marcello. What are your names? *Je m'appelle Marcello. E vous?*"

Nothing. It's as if they think he is trying to trick them into making a mistake for which they will be punished. He wonders how she got the tiny scar on her cheek. He wants to ask her but he doesn't want to make her aware of it and anyway he knows she won't answer him.

Sunlight sparkles in points of light on the flexing water. A branch torn loose by last night's storm floats on the tide past the boat. There is a lot of water traffic on the canal today and the boat is continually rocked. A tremor of emotion passes across the girl's face whenever this happens. He suspects there's some excitement in her fear. He would like to row them across the lagoon to the Lido, take off his shoes and feel warm grains of sand lodge themselves between his toes, perhaps build a sandcastle together. But public beaches are forbidden to Jews.

"*Uffa*. Try saying that. *Uffa*. It's what you say when you don't get what you want."

32

Everything blurs and quickens when Elisabetta opens the door to Marcello. She is unprepared for how important it is to her to have his approval. Her heart is still thumping in her chest when she leads him into the high-ceilinged room with its draped window and sharp smell of spirits and oils. The large canvas she has been working on stands at the far side of the room. For a moment she hates the sight of it. It's like she is seeing it reflected in a funhouse mirror. Every detail a distortion of the truth. It bears so little resemblance to her recent memory of it. The face-less sketched figure sitting in a cane chair looks like a ghoul. The detailed female figure standing behind appears lifeless, like a mannequin with dead eyes. The high sumptuous impasto on the forehead overworked, the white highlight in the left eye gaudy. Her face belongs to Marcello's sister. She used her sketches to capture the likeness. She feels now she might have taken an insensitive liberty which will offend Marcello.

She watches him walk up to the canvas. She folds her arms and squeezes them. She feels her future as an artist is under review and might be revoked. Her hunger for reassuring praise opens up a void inside her.

"I used a female model to paint the body and clothes," she says because the silence is unbearable.

"It's beautiful. It's Giulia. I can almost smell her."

Her relief is a new sunrise. The painting acquires sudden beauty for her eyes too. Her body wants to dance and spin, her voice wants to burst forth into song.

"My idea is to paint you sitting in the chair. To reunite you and your sister, if only in a painting. Does that make sense? And then few things anger me more than those grotesque caricatures of Jewish faces in the newspapers. I want to paint two beautiful Jewish faces. I want it to be a political protest as well as a beautiful painting."

When he turns to face her, she sees his eyes are moist. For a moment she thinks he is going to embrace her and instinctively steps back and picks up a sable brush.

"So, will you sit for me?"

"Your husband works for the secret police. I'm hardly going to say no, am I?"

She returns his smile but is hurt by all the implications of his joke. To disassociate herself from her husband is a constant imperative in her daily life.

She has to fight down the shyness of giving orders when she puts him into the pose she wants. And the further shyness of intently studying his face.

"Put your hands wherever they feel comfortable," she says.

He folds them in his lap. She watches him massage one thumb with the other. It's the only sign of any agitation in his body.

"I can see you're going to be a good model," she says. She uses a plumb line to measure the distance between his chin and the top of his head. Dips her brush into the pot of medium and into the dollop of black pigment on her palette which sits on a small table. She steps forward squinting and puts down a black mark on the canvas. She walks backwards to her palette, tilting her head from side to side, like a bird. Repeats the ritual over and over again. Her rhythm gaining in urgency and concentration. For a long time they don't speak.

Her excitement at the facility with which she puts down her marks is difficult to contain. Her neck is flushed, her fingertips tingle with this new power she feels she has at her disposal. Her hand dashes over the canvas. Every stroke of paint she puts down like a song she is singing. She marvels that her hand possesses knowledge that is independent of her conscious mind. Everything assumes clarity and connection. Immersion is absolute. She excels herself. She knows it's a fragile feeling, liable at any moment to dissolve back into doubt and torment but disciplines herself to make the most of it while it lasts.

She has set herself the task of getting at the reality behind the appearance. At any given moment the surface of life can dissolve and reveal a different reality beneath. People hide the truth of themselves behind conventions and bustle and make-believe. She does it herself. She wants to find Marcello's solitary self and give it eloquence. She is also convinced there is an emptiness at the heart of life. She feels it often. A presence that can be comforting as well as discouraging. She wants to somehow depict it as an atmosphere in her painting. Give it visibility, form.

It's a kind of heresy but there are moments while she is working on this painting that she feels she has been gifted with a greater talent than her father. She does not like to think of herself as competitive, especially with her father. But she is still at war with him. Still cannot overcome the deeply troubling dislike she feels for him. Nevertheless she still often finds herself wanting his approval. As if it will always be him who presides over her day of judgement.

During a break they talk about the war. The Allies have landed in Sicily. Fascist propaganda can't disguise the suspicion they are meeting with little resistance. Almost every night formations of unchallenged bombers can be heard in the sky above Venice. On their way through the moonlight to Verona, Milan and Turin. Turin especially has been extensively bombed.

"Secretly I think the majority of people are cheering on the English and Americans. We Italians are experiencing an identity crisis. Compelled to come out in support of the enemy. But so many of us don't understand why we are fighting this war. And we're tired of it. It's Hitler's war; not ours. That said, it seems somehow inconceivable that it will ever arrive in Venice."

"Is that what your husband thinks?"

"He rarely tells me what he thinks."

"And you're not very interested. It must be difficult to be married to someone in whom one takes so little interest."

"Can we talk about something else?"

"I keep remembering the consuming fascination toy soldiers had for me as a child. The unregistered hours I spent creating dangers and stories for them. Boys should be provided with different games to play."

"Boys with their toy soldiers and girls with their dolls. War and childbearing. It's depressing how we're groomed, isn't it?"

The intimacy of being so close to him while she is at her canvas in her heightened state of concentration. Brushing against him. There is a pocket of electric heat into which she steps when she stands beside him. She remembers when he kissed her. A volatile moment that rarely evokes the same emotion whenever she recalls it. As if she is yet to fully understand it. The truth perhaps is that she didn't return Marcello's kiss because he doesn't inspire confidence. She assures herself this has nothing to do with him being Jewish. He wouldn't inspire confidence no matter what race he belonged to. He's like a country that has an unstable government. She is still a virgin. She doesn't quite understand what went wrong in the marriage bed. Whether or not it was her fault. She wishes she had a mother or a close female friend to talk to. She is though glad of her husband's reluctance to talk about it. And the lack of impetus in him to try again. She suspects she might have inadvertently humiliated him. Now and again she remembers what Fausto said. It's true she can detect little desire in him for her. He appears oblivious to the sight of her in any state of undress.

He no longer makes her wince ten times a day with revulsion or embarrassment. She can look at the strained buttons of his waistcoat over his paunch without distaste. But she can never accustom herself to the reality of living with him, of sharing so many intimate rituals with him. That his face has become more familiar to her than her own is evidence that the world is critically out of kilter.

When she has been working for three hours she has a likeness of Marcello sketched on the canvas. She softens the edges with her fingertip.

"I can already see myself but with some hairline quality or flaw I don't recognise. I can't decide if you've made me look a little more like myself or a little less."

"I'll improve it tomorrow. I'm still feeling my way."

"I understand now that you've always seen me as an image."

"What do you mean?"

"It's a way you have of standing outside the moment. Like when you were measuring me with your piece of string. It's like you commit me to memory even when we're sitting in the same room. You have this way of removing yourself from the tide of the moment. As if you want to escape feeling. As if you don't want to know the truth about yourself."

She smiles but later will be unable not to take to heart this critical observation of his. Will ask herself several times how much truth there is in it. That perhaps it's a clue to her struggles to ever feel herself as womanly. She thinks this might be a trait inherited from her unknown mother. Everything mystifying about herself she imagines must be an inheritance from her unknown mother. She sometimes stares hard at the photographs she has of her mother, willing her to speak. It is strange she has never once felt any urgent need to look for her. She must after all still be somewhere out in the war-torn world. This detachment she suspects might also belong to her mother. Perhaps Marcello is right and she doesn't want to know the truth about herself. Once or twice she has thought of asking her husband to find her mother. It's a big part of his job after all to track down missing people. The thought of being in his debt dissuaded her. But she feels now they have come to a compromised understanding she might ask this favour of him. They give each other lots of space, serve each other little but leftovers, for which she is grateful. No longer does she face him as an enemy. He never makes her feel foolish or petty and she tries to do the same with him. In the light of what Marcello said she wonders now if perhaps she isn't excessive in the measures she takes to safeguard the privacy of her mind.

33

For once he takes no pleasure in the fear and tension his uniform causes. Staring up at him from his seat on the vaporetto is the German Jew he used to give Italian lessons to. In his shabby clothes and battered hat. With his son and young wife who he sees is pregnant. The wife looks at his uniform and then up into his eyes with a momentary flash of disgust which she quickly conceals.

Fausto has boarded the water bus with his companion Gino. A man who, despite the ever more severe food rationing, is always eating things wrapped in greasy wax paper. Venice has been inundated with refugees from bombed cities and with flocks of affluent people convinced it is the safest place in Italy to see out the rest of the war. It has become a mantra that no one will dare drop bombs on Venice and its cultural heritage. There is now unrest in the city caused by food shortages and sanitation problems due to the overcrowding. The anti-fascist movement is growing in numbers and becoming a little bolder. Anti-government and anti-German graffiti regularly appears on walls and crudely printed leaflets circulate the city. The prisons are ever more crowded. Fausto and Gino are under orders to check documents every day, to be on the alert for suspicious characters. He has grown tired of the coarse chafing repetition of the routines he has been forced to call his life. Of being always in the company of men who laugh uproariously at vulgar jokes, who swear every third word, who try to shout their mean little truths into being and do not ask questions because they believe they already have all the answers. So many of them are children in adult bodies. Seeking vengeance for classroom humiliations suffered. Instead of vitality they have brutality. He cannot find his voice amongst these mindlessly methodical men. It's as if they and their rote arguments are blotting him out. He knows if he is to find his way he needs to be rid of them soon. Especially given the way the war is going.

The vaporetto chugs out into the centre of the canal. Gino is holding Max's papers.

"This one's German and Jewish," he says, frowning as if this is a novel conundrum he has to puzzle out. Fausto despises Gino. He's a sadistic blockhead who once in the company of Fausto and a militia patrol tempted a black cat with white markings down from a wall with a piece of sausage and then with a movement as quick as a fish slit its throat. Afterwards he made fun of Fausto for feeling sorry for the animal. Gino always has an air of nosing the air like a hound. With only the lift of an eyebrow or the twitch of a muscle in his mouth he can show himself to be a force of heedless malevolence, of impending violence.

"Neither of which is illegal," he says and winks at the German whose lips are sore and his eyes watery. He's tempted to make his former neighbour pay for the look of disgust his wife gave him which is still making him feel dirty, as if the hairs on his body are furred in dust. "I know this man. He used to be my neighbour. And his only crime is to know more about German filmmakers than I do."

34

He likes going down to the bar with Elisabetta during the break from painting sessions. Enjoys being seen in public with her. He feels himself more noticed and respected when he is in her company. In the eyes of on-lookers they are a couple. A source of pride for him. He tries to get her to see what he sees. Tries to make her feel what he feels. Most of all though he relishes the release of spirit he always feels in her company.

He has told her about the fascist he pushed into the canal. He turned it into a comic anecdote in which all sympathy was on his side. Otherwise he hasn't given him much thought since returning from London. However, when he stands outside the bar looking into the man's face, it is like a forestalled moment that was always going to happen. He quickly understands that the man has been waiting for this moment. The high colour of his enraged face, the murderous hatred in his eyes. He manages to block the first punch but not the hefty shove that follows. He falls backwards and loses his balance. While he lies prostrate on the ground the man kicks him, shouting out his fury. A blow lands to the head before he can cover his face. Another to the body takes the breath out of him. He is aware Elisabetta is shouting. She is shouting out her husband's name. Invoking the prestige and power he wields. Some of the force withdraws from his attacker's fury. He takes more blows before his assailant is pulled away by his companion. The noises of the street return. Passers-by stare down at him. The humiliation he feels though is all in relation to Elisabetta who helps him to his feet.

Everything is a blur, adrenalin is drain-swirling in his body, blood is singing in his ears. He is sitting on the edge of the bath-tub, naked to the waist. Elisabetta is applying iodine to a cut on his face. The weight of her breast is resting on his bare arm. He can't tell if it's a contact she has willed or is even aware of. He can smell her shampoo amidst the stink of the iodine, the turps and oils on her clothes. He braves the sharp sting of the iodine on his cheek with only a faint wince.

"You're very thin. You're too thin," she says.

It is impossible not to recall the last time he wasn't wearing a shirt in her company. But he has the same urge to kiss her, to make her catch her breath, to open his heart to her. He feels he has never hated anything more than the wedding ring on her finger.

"The cut oddly suits you. I think I might paint it. It's like the part of you that you try to hide from the world."

He smiles but he still feels he is curled into a frightened ball on the ground. Belittled and humiliated. He concentrates on the warmth seeping into his body from the pressure of her breast on his arm, not wanting to miss a moment of its benediction.

"You mustn't let them get to you. They're nothing but thugs. You're much better than they are."

He gives her another feeble smile, another feeble nod of the head. Gingerly, he touches the beginnings of the bruises on his ribs.

"And you did push him in the canal."

"That seems a lifetime ago. My sister has died and I've sold women's knickers in a London market since then."

"I still find it hard to imagine you in London. I don't know why."

He can't help feeling with dismay that she doesn't spend much time with him in her imagination. She moves away. Replaces the bottle of iodine in the cabinet. The removal of her body's warmth casts a shadow over his mind and returns him to the indignity he has undergone. He gets to his feet and walks over to the mirror where he inspects his cut. In the glass their eyes meet. It feels like they are looking at each other in a near but far off alternative world. A shooting star of attraction passes between them. He is sure of it. In the mirrored world the intimacy between them seems feverishly heightened, a swirling constellation of connections. He has the feeling his and her alternate selves are urging him to perform an act of courage. He searches in her eyes for a confirmation. As if she senses he is on the verge of kissing her he watches her mirror image lower its eyes in the glass.

"I didn't tell you," she says, "my husband has found out where my mother lives. It's odd how my husband is becoming a benefactor in my life. First, he finds my mother then his name saves you from a hospital bed or prison. There was a time I never once believed anything good would come from him. I'm going to see my mother in two days. She doesn't know. I don't think I've ever felt so nervous in my entire life."

35

She steps off the bus into a sleepy sloping piazza. Beyond the towering pine trees bent back by sea winds there is a trail of sunlight over the Mediterranean. Eddied by the tidal swell the small boats at anchor in the harbour set up a mesmerising tinkling sound. Outside a bar on the wharf she watches the excited gesturing of old men brandishing pink newspapers and bright red aperitifs. A fisherman with a crooked cigarette clamped between his lips is mending his nets on the rocks. Green-shuttered houses with chalky pink, red and yellow ochre façades are clustered around the church in the piazza and rise up the incline of the hill in tiers of exuberant disorder. For a moment the beauty of the surroundings makes her sad that she can't make of herself something so simply irrefutable. Then her thoughts turn back to her mother. That this is the place her mother has chosen to make her home is new bloodline knowledge. She finds she can locate something of herself in this choice her mother has made. She can imagine herself relishing life here. As long as she had a studio to paint in.

After asking the location of the address her husband has written down for her she climbs up the twisting flight of steep steps towards the ruined Moorish castle on the rocky height above the village. To paint the world she walks through would require a palette of children's colours. The war seems remote here, like an invention of the newspapers. As she counts off the numbers of the buildings, breathing more heavily, she becomes uncertainly aware of her appearance. It surprises her how urgently she wants it to be pleasing to her mother. How anxious she is for her mother's approval. It occurs to her that she should feel angry at her mother. She doesn't though feel angry. She is too nervous. She is about to become less of a mystery to herself.

She stands on the doorstep of a house with a flaky rose-pink facade. It is incomprehensible to her that this woman facing her is her mother. In her highly agitated state she is unable to make any sense of the woman's face. Her mouth is set in a hard economical line and her wiry hair is lank and tied back.

"Cristina Del Monaco?"

There is a look of horror on the woman's face. And then annoyance.

"No. My name is Francesca," she says. "You must be Elisabetta. I spoke to your husband. Come in."

Almost every room in the apartment is on a slightly different level, divided by steps. The woman leads her into a dining room of nondescript weathered furniture. There are two botanical prints on the walls and an accomplished painting of a fishing boat in a pool of moonlight. The shutters are open and water reflections from the bay dance on the whitewashed ceiling.

"I explained everything to your husband. Did he not tell you?"

She shakes her head. She doesn't know what her face looks like, whether it wears an expression of perplexity, impatience or blankness.

"I don't know why your husband has created this awkward situation. I can't say it puts him in a good light as far as I'm concerned. There's no easy way to say this." Her voice takes on a sharpness. "Your mother died seven years ago. She drowned. It's probable she took her own life. Her personal effects were sent to her husband, your father. All this I explained to your husband."

For an hour she listens to the story of her mother's life in the fishing village. The woman constantly keeps her hands occupied with meaningless tasks. She seems to take pleasure in portraying her mother as an unbalanced woman from whom nothing positive could be gained. She hears how her mother eloped with a married man known locally as *il Poeta* who she met in Venice at a lecture on Byron and Shelley's poetry. "Shelley lived just across the bay here, in San Terenzo. It was his last home before he died. Your mother's boyfriend isn't really a poet. At least not a successful one. Calling him the *poeta* is a way people have of poking fun at him. She became something of a celebrity here. Everyone disapproved of her and I think she enjoyed the attention. From what I heard her husband, your father, gave her no attention at all. But the *poeta* eventually returned to his wife. He missed his daughters and his respectability. At this point your mother should have moved somewhere else. But she stayed. She moved in here with me. I needed the money. She worked for a while as a cleaner and then as a typist for an insurance firm in La Spezia. But she hungered for a more artistic life. She met another man who was a sculptor and a morphine addict." Several times the woman asks her if she is sure she wants to hear more. Elisabetta always nods. "One of the reasons she abandoned you was she didn't trust herself not to do you harm. She told me about this one night. She succumbed to violent irrational urges. She said the mere sight of a knife could bring panic into her mind. Another thing, towards the end she wrote to your father asking him to take her back. He refused."

She is dazed for a long time afterwards. She understands though that her mother is someone she needs to protect herself from. Only when she is sitting outside a café on the wharf does she become aware of her surroundings again. Two old men are engaged in a good-natured argument. There is the vigour of the sea tides in the way they develop the logic of their arguments. A man wearing a long black coat slung over one shoulder catches her eye. His probing look disarms her. It's like a door he is opening into his private world. For a moment she wonders if he might be the *poeta*.

She calls her husband from the hotel lobby. Little she feels can she find words for. Except a mounting tide of anger at him for withholding what he knew.

"Forgive me," he says. "I didn't have the heart to tell you myself. It was cowardly of me I know."

The longer she lives with him the more mysterious become his silences. It's the opposite of what she expected from marriage. And the longer you know someone the easier it becomes to feel pity for them. She refrains from calling her father. That he has once again kept her in the dark makes it still harder to feel any affection for him. She finds the only person she wants to talk to is Marcello. Someone of her own age. She is sick and tired of this older generation that has led the world into war.

On the balcony of her room she looks out at the black surf-threaded sea which took her mother's life. She wonders what she herself was doing, oblivious, when her mother sank down beneath the surface of the sea. Something mundane no doubt, like watering the plants or washing her tights at the sink. And as she thinks this she realises somewhere in the world someone's life is coming to an end at this very moment. The momentous is always latent in the banal. It's a premise she needs to always keep in mind when painting.

Her eye is attracted by the flashing tendril of light from the lighthouse on a nearby island. It moves slowly over the darkening sea. A small fishing boat is momentarily set aglow with otherworldly translucence. It is being rowed without hurry to shore by a single figure. She recalls the painting in the apartment and for an eerie moment experiences the moment as some kind of cryptic message from her dead mother.

36

Manuela falls short of Marcello's ideal. And he feels it is important to his morale in this time of war to hold fast to his ideals. He is critical of her heavy-lidded eyes, her thin lips, her sharp nose. But there's a magnetic charge about her insistent determination to make herself felt. She reminds him of Beth in London. He met Manuela at one of the Jewish institutes in the former ghetto. Because of the charity work he sometimes helps his mother with he now has more contact with the city's Jewish community. There are times when he can't help hating all Christians and wants only to be in the company of people of his own religion. But when this is the case and he is surrounded by fellow Jews he often feels alienated, weary of listening to the same mantras and fears. First and foremost, he feels he is Italian.

He has been thinking obsessively about Elisabetta. The flush of warmth that courses through his body when her arm brushes his shoulder. Her pinned up dark hair exposing the back of her naked neck when she stands close to him busy with her paintbrush. He thinks the world might become an extension of her embrace were she ever to press him against the heat of her body. As if all his boundaries might be redefined. The sight of her in her painting smock streaked with paint is somehow like being given a glimpse of her in her underclothes. Perhaps because he knows she has stripped off a protective layer when she paints. It is when she is most nakedly herself in the world. Her painted image of him with the small cut on his cheek glows with an attractive quality. That she attributes a glamour to his appearance has buoyed up his self-esteem. Sometimes it is easy to forget she is married and he finds himself looking forward to the future. Thus he can dislike Manuela simply because she isn't Elisabetta. Now, for example, as he punts his boat down the blacked-out Grand Canal, he feels it ought to be Elisabetta and not Manuela who is sitting with her bag in her lap in his boat.

"Are we breaking the law? It feels like it, doesn't it?"

"Everything we Jews do now breaks some law," he replies.

"How come I've never once seen you at the synagogue? Don't you feel guilty?"

"I feel guilty a lot but never because I don't go to the synagogue."

"My father makes me go. He was an enthusiastic member of the fascist party. He even donated money to government charities. His favourite word now is economise. Everything has to be done on the cheap. He's had to sell most of his securities. Do you get phone calls at night and no one speaks when you pick up the receiver?"

"No."

"We do. It's creepy."

She has dressed up and scented herself for him tonight. She has curled her hair with an iron; powdered her face. She wears a lilac dress with a silvery sheen. It strikes him as baleful that she has made so much effort to so little avail. But perhaps that is the story of every life. He realises he does with Elisabetta what Manuela does with him – tries to talk her into changing her mind. He wonders if talk ever changes anyone's mind. Our struggles to argue our truth into consequence against an opponent are when we are most naked. He has to keep reminding himself not to be unkind. So generously does she appear to be offering herself to him that it feels like a sin against the principle of life to put up resistance.

The moon bobs about on the black water when they are out on the lagoon. There is the smell of seaweed. The plash of the tide against the boat's hull. The occasional glimmer of spume.

In the distance the lamps of two isolated fishing boats. They make him think of beauty that's out of reach. Of meaning on the far side of language. He puts down the oar and sits beside her. When they kiss he is thinking of Elisabetta. He is taken aback when she undoes the buttons of his trousers. The rocking back and forth of the boat mirrors the agitation in his mind.

It's all, this new knowledge, over very quickly. A sordid event in both his mind and body he almost immediately wishes had never happened. He marvels at how much strength the act has taken from his limbs while he manoeuvres the blade of the oar through the water afterwards, his legs and hands jittery. He is ashamed of the callous nature of his feeling for Manuela but he also senses this callousness seems to increase her attraction towards him. The unfathomable mystery of women! Over-eagerness on his part drove Elisabetta away; his lack of amorous feeling for Manuela makes him more compelling to her.

In the following days he sits every day for Elisabetta during the siesta. He stops helping his mother with the charity work and knows he upsets her as a result. But he doesn't want to see Manuela. He has no desire to repeat the experience. His lack of enthusiasm makes him feel mean. He also feels ashamed of himself in relation to Elisabetta. As if he has betrayed her. Ridiculous seeing as she's married to someone else. But it is an ideal he has betrayed and he can't help deeming himself belittled as a result.

He doesn't want these painting sessions to ever end. He often finds himself wishing he could put out his hand and arrest the moment in its flight. Her smile reminds him of a flower whose folded petals only disclose the promise of the withheld pollen. Her shy smile, never delivered with her shoulders thrown back. She seems incapable of throwing her shoulders back. There's a loneliness in her, as if she's watching rain from behind a sealed window. This loneliness gives her an untouchability, a freedom he himself does not possess. At the same time he marvels at her ability to engage him so entirely, to galvanise him so animatedly into consciousness of her. He tries to impress her by talking in English, by speaking of the three hours he spent in Paris. He tries to glean her sympathy by talking of Giulia.

"Giulia once said you can gauge the level of your attraction to someone by how willing you'd be to soak in their dirty bathwater."

She pulls a face. Is she imagining immersing herself in his dirty bath water or her husband's? He doesn't tell her how seductive he finds the thought of plunging his naked body into her clouded bath water. The enforced polite formality of conversation is maddening. Always he is compelled to say the next best thing or deliver his meaning in code. Our submission to the rules of tact hinders so many of our true desires. Pleas have to shine in his eyes rather than come forth from his lips.

He feels the shared history they are acquiring makes him more known to himself. That it is an important part of his future. While she paints him he is able to watch her without looking at her, as if standing outside his body. It's like a small act of magic. And when she is standing by his side with her paintbrush extended he sometimes catches the smell of her among the oils on her palette. He feels he understands why smell is so important to animals. He would love to have her smell as part of his everyday life. It's another of those things he can't tell her. He has looked for signs wrought in her body by the carnal knowledge it now has. Her hands look no different. He knows them in all their detail, the long beautiful tapering fingers, the shine of the nails, the bones at her long wrist. Her hands for him leave a brightness on everything they touch. She still walks with the same slightly dreamy gait and there's still the little skip in her stride when he says something that pleases her. Outwardly she is the same. So he marvels at how well she conceals whatever inward changes have taken place since her wedding night. He is always on the lookout for some sign of her intimate life in the apartment. But he is struck by how little trace of her presence there is in her home. What he sees is little more than a collection of bare facts, mostly pertaining to her husband. The bedroom door is always closed. There is a photograph of her husband in a fascist uniform on the mantelpiece in the sitting room. He can't help feeling union for her with this nondescript ageing man must not be dissimilar with what he experienced with Manuela out on the black lagoon.

She has taken off her shoes and there is a hole in the heel of her stockings. His eye keeps going to it, as if it is an opening to her secret life. Then he finds himself looking at her hands again. He imagines those hands at night, in darkness, moving across a sheet, seeking contact. He would love more than anything to be intimate with the touch of her hands, to know their weight and ministrations. He imagines his body becoming wet clay for her fingers. On a sudden impulse he holds out his own hand to her. She is mystified by his gesture. He takes hold of her hand and caresses it. There is no response from her fingers. He removes the hated wedding ring from her finger and places it on the arm of his chair. She looks at him questioningly. He doesn't know what has prompted his gesture or what meaning it has. He lifts an eyebrow. Sometimes the creation of a mystery is an end in itself. He feels he has done something that she will remember.

37

There are times when she enjoys all the necessary preparations for painting more than the act of painting itself. The making up of her mediums for example when, feeling like a medieval alchemist, she leaves several bottles of the carefully measured combinations of oils to thicken on the windowsill in the sun for different lengths of time. She affixes a label to each bottle with details of its ratio of components and the time it has spent warming in the sunlight. Each bottle will eventually produce an elixir of a slightly different consistency with which to move the paint around on the canvas. She enjoys preparing canvases too, sitting on the wooden boards hammering tiny nails into the stretcher bars. She's not so fond of the sickening stench when cooking up and stirring the rabbit-skin glue but otherwise she enjoys the labour of priming a canvas. She takes pride in all this work, including the grinding of pigment. She is at work now with the pestle, working up the black pigment on the tray into a creamy consistency, when the telephone rings.

It's her father. She hasn't told him what she learned about her mother. She wants to forget her mother. Make her become inconsequential. No good can come from the knowledge she now possesses. He complains about how long it has taken to get through to her. The war for him is a medley of minor inconveniences he takes personally. He then spends a few minutes asking her polite questions and feigning interest in her answers. The slyness of the charade puts her on her guard. She waits for the real reason he has called. There will be something he wants from her. It annoys her that he thinks she is so easily fooled. Eventually there is a pregnant silence. Then he clears his throat. "Zecchi has run out of the weave of canvas I like. This damned war again. But I couldn't help noticing when I came to dinner last week that you have a primed canvas exactly the size I need. 140 centimetres by 115. It's become a source of great anguish to me that I can't start on the picture I want to paint. In fact, I've had trouble sleeping the past few nights. You know how anxious I get when I can't work."

"I've already started work on that canvas."

"You don't think you could go back to drawing for a while?"

"You want to paint over my picture?"

"Unless you still have more of that canvas you aren't using?"

"Zecchi has got other weaves of canvas."

"But you know I'm a creature of habit."

An image of him as a vulture enters her mind. Circling overhead with scheming greedy cold eyes. Her hands are trembling with fury. She puts down the receiver on him.

38

Fausto dishevels his hair and puts on blue overalls and a pair of old scuffed shoes he has been saving for a moment like this. He looks at his new gold tooth in the bathroom mirror. He wanted to make himself more noticeable, more memorable. Now he realises this was a mistake. Better to have gone unnoticed and been forgotten. It has become a liability. A distinguishing mark that might give the lie to every story he tells. He checks his gun and slips it into his pocket. Then he goes out into the streets where the celebrations are in full swing.

Mussolini has been arrested. Fascism has come to an end. The night is ablaze with lights. A man is singing *Tosca* at the top of his voice up in a roof garden. Forbidden voices on the radio can be heard from open windows. Voices shout out slogans outlawed only a few hours earlier. Mussolini is mocked and abused. Every fascist poster is torn from the walls. All the noise agitates the pigeons and gulls up in their crannies among the rooftops. They continually rise and descend again in a raucous clapping of wings. The gulls shriek. People are ringing on door bells and shouting the tidings up at the shuttered windows. No one is wearing a uniform; no one is wearing the fascist party pin. He smiles at almost everyone he passes as seems to be the protocol. Before long all the high excitement wearies and irritates him. He can't participate in it and it begins to strike him as naive. Adults behaving like unchaperoned children. He makes for the alleyways near Santo Stefano. The tumult of jubilation is further away here. He only has cats for company. He can collect his thoughts.

It's clear he has aligned himself with the wrong side. But his mood is one of sudden excitement. A surge of adrenalin makes him jog up and down the steps of a small bridge. He feels rash and boyish. Buoyed up now that he faces a threat that is finally real and pressing. His resources of guile will be tested. Risk creates energy, it makes the body feel more alive. And he can rid himself of the mind-numbing company of the likes of Gino. It infuriates him that people pair him off with such a blockhead bully. He often has a violent desire to publicly shame Gino's stupidity and cruelty. He can't think of any obvious enemies he has made. He doesn't need to flee Venice. Just as well because he can't bear the thought of returning to the chafing mediocrity of his family home. Only Volpato knows the part he played in the arrest of one or two anti-fascists. For a moment the idea of going to his apartment and shooting his former boss blazes into his mind as the most sensible idea. He imagines everyone has killed someone in thought at least once in their life. He would like to know if he is capable of killing someone in deed. He often sits holding his pistol in his lap. His finger itching to pull that metal trigger of power. Who would miss Volpato? He's probably not inspired a single spark of love in anyone since he was a child.

He eventually enters Piazza San Marco. He needs to gauge the mood of the populace. He half expects to see the bloodied bodies of renowned black-hearted fascists strewn over the paving stones. But there is no sign of violence. He resumes the exchanging of smiles with everyone who catches his eye including a bearded young man with an empty trouser leg swinging along on crutches. There is a man standing on a table outside Caffè Florian. He is denouncing fascism and is cheered.

Under the arcade in front of a shuttered shop he does his Mussolini impersonation for the amusement of two old women. Lifting his chin and pumping out his chest and making fists of his hands. "I come among you to look you firmly in the eyes, feel your temperature and break the silence which is dear to me," he declaims. Then he begins squawking and dancing like a panicked rooster. He performs the mad dance until it risks taking possession of him. Until there's a madness in his mind he is on the verge of losing control of. It's the sight of Marcello among the crowd by the towers of sandbags in front of the basilica that returns him to his senses. He is engaged in an intense conversation with a girl he doesn't recognise. He feels a need to know if Elisabetta has confided to him what she knows about his OVRA activities. He waits until he can come up with a good opening line.

"Doesn't it feel like we've all been let out of the asylum," he says. "Perhaps you don't remember me? I'm a friend of Elisabetta's."

He senses he has interrupted some kind of impassioned lovers' tiff but he doesn't like the disdain with which the Jew dismisses him.

"It's no wonder everyone's face looks like a mask," she says, the bitter taste of the unsweetened barley coffee still a lingering unpleasant taste in her mouth. She steps up onto a chair and takes down the blackout curtain from the window, tossing it to the floor and leaving it there. She is too annoyed to fold it up, to concern herself with the niceties of neatness and tidiness. Her husband at the dining room table lowers his copy of *Il Gazzettino*. She looks at the knot of his tie and the buttoned crisp collars of his shirt. It's like he is strait-jacketed into his clothes. Only late in the evening does she ever see him without his tie.

"What do you mean?"

"The enforced secrecy of what they really think about fascism has put a glaze over their faces," she says, sitting back down at the table. "For thirty days there was widespread jubilation that fascism was over. Now, all of a sudden, there's this charade that those thirty days never happened. Everyone's a loyal fascist again. More than ever that newspaper treats us like we're children. An eighteen year old is given a ten year prison sentence because he's overheard making the remark that if men stopped enlisting, the war would be over sooner and the *Gazzettino* writes up the story as though the prison sentence is the height of reason. We're living in a country where an offhand remark is seen as a political manifesto, an expression of doubt an act of seditious revolt. We're being governed by madmen and criminals. We've all become puppets. You've chosen the wrong side. You know that, don't you? Yesterday, the Germans marched off all the young apprentices from the Celestia engineering firm. They're only fourteen and fifteen years of age. They're sending them to Germany. The Germans aren't our friends. We should be fighting them. They've occupied our country. They want us to live in fear. They see us as their slave workers. And all this vile race hatred they spew out. How can you align yourself to these Nazis?"

"I don't. But perhaps you're oversimplifying everything," he says in a low and strained voice. "In the first place, fascism prevented us from being occupied by the Nazis in 1940. That would have been easy for them. At least, thanks to fascism, we've had three years of relative autonomy and peace. And if people are as passionately opposed to fascism as you suggest you also have to say they've been cowards for cowering under it without protest for so long. You get what's coming to you in life unless you put up a fight. To do a bad thing is no worse than standing by and allowing it to happen. Most of us have a viewpoint; few have a standpoint. A viewpoint is often dictated by fashion, a collective agreement to make things easier for ourselves, to fit in, to become a functionary and not ask many questions. Those with a standpoint are the ones who make life difficult for themselves by speaking out against the grain. I've only ever had a viewpoint. I suppose I don't feel very strongly about most things. Truth be told, I've never felt passionately about fascism one way or the other. To my mind it was preferable to communism which seemed the only other option. That's all. And I can't say your outburst of passion is entirely convincing. At heart you're like your father. Happy with the world as long as you're left alone to paint."

She stops herself before voicing a protest. Instead she reaches out to alter the arrangement of the four forlorn flowers in the vase on the table.

"As for my work, I've always been fascinated by secrets. It goes back to my childhood. My brother and sister kept secrets from me. They told me lies. I lived in a world of secrets and lies. I felt belittled. There is control in knowing things the other person does not know. It's one way of shedding light on darkness. And I've always loathed darkness."

It is unprecedented for him to speak of his inner life. For him, talk is less a quest for intimacy and discovery than an attempt to arrive at absolution. For this reason conversation between them has always been hard to keep alive. He retains a professional manner at home. He behaves as if the outer world is of more consequence to him than any inner world. But it's what people hide not what they show that's important to his work. She realises what she does in the act of portrait painting isn't entirely dissimilar. She too makes a show of being interested only in appearances but in truth is seeking out the secret beneath the surface.

"The more secrets you discover about other people the safer your own secret seems?"

"What do you mean?"

"Luigi!" She smiles across at him.

He is shocked by her speaking aloud his name which she so very rarely does.

Her husband cannot bear anyone to laugh at him. It is a shortcoming of his. To her mind it's a sign of generosity when a person allows you to laugh at them. Luigi is never able to laugh at himself nor does he allow other people to laugh at him. Her father is the same. Marcello, on the other hand, can enter into the comic spirit when he is teased.

"Anyway, won't you be made redundant when the Gestapo arrive?"

"I don't know."

"Well, at least you're too old to be called up."

She sees he is both hurt and frightened by her glib remark and surprises herself by feeling a desire to offer him some small gesture of comfort.

"Anyway, it would appear the Gestapo has already arrived. Look at this."

He shows her the notice in the newspaper ordering all Jews to report to the civic authority within twenty-four hours. Her thoughts immediately turn to Marcello.

40

The sinister red and black Nazi flag is draped over palaces along the Grand Canal. Its reflection rippling on the water. He is punting towards the Rialto bridge when his *sandolo* is violently rocked by the wake of a speeding German police boat. Its odious pennants ice his blood. When he needs to clear his mind his first thought is always to take the boat onto the waterways. To be on the canals, working the blade of his long oar through the reflections on the water, easing his way under arched bridges, in the company of gondolas and barges, gives him a sense of autonomy and peace he feels he needs as much as food. It seems this freedom too is to be taken from him.

Now, after mooring his boat, he sees a pair of German police officers walking towards him and his legs turn to liquid. They appear otherworldly in their crisp pressed uniforms, alien beings whose behaviour cannot be predicted. It is hard to believe he and they are of one and the same flesh. It is impossible for him to see any individuality in them. They are components of a collective; cogs in a murderous machine.

The shop he has chosen is in a junction of Rio San Treviso and the Grand Canal. He walks past a series of pasted death notices on a wall, the printed black cross and typescript on sullied white paper. He cannot rid himself of the disgust he feels for himself. In his pockets he has his father's silver war medals and three pieces of his grandmother's jewellery. He stole them in the middle of the night. Crept about the apartment in his bare feet perpetrating a crime against his own family. He imagined the ghost of Giulia was watching him when he held the valuables in his hands and almost put them back in the safe. But the quandary he is in allows him no peace. An unprecedented shame and dread has taken hold of him. Manuela is pregnant. He finds it hard to believe such a sordid act has produced new life. And he feels guilty at the fervour of his unwillingness to spend the rest of his life with her. He is tormented by the nagging suspicion he might not be a nice person. And he has managed to convince himself that the poison panicking his head and blackening his heart will only be expunged if he can acquire the money to pay for a termination. Even though he is yet to convince Manuela this is the best solution. And abortion, like contraceptives, is illegal in Mussolini's Italy. "He who is not a father is not a man," says Il Duce.

Before entering the pawnshop he doesn't register the two young men with hardened faces looking at him, though he will recall their presence afterwards. Inside the shop his hands feel grubby when he extracts the jewellery and medals of which his father is so proud from his pocket. He lays them on the counter. The small old man with an oval shaped bald patch and tortoiseshell glasses perched half way down his nose inspects each item, makes a great show of studious calculation and finally offers 450 lire. Marcello has no idea if this is a fair price or will be enough to pay for an abortion. He feels shabbier and shabbier at the counter. The shame of what he is doing rising up like a flood tide. This is an act, he recognises, that will change him so fundamentally that even his handwriting might no longer be recognisable as his own afterwards. He cannot betray his father in this way. He has chosen to perform this cowardly crime so as to avoid the humiliation of talking openly with his parents about his situation. This is what he decides he will have to do. He will sit down and tell his mother and father he has got pregnant a girl he does not love. He will have to live with the disappointment in him this will cause his parents. He leaves the shop with the valuables returned to his pocket. His blood is beating with a broth of both relief and dread. Outside, as he walks down an alley with blackened walls and peeling plaster towards his boat, his hat is knocked off his head from behind. The shock of it causes him to bite blood from his lip. For a moment he feels like a spilled suitcase, all its contents exposed. He swivels round to face the two youths with hardened faces he only now registers as having seen earlier. His eye goes to the knife pointed at him. The world is suddenly silent and overbright with consequence as if he is at the very heart of the universe for a moment. He has a ghostly ruined feeling as one of the men riffles through his pockets and takes his father's medals and grandmother's jewellery. The ordeal seems to simultaneously last an eternity and be over in a flash.

That evening he and his parents are eating what tastes like flavoured water for the fourth day in a row. The smell of it makes him nauseous. He feels isolated on his chair. He sees nothing beyond what's going on in his mind. It's a constant struggle for him to hold an appearance of composure. Every small comfort of his old life is denied him.

There has been no word from Flora in London for months and his mother and father discuss this. They also discuss a local baker arrested for using canal water to make his bread.

"Thankfully I've never bought his bread."

But mostly they discuss the notice in the newspaper today ordering all Jews to register with the civic authority within twenty-four hours.

"I still think we should go to Rome tomorrow," says Mother.

"And where will we stay? You still haven't been able to get hold of Gina on the phone. I don't know. I don't like the thought of leaving our home and shop unattended. Who knows what might happen in our absence. And the train journey will be dangerous. They strafe and bomb trains. And we don't have a transit visa."

"You're surely not suggesting we stay here?"

Marcello suggests hiding in the former lunatic asylum on an island in the lagoon. He speaks aloud to distract himself from the ache of dread in his body. For a moment he associates the lunatic asylum with his state of mind and pictures a wild bitter wind sweeping through roofless ruins.

"There are already German police boats patrolling the lagoon."

"I was joking."

"You didn't sound like you were joking."

"Well, it's not easy to sound jocular these days."

"What about Switzerland? They say if you can get to the Italian Alps you can pay a guide to take you over the border. But we need to leave tomorrow, Alfredo."

"We can't just take off. There are things I'll have to see to first. For one thing, we'll need fake identity papers." It is an infuriating habit of his father to try to complicate the simple truth of what he knows.

"We don't have time. We can pretend we're a bombed-out family from Verona or Milan. Everything lost in the carnage. We'll have to concoct a story."

Marcello has often marvelled at the ability his mother has to donate her full attention to the worries of others, especially evident when they were engaged together helping at the Jewish aid agency. He feels a momentary urge to throw himself at her mercy. To break down and confess his crime. It's the presence of his father that holds him back. Marcello sits facing Elisabetta's painting of him and Giulia. It came as a great surprise when, beautifully framed, Elisabetta gave it to him as a gift. It moved his father to tears when he brought it home. To Marcello it conveys with heartbreaking lucidity how inescapably we are all locked in our parallel private solitudes. Never has he felt this more than now.

His father returns with a map. He opens it out on the table and begins tracing lines on it with his finger. It reminds him how lovingly his father handles paper money. He feels a moment's sadness for this rupture with his father, remembering times when he was able to participate in his father's excitement after a day of good takings in the shop. Increasingly in these fraught times the purpose of memories seems to be to break the heart.

"How much do you think we'd have to pay a guide?"

"We've got your mother's jewellery."

Marcello's blood runs cold. His heart races. He feels his face has swollen and is sliding about on his skull.

His father gets up from the table and leaves the room again.

"You don't look well tonight," Mother says. "What's wrong? I know when you're troubled. Your hand goes constantly to the back of your neck."

He stands up and walks over to the painting. He can't bear to meet his mother's eyes. He is about to confess when his father blusters back into the dining room. His eyes are ablaze, his jaw is tightened. "It was you, wasn't it?"

"What are you talking about, dear? What's wrong?"

"My war medals, my mother's jewellery. All gone."

"Of course it wasn't him."

"Look at his face! Guilt written all over it. Where are my two daughters? I want my daughters. Why has life left me with only this disgrace of a son?"

"Marcello?"

He marches out into the hall and opens the front door. The beat of blood behind his eyes blinds him to everything but the urge to be where no one can see him.

"Marcello! You can't go outside. There's the curfew."

He ignores his mother. There is no logic in his thinking. His only thought is to seek out the refuge of his boat. In the narrow alley he is engulfed in the thick swell of shadow. He reaches the canal. The moon is a faint glow behind a featherbed of clouds. He is about to climb over the railing and jump down into his boat when a harsh echoing voice startles him.

"You!"

The quicksilver beam of a torch shoots out of the darkness, ensnares him and brings him to his senses. He steps out of the pinioning shaft of light and runs back to the apartment building.

The cobbles pounding up through the soles of his feet. The spear of torchlight wobbling in front of him, creating a grotesque shadow show. His body is awaiting the crack of a gunshot. He sprints into the alley and its concealing thick shadow. His hands are shaking when he fumbles with the key, trying to locate the lock in the darkness. The metallic footsteps are coming closer.

41

In the early hours of 5 December, when the canals glint with wafer-thin sheets of ice, the roundup of the Jews in Venice begins. The Germans are keen to involve Italians in the operation. To avoid being sent to work in a factory in Germany Fausto has joined a Republican secret police unit. He is not required to wear a uniform. Today is his first day working in liaison with the German SS police. Snowflakes fall on the sleeve of his coat as he stands in the alley outside the targeted building while an SS police officer thumps on the door with the butt of his rifle. A dog begins barking and one or two lights show faint through the slats of the shutters. He knows it's the Zecchi family they have come to arrest. He recognises the building. He thinks back to when he followed Signora Zecchi and his encounters with her son. He is not looking forward to meeting Marcello's eye. He claps his gloved hands together to chase away the chill underneath his skin.

The concierge, in her dressing gown, opens the door. Fausto's Italian companion does the translating. She tells them she hasn't seen the Zecchi family for two days. The most officious and self-satisfied of the Germans tells her she is a liar. She straightens her spine. Then refuses to hand over the keys to the apartment. Eventually it is agreed she will accompany them upstairs. Fausto is relieved he won't have to look Marcello in the eye. Unless the concierge *is* lying. As he makes his way up the final flight of stairs he is forced to admit how tired, annoyed and angry he is. This is not what he wants to be doing with his life. It's as if he

201

has lost control of all the pieces on the board, as if he has been outsmarted by a superior opponent.

The concierge opens the door. They enter the apartment and its sketch of the story of a family's life. The officious Nazi shouts in German at Fausto and his companion. He treats them like they are slow-witted lackeys.

"Now what's he in a stew about?"

"He wants us to search the apartment. Make sure no one's hiding."

Fausto walks into a bedroom and sits on the unmade bed. There is a model ship on the bedside table. He picks it up as if it might restore some childhood memory of his own. But no feeling arrives. Instead he has the sudden sensation he can detect a breathless presence underneath the bed. He decides he will not give them away. He likes this idea. Of secretly colluding against the two odious Nazis. He is primed to see a terrified face when he kneels down on the rug and peers into the shadowy world beneath the bed. But there is no one there.

When he returns to the living room he watches the more subservient of the Germans steal things. A fountain pen. A thimble. A paper knife. He takes two puppets from a cabinet and holds them up to his sidekick – a costumed mermaid and pirate made of painted wood. He stuffs them in the pockets of his great coat with a show of uncertain defiance. He then opens the violin case. Holds the yellow varnished instrument by the neck and plucks a discordant note from the strings. Fausto knows before it happens that he is going to stamp on the carved instrument. Children let loose in an abandoned house will smash or steal everything they find.

Before they leave, Fausto stands in front of the painting of Giulia and Marcello hanging in the dining room. He has not seen Giulia since they were at university together. A period in time that now seems carefree and blessed. He has the creepy feeling as he meets Giulia's eye that she is summoning him from the other side of life.

He waits until the Germans have begun descending the stairs and then demands the keys from the concierge. The woman is reluctant to part with them and he has to shout at her.

There are five Jews huddled up in the launch, including an elderly couple in threadbare clothes and two children, a boy holding a bear and wearing a cap and a girl with a tiny scar on her cheek and a red ribbon in her black hair. The launch bounds into the choppy water of the lagoon on its way to the women's prison on Giudecca. The German shows the puppets to the children. He says something that sounds cruel. Fausto is pleased the girl gives the German so little attention.

"This girl is your superior in every way, despite all the drivel that comes out of your fuhrer's mouth," he says, smiling at the German and hoping none of his companions speak Italian.

The German throws the two painted wooden puppets overboard. Another of the Nazis, rubbing his hands together, laughs. He tries to catch Fausto's eye. He wants to encourage him to join in with the laughter.

In an ideal world – or a film - he would now choose for himself the role of heroic saviour. He would find a way of rescuing the two Jewish children, carrying them off to safety. He would shoot the four Germans without any qualms. He dislikes the Germans. They are an enigma to him. He finds them either humourless or imbecilic in their ideas of fun. And they seem to have a screw missing. Where is the honour or courage in hunting down old men, women and children? It makes no more sense to him than it would to execute a mission to take captive all the stray cats of Venice.

An hour later he stands with the Germans outside his old apartment building. He hopes Max and his pregnant wife have had the sense to escape. The fervour with which he hopes this surprises and unsettles him.

"What do you think happens to these Jews?"

"Nothing good," says his companion.

42

She stands shivering on the pontoon. She has just spent an hour in the church of the Madonna dell'Orto studying the Tintoretto altarpieces. Seeking inspiration, seeking sanctuary. The icy wind now beating against her face makes her eyes water. The earlier snow swept in from the Dolomite mountains to the north has ceased to fall but the temperature has not risen. The long awaited vaporetto, foaming at the prow, eases towards her through the mist. She has been unsuccessful in her quest to find canvas, linseed oil and resin. Marcello's family shop has been closed for over a week. When she saw the padlocked iron shutters in place over the door and window she found herself wondering if they would ever return.

She steps aboard the crowded vaporetto which are now scarce and run by the Germans. For a moment she welcomes the warmth of the press of congested bodies. She is crushed in the aisle between a woman who smells of fried onions and an old man who has an unlit Tuscan cigar between his chapped lips. Every face looks austere, pinched, wary. No one speaks.

The boat chugs out into the middle of the Grand Canal. Through the condensation and silvery frost on the window she watches a funeral cortege pass by. The array of mourning gondolas keeping close to the high poles to which boats are moored and the palaces over some of which are draped Nazi banners, billowing and fluttering. In the mist the spectacle appears ghostly. She crosses herself. She thinks of how long it has been since she took confession. Her inability to forgive her father is perhaps a sin. But what most bothers her is the constant regret she feels for making a gift of her painting of brother and sister to Marcello. It is mean-spirited of her. But it is by far the best piece of work she has ever done. And now she has no evidence of her accomplishment. And it's as if by separating herself from it she has also separated herself from the source of inspiration which enabled her to work so joyously and fluently. She is dissatisfied with every new painting she completes. There's something missing in the depth, gloss and lustre of her colours. Her brush strokes lack some subtlety of truth. And now she has run out of canvas and the ingredients that make up her medium. She misses the smell of her sun-thickened oils. The smell which most makes her feel rooted in the moment. She has been told there is unlikely to be any more painting materials until this war ends. She sometimes forgets there is a war. It can be a surreal feeling to know a devastating war is waging throughout Europe and yet see no evidence of its violence here in Venice.

The tight press of the passengers gives off a sour sickening fume. She is relieved to step off the vaporetto, her legs unsteady with the ghost motions of the boat. She has decided to try to find Marcello's home. She asks one of the women queuing for water at the well in the campo if she knows the address of the Zecchi family.

"Number 221 but I doubt if you'll find anyone there."

The concierge at number 221 tells her the Zecchi family have left but that a young man is living in their apartment. The woman studies her closely for a moment. Elisabetta senses she is about to discover whether she appears trustworthy or not. More often than not out in the world she forgets she is a married woman. She assumes people see a naïve teenage girl when they look at her. It often startles her when she catches sight of her wedding ring, becomes aware again of the tight pinch of its discordant presence, as if she is waking up from a dream. "One of this new breed of policemen who don't wear uniforms," says the concierge, making little effort to disguise her distaste.

She knocks on the door. After a long wait it is Fausto who opens it. His trousers are held up by a single strap of his braces.

"What are you doing here?"

"Living rent free if you must know. A question of economics. Why let an empty apartment go to waste? You look like you want to stride past me imperiously. I'm not sure moral indignation suits you," he says after smiling at her. She registers the new gold tooth and then watches him vigorously scratch his head. She walks past him into the apartment. She is struck by the forlorn look of all the household objects, the gumboots and umbrellas and coats by the front door, the open violin case with its red velvet lining, the framed photographs in the sitting room. How little value everything seems to possess. She sees the gold-leaved cherry-wood frame leaning against the wall. It is empty.

"Can I offer you a coffee. Coffee in name only of course. And I've no sugar to sweeten the bitter muck. For a moment when I wake up I have the taste of real coffee in my mouth. It's then I realise there isn't much difference between habit and happiness. Have you noticed the drinking water tastes different these days? It's had an unpleasant aftertaste since the Germans arrived."

"I still don't understand why you're here. What right have you got to move in to someone else's home?"

"Stop being naïve. They're Jews. Jews have less rights now than pigeons." He gathers up a pile of letters on a table and stuffs them inside an open drawer in the sideboard. She notices the gun on the table. She looks down at the gramophone records in their sleeves strewn over the floor. "Now that the Italian film industry is based in Venice I've become good friends with Osvaldo Valenti. I was on the set of his new film yesterday. He says he'll give me a role in the film he wants to make. I supply him with his morphine. He's an addict. I get the morphine from a medic at the hospital. I've got leverage over this medic thanks to work I did with your husband. I took him his file. I now get excellent rates."

She is turning the pages of an illustrated book on snakes she has picked up from the floor. "Why are you telling me all this?"

"Just making conversation. What do you want me to talk about? The sawdust bread we're expected to eat? The accumulation of garbage everywhere?" He begins to impersonate a woman gossiping to a neighbour, the kind of dialogue frequently heard nowadays. His hands planted on his hips. "And don't talk to me about the quality of these new blocks of toothpaste. They dissolve into moon dust the moment you run water over them."

In a corner of the room she sees the corpse of a brutalised violin. She walks over to it and stares down at its broken and splintered neck, its loosened strings.

"I didn't do that, if that's what you're thinking. But it's an image that tells you everything you need to know about the Third Reich. Don't you think?"

"Have you seen the painting that was in this frame?"

"I wondered about that. I suppose they must have taken it with them. What was the painting of?"

"It was a painting I did of Marcello and Giulia."

"You should feel flattered they took it. Must have been one of their prized possessions."

She looks again at the gun on the table. It sits beside a mess of strewed paperwork.

"Looks like you've been doing some detective work," she says. "Isn't their home enough for you?"

"Any more insubordination and I might have to arrest you. And you don't want to be arrested. They torture prisoners at Ca' Littoria. First they dehumanise them, then they do awful things to their bodies. Sometimes I try to imagine those prisoners as children – how unfathomable it would have been to them then to know this is what lay in store later down the line. I remember once reading a poem. It went something like this. I have always known I would take this road, but yesterday I did not know it would be today. I expect something of the kind awaits me too. And you. I've had to witness some barbaric acts. And the perpetrators enjoy it. The principle torturer was once a waiter. They think I'm squeamish. I'm known as the princess."

"Because you believe you have a conscience?"

"I don't recall saying that." He sits down on the desk and picks up his gun. "Do you know what I think? I think you're in love with Giulia's brother. I used to think I was lying to your husband when I told him how lovestruck you appeared around the Jew but I see now I was telling the truth without realising it."

"Don't call him the Jew. His name is Marcello," she says. His name in her mouth is both delicate and sharp. She recalls how Marcello always used to brighten when she called him by his name.

"It's strange how our paths keep crossing," he says, peering down the barrel of his gun. "Anyone would think fate is pushing us together. But you and I are very different. I don't venture so deep into my mind as you do. But I like violent emotions. You do everything possible to avoid them. How are you anyway? You haven't been to a hairdresser since I last saw you. How's your husband? I saw him in the public gardens a few days ago. Locked in conversation with a pouting young man."

She looks over at a framed photo of Marcello. She thinks her painting captured some essence of his likeness more eloquently. She decides she will search the rest of the apartment for her painting.

"Where do you think you're going?"

"I want to find my painting. It was in that frame."

There is no sign of it in the apartment. On her way home she thinks of the mysterious fate awaiting every completed painting. In all probability it will outlast the flesh of the artist. It has a much more fraught and lengthy destiny. What will happen to it? Will someone look after it, treasure it even? It's important to her that this painting survives her. Sooner or later the war will arrive in Venice. She might die before she can accomplish anything better.

She crosses herself with holy water when she enters the church of the Frari. She stands in front of Titian's *Assumption* for a long time. Willing herself to learn as much as she can from it. For a moment she is holding the ghost of a paintbrush in her hand, a rush of love in her fingers. When she sits down in a pew she finds herself remembering Marcello with a new intensity of detail. In the church with its smell of incense and snuffed candles it is easy to think of him as already a ghost. The further away he appears the more attractive he becomes. She asks herself if perhaps Fausto is right. It's true she came to dislike Marcello's independence from her, didn't like thinking about it. That other women might interest him, make him laugh, warm his blood. While painting him she came to view these accolades as hers.

There is a heaviness in her legs as she climbs the steps of a bridge. The image of Titian's virgin is bright in her mind. Does she want to go through her life as a virgin? To have no memory of love. The only time she ever drops her guard is when she is working, when she is painting. She takes a deeper breath. The low tide exposes a tapestry of green slime and mud on the bulwarks of the canal she walks alongside.

43

Marcello turns to face the footprints he has left behind in the expanse of snow. He is struck by the eloquence of what he sees. All the loneliness he feels is conveyed by the tapering trail of marks in the snow. He stares at them through the streamers of his breath on the crisp thin air. His aim is to arrive at a precipice. He wants to make visible what he has felt for three days - that death is a single misplaced footstep away. And he wants to know if he still has the will to carry on living.

The constant effort of keeping fear from overrunning all the mechanisms of his mind has exhausted him. Thoughts are too loud in his head. The train journey to the Italian Alps took more than two days. He has never thought it a good idea. But they have been lucky so far. At Santa Lucia station the checkpoint was manned not by German police but Italian fascists. They showed little interest in his family's papers. So far he has not had to answer back to a Nazi. But he is conspicuous as a young man not in uniform. They are now staying in a hotel in the small ski resort. They don't have false papers. The owner knows they are Jewish. There is a reward of twenty-thousand lire for reporting Jews. They have to trust he is a decent man. There is a new yearning in him to believe there are still kind people in the world. Kindness is often no more than the exertion of imagination on another's behalf. Not much to ask for. Giulia once told him she would like to feel at peace with the human race. Perhaps she is lucky not to have learned how threadbare and desperate such a hope would become.

He is unused to walking long distances. The ache of the muscles in his legs is a novel sensation. Life has new surprises every day. This is the first for a while he is able to smile about. He stands watching crystal clear water cascade down a cliff face. The drumming noise of it creating a welcome silence in his mind. The moment is innocent. If only he could halt the onrush of time. Only the bitter cold is unkind. He follows the trail into a spruce and pine forest. The sharp tang of the air arrows deep down into his lungs. His shortness of breath as he climbs uphill reminds him of Giulia's struggles to breathe. It is almost inconceivable to him now how complacently he took all the simple old freedoms for granted. The pleasures and indecisions of buying a new hat for example. An ache of nostalgia grips him for the time in his life when he was able to believe a new article of clothing could endow him with heightened possibilities of romantic adventure. Those far off days when he enjoyed looking at himself in mirrors, when his expectations of the future were of a world in which he would be ever more attractive and accomplished, ever more worthy of respect, of love.

He returns to the hotel exhausted and chilled to the bone. His father, whispering, tells him a German staff car with flags on the front fenders has arrived at the hotel. Three Nazis have occupied rooms on their floor.

He sits down on the bed in his parents' room. He prepares himself for another clash with his father. Relations between them have been tense. His father made little attempt to disguise his disgust that his son had got a girl pregnant he does not love. And that instead of acting with maturity and taking responsibility for his actions he behaved like a panicked child. His mother, on the other hand, was more sympathetic. He confided to her his feelings for Elisabetta. He felt the need to convince her he is not a callow callous young man without worthy sentiments.

"We'll have to trust this Alberto then. There's no other choice."

"Keep your voice down," whispers his father with irritation. He loosens his tie. "You don't trust him any more than I do. At least that's one thing we can agree upon."

"Marcello's right, dear." His father flinches at the touch of his wife's hand, as if so tense his body cannot withstand any form of physical contact. "We no longer have a choice. You must go and find him and tell him we need to leave as soon as possible. Tomorrow if possible."

This Alberto was wearing tan riding breeches and high glossed boots like Mussolini when they met him. Marcello thought he detected a darkness in the depths of his eyes while he listened to him explain how perilous and arduous the climb would be in places and how he would hand them over to a Swiss guide close to the border for the final stretch of the journey.

In the dining room that evening the three Nazis in crisp uniforms are sitting at a table to Marcello's left. He has to turn his head to see their table. Which he can't help doing frequently. The Germans exert a magnetic force over him. They hold the fascination any murderer does. There's a desire to seek out some disclosure of the evil beneath the veneer of normality.

His father kicks him under the table. "Will you stop staring at them," he hisses at Marcello.

But it bewilders him that he has so much significance for the Nazis. In truth he feels he is wholly irrelevant in the grand scheme of things.

44

Marcello puts on his black turtleneck jumper. In the mirror he could pass as a fascist. It once again occurs to him that he is being persecuted for beliefs he doesn't hold, things he knows nothing about. Chanukah, Rosh Hashanah, Yom Kippur, Passover, Purim. All as meaningless to him as angels, virgin births and holy water. He knows next to nothing of the language and culture of Zionism. He doesn't even understand why his parents had him circumcised given how little relevance was given to religion in his upbringing. And wonders now why he has never asked.

The carpeted stairs respond to his weight with groans. He is overcome by the strangeness of what his life has led to. He finds this is both a moment that was always going to happen and a moment that doesn't belong to his real life. The lobby is deserted. There are potted ferns along the wall opposite the unattended front desk. Outside the sun hasn't yet risen. The straps of his heavy rucksack are already chafing his shoulders. He looks at his watch. He is early. He hasn't slept all night. He laid awake with a feeling that side by side with the world we live in is another world into which we might fall at any moment. Sometimes this other world seems much closer. And it's a darker, more violent world. The shadows on his wall thrown by the moon seemed to belong to this other world. Outside his window he pictured slugs oozing over the garden path to the lettuce plants or the drain or the rubbish bin. Then realised he was no longer living in London even though the smell of the London house was

213

thick in his nostrils. Outside the window he pictured a black cat that became Luna emerging stealthily from the dark and jumping up onto the roof of the garden shed. Inside the shed, neatly arraigned, all kinds of garden tools he had never seen before. Once again he was back in London. Then he saw his mother playing the violin. Except the music she played seemed to be a composition he had made up in his own mind. He and Massimo performed a comic dance they copied from adults and then exaggerated every shift of the hips, every extension of the arms. He remembered how easily delight and surprise come to children. And then his father carried him against his shoulders. He could feel in his limbs the physical sensation of being held by his father, how snugly and safely he fitted his small body to the shape and warmth of his embrace. Giulia was there, jumping over the waves and then she was holding Luna to her face, rubbing noses with the lost cat. She smiled and then a bottomless loneliness glazed over her eyes and her face became cadaverous and her breathing laboured and her fingers fretted at the red ribbon at the neck of her nightdress and the beating of her heart seemed to vibrate through the entire bed.

Memories came in snatches. They didn't have a beginning or an end. Often he relived just a broken off fragment of a moment of wellbeing or adventure or loss. Sometimes these vignettes were an invention but no less authentic in their emotional charge. Like when he saw himself punting Elisabetta in his boat. Enjoying the sensation of the strength and agility in his shoulders as he pushed into each new stroke. He does not know who he might become if he never has his boat to return to. The mental images he possesses of Venice's waterways are as clear as his image of his own body. He misses the canals. He misses water. The lights carried by water. Water opens up perspective. Water makes everything clear. He wanted to tell Elisabetta this. He and Elisabetta, he knows, have forged a companionship which has an essence of its own, a unique sequestering quality which can heighten the passing moment. He can sense this is true for her too. He pictured her bedroom which he has never seen. All her clothes strewn on the floor. Then she was standing before him barefooted, emblazoned with light. The moment he has longed for but which never arrived. At a certain point in the long night he realised something. There are no full stops in the human mind. There is no final draft. Everything that happens continues happening. It has an existence outside of time.

On the far side of the bridge under which the water surges there is no sign of the guide. Marcello finds it hard to believe that the bed he climbs into tonight will be in Switzerland. That there's a line drawn out on the earth that he only has to step over to ensure he will no longer be hunted down, like an arbitrary rule in a children's game, strikes him as indication of the insanity of politics, the heartbreak of cartography. And then he thinks of his failure to cross Elisabetta's borders, to make a new map with her of shifted boundaries and marvels at the liberating or crushing power to be found on the threshold of every frontier. He looks at his breath on the chill air. It seems to have a message for him as if it is the manifestation of words he dare not speak.

Mother and Father arrive with their bags. A black woollen scarf is wound twice around his father's neck. He looks frail and hounded. It pains Marcello to see so much anguish disfiguring his familiar face.

"I'm only going to give him half the money up front." His father, he knows, is trying to make believe he still has some control over proceedings.

His mother surprises him. There is a galvanised poise about her like she has before she begins to play music. Sometimes he has the feeling his mother is secretly thriving on the danger they are in. As if the high emotion is a relief from the monotonous banality of household chores, from the nagging disappointment of her failed musical career. He unfortunately takes after his father. He is timid and easily depressed. He overthinks. There is no longer any denying it.

The guide arrives five minutes late. He apologises. His smile is tight. His eyes elusive. His rucksack looks half empty.

Negotiations take place. Father gives him half the agreed sum. They walk away from the town. He hears the lorry before it comes into view. The noise of its engine seems to gather the early morning around it as if it is the day's heartbeat. Marcello's entire body is as if plunged into darkness for want of a flame. It's his first vivid premonition of extinction.

Two German soldiers jump down from behind the tarpaulin with rifles at the ready. A man with the face of a weasel wearing a long black leather coat and buckskin gloves climbs out of the passenger seat. He says something to one of the soldiers. The soldier frisks Father and removes his wallet. The weasel counts out ten banknotes and hands them to the guide.

"Look me in the eye," says Father, taking a step towards the guide. "Don't look away. Don't look away, you cowardly dog. Face what you've done. I want you to remember my face. And the face of my wife and my son."

It is the first time in a while Marcello feels pride in his father.

45

Fossoli transit camp, February-March 1944

Mother and Father have become like two young lovers again. Every day they meet at the barbed wire fence which separates the men from the women in the camp. Marcello is allowed to join them for a while but is always eventually sent away by his father who has become still more possessive of his wife's company now that it is limited to less than an hour every day. He learns from his father they talk a lot about the past. They have a rich shared history to bring into play. They are the keepers of treasures. He himself feels in possession of no such hoard of treasures. His life has barely begun. And yet it is being consumed day by day to no avail. He returns again and again to this feeling. He learns as never before how important is the body's need to be touched. The press of his mother's hand reaches directly to the heart and soul of his being. Awakens and replenishes the healthy animal in him. He hopes the touch of his hands has the same effect on her. It's such an easy gift to give. He doesn't understand why he hasn't understood this sooner.

He now has a number. It is sewn onto his shaggy black jersey. He has a yellow star. This too is sewn onto his shaggy black jersey. On arrival he had to strip naked and submit to the prodding of a man in a white coat with a stethoscope. He had to stand naked beside his naked father in a shower. An unprecedented humiliating experience for both of them. He and his father share a bunk in the hut. Sleeping head to toe. This pressing intimacy too causes mutual embarrassment. It highlights the realisation that, of the same bloodline though they might be, his father is a troubling stranger to him. Never has he made the effort to look deeply into his father's heart. Empting his bowels without the privacy he is accustomed to is another humiliation he still has difficulty resigning himself to. He makes a habit of visiting the latrines in the middle of the night. More than once he has walked out into a white mist of falling flakes and crunched footprints into a virgin covering of snow. These trips out into the middle of the night when he looks up at the bewildering astrology of the night sky have become a momentary escape. He is able to take a step outside time. The magic white light of the moon gradually spreading under his gaze. There are moments when he feels he knows something he cannot possibly know.

Another thing he can't get used to is being shouted at. Never can he accept these men in their dress uniforms have earned the right to bark orders at him. They incite a will to violence in him he did not know he possessed. The knowledge he might be capable of murder. Every morning and evening there is a roll call. Everyone in lines trying not to fidget. The bitter cold quickly penetrating up through the soles of shoes, biting at fingertips. Upper lips drawn back in grimaces on every face. Eyes watering, noses running. The roll calls are pointless. No one ever escapes. The landscape is flat and barren on all four sides of the camp. Swept by raw winds. It is an empty sight. There are no hiding places.

Spacious days, unused days, empty days of purposeless leisure. It is bewildering to be so bored and yet at the same time conscious of participating in a page of history. Every day he feels himself lose another attachment to the past. Every day he realises memory is both the best and cruellest friend we will ever have.

Outside the hut, where there is always a line of washed clothes, Father shares his memories of his children, something he has never before done. Marcello marvels at all the fragmented images his father possesses of him that play no part in his conception of himself. All of us, he thinks, are a multitude of unfinished stories told by different narrators. His father has begun to walk with a slight limp and Marcello knows a new access of tenderness for him. It is a gift to feel love for his father. As if he is finally able to see into his heart.

A highlight of every day is often the appearance of the cat. It patrols the camp with a regal sense of entitlement. Marcello would love to tempt it into his arms. Just one infusion of its pulsing warmth against his chest would return him to a kinder world. He is jealous of it too, the carefree manner in which it yawns or cleans its ears, the ease and impunity with which it can slip outside the camp. To catch sight of the flight of a bird is another source of wonder. He tries to follow their journey in his imagination. The hunger for a new horizon more pressing than the hunger for food.

At the fence he searches among the women for a face he might fall in love with. A young woman to spin protective fantasies around. The landscape seems to blossom when the women all gather together behind the fence with their soft voices and expressive bodies. He loves to look at their faces. The young and old alike. He remembers what Elisabetta once said about the infinite beauty of people's faces. He always returns to Elisabetta. Often he finds himself imagining standing outside the large heavy door of her building and is overcome by the magical properties her home now has in his imagination, as if it has been removed to a mythical kingdom.

It pains him to see the two children he took out in his boat in the camp. And that they too are separated and meet by the fence every day. Every time he watches the girl reach through the wire to touch her brother he is disgusted anew by the baseness of human nature that can devise such senselessly cruel prohibitions. He has discovered their names. Boris and Hanna. He is not alone in taking Boris under his wing. There is an unspoken competition among some of the men to be his favourite. To be liked and trusted by the boy is a means of feeling better about oneself. One afternoon when Marcello is piggybacking Boris across the yard an Italian guard with prominent teeth approaches and opens his palm to show a handful of coloured mints. He puts them in the pocket of Boris' jacket.

"He reminds me of my own son. I suppose you must hate me," he says, a flush coming to his cheeks. "I don't blame you. I'm not proud of myself. But what can I do? I'm just one man. If I had an army I'd free you all without a moment's hesitation. But as things stand I don't have the courage to stand alone and disobey."

Marcello nods. He could say what he feels, that passivity is akin to complicity, that a chain of command can be undone by breaking the links, but he has no desire to make the man feel worse about himself. He senses he is essentially a kind man somehow tricked into doing an unkind job.

There is no sign of Manuela in the camp. He is thankful she has escaped the Nazis. It remains inconceivable to him that he might before too long become the father of a son or a daughter. He thinks he would like a daughter. But then he pictures himself teaching a small boy to punt the *sandolo* on Venice's canals. The innocence of the image seems an infinity away from the world he is forced to inhabit.

They have been in the camp three weeks. The weather is warming. The hope they will be allowed to stay here until the war is over is a fragile thing everyone handles with trepidation as if it might lose its heartening power if given too much attention. This hope is shattered with the announcement at evening roll call that they are required to pack for a twelve-day journey.

There is singing and prayers are sent up to heaven inside the hut while he sits in a corner composing his note. All the time he is immersed in the act of writing he is protected, outside of time. He understands the attraction of creative work. How it takes you outside of yourself and outside of time. Like being a child again fully immersed in a game, oblivious to the outside world. He has a story he wants to tell. His thoughts continue to run forward. He only has two thin pages he surreptitiously tore out of a Rabbi's Hebrew prayer book. The guilt of the act remaining a shadow at the back of his mind. He has to write over the text. He tells Elisabetta he has escaped the camp. With the aid of a kind Italian guard. His imagination gives the story more detail until it begins to become true as a feeling. He tells her this story because he wants to imagine it as a truth and because he wants her to expect his reappearance in her life. He wants to keep her in a state of expectation, to make her think of him as a pressing presence which will return soon to her life. He wants to make her feel on his behalf. He wants to make her ache on his behalf. He recalls Tintoretto's *Crucifixion*. It's the three women at the foot of the cross that bewitch him. He can't help thinking this is how he himself would like to be mourned.

He writes her name and address at the head of the page. He blocks in every letter of her name and address as thickly as he can with the blunt stub of pencil. Then he goes outside to the latrine. It is a few minutes past midnight. There are the lights of candles outside the women's camp and huge grotesque shadows moving over the pools of light. He hears ghostly women's voices singing. For a moment he mourns his lack of religious faith. The night sky is ablaze with stars. The information encoded in those lights shrinks him to the size of a particle. He feels like he is standing in the most intimate corner of the night. The chill air and the sharp smell of turf sends a shiver through his body.

There are many more Germans at the roll call the following morning. Most wear a look of disgust on their faces. There is no sign of the Italian guard he wants to pass his note to. The roll call takes forever. Then they are shouted at by the Germans and taken in trucks to the railway station at Carpi. He catches Mother's eye on the platform amongst all the panicked faces and tries to shove his way towards her. He knows a feral hatred for all the people blocking his way. The raucous shout of a German voice makes him look over his shoulder. His father is kneeling on the ground with blood streaming from his nose. For a moment he is caught in two minds. Then he turns back and helps his father to his feet. He sees Boris' cap and teddy bear abandoned on the platform. They are being kicked about by all the shuffling feet. The urgency with which he hopes Boris has managed to find his sister quickens his heartbeat. There is no way of reaching Mother now. They are forced to enter different carriages. Boris is inside, without his sister. It's a moment that moves him to a place in his mind he doesn't know and doesn't want to know.

He will eventually throw his note to Elisabetta out of the narrow slit in the cattle truck door before they have crossed a border into another country. He imagines rain or snow or dew turning it to illegible pulp before anyone finds it.

46

Fausto reigns in his distaste and kisses the girl on the Rialto bridge. A mosquito whines close to his ear. As a rule he avoids public displays of amorous behaviour. It's something he considers vulgar. But the girl is unattractive and the desire he brings up into his eyes is entirely fake. As is everything he has told her about himself. "Love for me is being able to share every thought that passes through my mind," he told her while sitting by the water. "If we bury our thoughts we never retrieve them, which is why love is so necessary in our lives. Without love we are compelled to create a forgery of ourselves, a copy of the lost original." In truth, he suspects her of knowing insurgents, the discovery of which would grant him power. While walking her home he tells her he is making a film with Osvaldo Valenti.

"Isn't he a fascist?" she says with disgust.

The next day, in his spare time, he positions himself discreetly close to her home and then follows her. He does the same three days later. Both times she enters a tailor's in the Santa Croce district. The door of the premises magnetises him. He is certain plots are being hatched behind it. He notes the shifty vigilant nature of the people entering and leaving. He can tell they all possess dangerous secrets. He begins to recognise the same faces. Excitement in him mounts as he realises he has almost certainly discovered a coven of insurgents. The power he has over these men makes him dizzy. One word from him and they would be subjected to insufferable physical torments. He begins to see their faces as they might look after the torture implements at Ca' Littoria have been used on them.

Today he is baffled to see a companion of his enter the shop. Cesare remains inside for half an hour. He follows him when he leaves. He trails in his wake over two bridges. Then Cesare suddenly swivels around by the side of a narrow canal.

"Why are you following me, Gentile?"

"You tell me," says Fausto, approaching him with a smile.

"What are you, a private detective?"

"What's going on, Cesare?"

"Something you're liable to fuck up with your amateur sleuth work."

"Tell me."

"It's top secret but what if I told you I was a double agent?"

"You would say that."

"Report me if you don't believe me."

"I think you're keeping your options open. Very clever of you."

"Carry on with this line of argument and I might have to report *you*."

"You're no more a committed fascist than I am."

"How do you know, Gentile? Fascism is just an ugly part of human nature to which we're all susceptible. The desire to put everyone we don't like in a prison camp. I'm not above such base motivations. But supposing I said I enjoy the risk. I don't give much thought to what these people are doing. I certainly feel no righteous indignation. I don't even feel much desire to stop them. But I find it exciting to enter into their midst. It's like I'm fate. I've got them all on strings. Do you know what I think about the war? I think it gives us the opportunity to play out the games we loved as kids. The trouble is, the hapless kids are given the shitty roles. So you don't want to be one of those hapless kids."

"Do they know you work for the GNR?"

"Of course. That's part of the fun. They desperately want to trust me and when you want something bad you always trample down your doubts. No one is honest with themselves when they want something. Like when you're in love, Gentile. Not that I can imagine you've ever been in love. Perhaps that's what brings closer the possibility that you will end up one of the hapless kids. Your lovelessness. But listen, Gentile, you have to stop hanging around here. I spotted you when I came out. Someone else will do the same before long. They're all as jumpy as cats. Because they've got something explosive in the pipeline."

47

"Tonight you can prove to me you're not a faggot, Gentile."

They are walking between rows of closed shutters and bolted doors in the vapours of light provided by Gino's flashlight.

"Most indebted to you, kind sir," says Fausto, adjusting the belt around his waist. They are both dressed in plain clothes, as instructed.

"Much as I'd love to do it myself, I've decided to give you the honour of liquidating this traitor. Let's find out what you're made of. 8 July, 1944. Remember the date, Gentile. The day you became a man."

Fausto makes a mocking face, silently mouthing Gino's words. His stomach lurched at the briefing when he found out what he had to do and who he had to do it with. He and Gino are one of ten execution squads sent out into the night to murder suspected anti-fascist insurgents, all resident in the Cannaregio district, as a reprisal for the assassination of an important fascist marshal in the area two days ago. The order is to arrest these men, take them out onto the street and shoot them in the back of the head, leaving their bodies where they fall.

"I'm not sure you've got the balls."

"You're never going to let me forget I once felt sorry for a cat, are you?"

"It's not just that. There's something about you, Gentile, I don't trust. I don't think you're committed to the cause. I don't think you're a true patriot."

Fausto has often fantasised about using his gun. But he

realises now it was cinema in his imagination whenever he released a bullet from the chamber of his weapon. The victim would always get back to his feet after he fired his shot and the cameras stopped rolling. Now, within ten minutes, he will have to shoot a man who won't ever get back to his feet. The prospect makes him dizzy with fearful reluctance. It is baffling when he thinks of the countless other situations his life might have taken him to instead of this one. He realises how pitilessly imprisoned we are in the day to which we awake. He tries to convince himself that if the intended target has any brains he won't answer the door. No one in the building will. Who nowadays opens their door at two in the morning? He and Gino have a licence to leave if they can't get into the building. This is what he has to hope.

The gentle slop of the tide against slimed stone can be heard as they cross a wooden bridge. Gino shifts his flashlight up at Fausto's profile. "You've gone very quiet, Gentile."

Fausto begins quietly humming *Nessun Dorma*. "Is that better?" he says. He continues humming the aria until they reach the building.

Gino presses the bell. Fausto can hear his own breathing in his ears. There is a dampness under his armpits. The stink of a drain makes him feel nauseous. A light appears at a third-floor window. Then the shutters are thrown open. He is furious with the man when he appears at the window.

"Giuseppe Bonicelli? We have orders to bring you in for questioning. Get dressed and bring your papers."

"What have I done? I haven't done anything. I'm a teacher. I teach geography to eleven year old kids."

"You can explain yourself at the station," shouts Fausto, his neck muscles aching with the strain of having to stare up high above his head.

The man continues pleading his innocence until Gino shouts at him.

While waiting outside Fausto unholsters his gun and releases the safety.

"I'll walk with him by my side," says Gino. "You walk behind. When I stop, you do the deed. One headshot."

How trivially routine he makes it sound, the ending of a man's life. Fausto finds himself hoping the ending of Gino's life meets with an equal measure of indifference.

The man eventually appears downstairs. He stands in the doorway, clearly reluctant to leave his home. Fausto notices he has buttoned his shirt crookedly. There is a crackling in the exposed wires on the damp wall behind him and then the light expires but Fausto has registered every detail of his face and it already haunts him. Behind the glaze of terror he has a kind face.

"Look, I was once arrested for telling a harmless joke in the school staffroom. An overzealous colleague reported me. That's all. That's the extent of my criminal activities. I was released after an hour without being charged."

"What was the joke?" asks Gino.

"I can't remember now. It was two years ago. But you've got the wrong man. I've done nothing wrong. I swear it. I swear it on my little girl's life."

Gino grabs hold of the teacher's genitals and squeezes hard. The teacher lets out a shrill yelp. "Tell me the joke."

"Okay. But it's not really a joke and I was just repeating something I had heard."

Gino tugs and twists at the teacher's trousers again.

"There are three things that don't go together: honesty, intelligence and fascism. He who is honest and fascist isn't intelligent; he who is intelligent and fascist isn't honest; he who is intelligent and honest isn't fascist."

"So you're telling me I'm stupid?"

"I recounted something I heard. That doesn't mean I believe it."

"You think you're so clever. You think you're better than me. Admit it. I'll tell you what you are. You're a little man. A little man of no significance. Look at you. You're shaking with fear."

Gino hawks up some phlegm and spits it in the teacher's face.

Fausto's mind is racing. But one idea keeps returning. And with growing lucidity and persuasion. *Okay Fausto. We've reached a critical junction and you need to make the right decision here. And I think you know what this decision is.*

They walk back the way they came. Gino holds the teacher on the upper arm. Even in the thin nimbus of Gino's torch Fausto can see the teacher sways about like a kite. Every so often he again proclaims his innocence. His voice cracking with unrelenting fear. He keeps looking over his shoulder. Fausto knows it is to him the teacher is appealing. He recalls all the times Gino has insulted and tried to humiliate him. He recalls Gino's face when he slit the throat of the cat. The flash of cruelty that so frequently appears in his eyes. When they are by the side of a short narrow canal Gino stops. The moment seems to fill the entire night, reach up to the stars overhead. The scale of everything changes. Fausto aims the gun at the back of the teacher's neck. He has to steel himself to keep his hand steady. Then he shouts out a word he invents and belongs to no known language and swivels his arm and fires. The noise of the explosion ricochets off the walls followed by the sound of flapping wings. Fausto tries to ignore the gurgling noise he hears by his feet. Gino's torch rolls over the cobbles and falls into the water where for a moment it creates a ghostly pathway.

"Please," says the teacher. "I don't understand what's happening."

"Count yourself lucky you've got a kind face. Now go home, pack some things and leave. You need to disappear."

Fausto sits on the floor. He is wearing a vest and a pair of trousers which belong to Marcello. The trousers are too long in the leg and remind him of when, as a little boy, he dressed up in his father's clothes to make his mother laugh. It's a wonder to him that he was ever so innocent. He has retrieved Elisabetta's painting of Giulia and Marcello from under the bed where he hid it because the expression in Giulia's eyes seemed to tug him towards the world of spirits. He thinks now it was absurd of him to believe a painted image could come alive and reproach him. The edges of the canvas are beginning to curl at the edges. Perhaps it's the recollection of his good nature as a child that makes him want to restore it to Elisabetta. And a newly discovered desire that someone in this world should think well of him. In his sequestered isolation he has become more susceptible to nostalgia and sentiment.

He has been hiding for two weeks. Has barely left the apartment. Talked to no one. There has been no running water for two days and the electricity failed last night. The darkness and silence in which he sat erased all the contours by which he recognises himself. He has entered into a different world, his head still adjusting to the changed nature of reality. It's like he has emerged from a darkened cinema and the film is still more real than he is to himself. Every unexpected noise from the outside world makes him realise how precariously he is holding himself together.

He assumes the fascists are conducting a manhunt to find

him. It's fitting he's hiding in a former Jewish household because to all intents and purposes he has to think of himself as a Jew now. He thinks back to the two children he escorted on the launch to the prison. They both have angelic faces in his memory. Angry avenging angelic faces.

"You can't say your present fate doesn't serve you right," he said to his lathered face in the bathroom mirror while shaving.

He read in the newspaper, reduced now to a single sheet, that five of the ten assassination attempts were successful. Except they were reported as inexplicable murders. The fascist authorities did not claim responsibility for them. The shooting of Gino was also reported. There was no mention of his own name. Gino isn't dead. Fausto waited for the news that he isn't a murderer to change how he thought about himself. But no change took place. It's the two children in the boat who haunt him. No matter how many times he manages to convince himself he was not responsible for their fate their stricken faces return to unsettle him in the dark.

As he gets to his feet now a terrific explosion rocks the building. Already dizzy with hunger he feels the floor sway beneath his feet. There is a light rain of falling dust. For a moment he has no idea what to expect next, as if all the laws of reality have changed. After his body and mind have absorbed the shock he realises this is a good moment to leave the building and get some food. People will be too agitated to take much notice of him. He picks up the painted canvas and leaves the apartment.

The streets are charged with excitement. Word is passed that bombs have destroyed the basilica of Saint Mark's. "The sacred heart of the city." He passes an old man who sits on the pavement in tears. His battered hat resting on his knee. He has only been inside the basilica once. A vague image of its dizzying engineering and all its mosaics flashes into his mind. And then it is reduced to an ugly mound of smoking rubble.

High overhead two seagulls call to each other.

It is a city of unfriendly faces in his new state of mind. He doesn't know where Elisabetta lives so goes to her father's studio.

"Hello Maestro."

The artist stares at him as if he might be a figment of his imagination. He has aged since Fausto last saw him. There is more grey in his matted hair. Broken blood vessels in his pinched cheeks. Breadcrumbs in his beard. Paint engrained in the chapped skin of his hands and beneath his fingernails. He looks as though he hasn't washed for a week. Fausto suspects he is the first person he's been called upon to converse with for days. Something they have in common. Two survivors of a shipwreck facing each other.

"What was that explosion, do you know?"

"They say the basilica of Saint Mark's has been bombed."

"Who would do that?"

"Beats me."

"What's that canvas you're holding?"

"It belongs to your daughter."

"Where did you get it?"

"Long story."

"Come in," he says.

In the studio motes swim about in the shafts of north light. Crushed tubes of paint sit on every surface. The smell of oils and varnishes thickens in the air. A wave of wistful nostalgia sweeps through him. It now seems to him, against his better judgement, that he was happy here. In those days he possessed the conviction of writing his own scripts, a conviction, he realises, he no longer enjoys.

He invents a spurious story about how he came into possession of the painting.

Del Monaco takes the canvas and lays it on the floorboards. He weighs down the curling edges with glass jars. Then stands over it, studying it closely. "My daughter did this, did she? It's not bad. Of course I taught her everything she knows. It bears all my hallmarks. Nice handling of the hair here. My daughter isn't talking to me. She's shown me nothing but ingratitude lately."

"The war is driving everyone a bit mad," says Fausto.

"The war *is* driving everyone mad. You're not wrong. I can't get hold of the materials I need to paint. That's what's driving me mad. My daughter though has shown a cruel mean side to her character I didn't know existed. She's made me feel things I don't have time for. A man should live in his work, not in his feelings. Women can never understand this. You've seen her, have you?"

"I saw her briefly."

"Give me a hand. I'm going to put it behind the painting I did of you as Saint Anthony which is slightly bigger. Do you get the joke? Saint Anthony is the patron saint of lost things. Saint Anthony will be the custodian of her lost painting. I'll give it back to her when she apologises to me."

He helps the artist take down the painting from the wall and remove the frame. He is perplexed Elisabetta's father evidently has no cognisance of how childishly he's behaving. It always baffles him when people are incapable of seeing themselves from a perimeter. He watches him smooth out Elisabetta's canvas on the board behind his own painting with a cunning smirk on his face. There is a busy brittle pleasure in his voice. The man has clearly gone a little mad. As if too much solitude has worn down the varnish of his social identity.

When Elisabetta's painting is concealed behind his own painting he replaces the frame but does not hang it back on the wall.

Fausto leaves the studio, pulls his hat down low on his head and buys what groceries he can find. He learns it is the GNR's headquarters in Ca' Giustinian that has been bombed. In his mind all the mosaics of the basilica reconstitute themselves from the rubble to the towering walls, like a film running backwards. Then, as he is walking down Fondamenta dei Tolentini, someone calls out his name. He is sure his heart stops beating for a second.

Cesare is carrying a rucksack. His hat is battered; his tie is askew. He looks frightened, hunted.

"I need your help, Fausto. I need somewhere to stay until I know what's happening. They're looking for you, you know. They say you shot Gino. I don't blame you for that. Both of us need to get out of the city. I can help you."

Fausto frowns.

"Look, it would be easy for me to follow you and, unless you never go home, find out where you live. I don't want to do this, Fausto. I like you. But I'm in desperate straits. I'll explain inside."

Back in the apartment Cesare tells his story.

"I passed on all the information they needed to stop this attack. I'm willing to wager it was carried out exactly as I told them it would. So why did they allow it to go ahead? Effectively, they've given the green light to blow up their own headquarters. There's no possibility Zani or Morelli or any of the other fascist bigwigs were in that building today. Zani and Morelli were worried the moderate fascists were getting more and more support. My guess is they needed an outrage. Innocent victims. A couple of female secretaries with young children would be ideal for propaganda purposes. They'll now use this to their advantage. To carry out purges probably. To satiate their unquenchable bloodlust. But now I'm the sole possessor of their dirty secret. On the good side, my credentials with the anti-fascists are still intact. My plan is to join a partisan band near San Donà di Piave. Why don't you join me? The fascists are going to lose the war. It's only a matter of time now. I don't believe Hitler has these secret weapons everyone's putting their faith in. We need to show we've fought on the right side when the war ends. There will be a lot of bloodletting."

49

Elisabetta has learned plans are afoot to carry her father's casket into the basilica of San Marco and hold the funeral service there. It's an honour he always secretly wanted. To be celebrated as one of Venice's most gifted sons. Instead though he is to be celebrated as a martyr to the Nazi-fascist cause along with the other twenty-two victims of the Allied air raid on the city.

"That's not what I want. It's certainly not what he would have wanted. It's sickening they're going to use my father's corpse for propaganda purposes. His funeral should take place in the Frari. That's our church."

"I'm sorry, Elisabetta. There's nothing I can do."

Her husband now works for the UPI (the political investigations office of the Republican fascists). He was inside Ca' Giustinian when the bomb exploded. His hearing was impaired afterwards. She has little idea exactly what his work entails. He never talks about it. Only that it consumes most of his energies. She suspects, like a spider, he creates webs in which to capture prey. What she does know is that there was no excuse for what the Allies did, described in the *Gazzettino* as a "ferocious terrorist attack". The target of the air raid had been the German hospital ship moored in the basin near Saint Mark's. Wounded German soldiers have been flooding into the city from the front. Men with charred faces and shattered limbs are carried down the steps at the station of Santa Lucia every day. She has witnessed the spectacle herself while searching for salt which can't be found anywhere. After the hospital ship had been hit, fighter planes swooped low over the lagoon and strafed two vaporetti. She still doesn't understand what her father was doing on a vaporetto headed for Chioggia. He rarely stepped on board any boat. She can only imagine he was desperate to find painting materials.

Only when she sits on his bed does the full force of grief hit her. She picks up a pair of his shoes and cradles them in her lap. His face goes in and out of focus before her wet eyes. She sees pain and incomprehension on it. Pain and incomprehension caused by her. She longs for another half hour of his company. In half an hour she might make amends for the wrong she has done him. She could tell him how thankful she is for all he has given her. Half an hour. It seems so little to ask for in the context of an entire life.

Did he think of her the moment before he died? She can imagine him asking himself who would look after his paintings after his death. And not feeling sure of being able to trust her. "What an awful daughter I've been," she thinks. "Never as indulgent with others as I am with myself. Selfish! Always selfish! Even now I'm being selfish. I want you back so you can make me feel better about how I treated you."

She sits down on the floor, her back resting against the frame of his bed. She aches to do him justice. She wants to feel until she breaks. Surrounded by the things he touched every day, nestled in his distinctive smell, it is incomprehensible to her that he will never again return to this room. The realisation will not take root. The atmosphere of his presence thickens around her. She knows her father was a difficult man to appease. But it appals her now how eager she was to censor him and cause him pain. With what casual dismissiveness she was prepared to disappoint him. As if she herself were some kind of perfect being. "I was the worst kind of fascist," she thinks.

Outside the window snow is falling through thickening mist. She lets her mind drift with the flakes, until she feels abandoned in some unreachable place, like a ghost ship. Never has her life felt so loveless. It's the most damning criticism she has ever faced.

She returns to his studio through another snowstorm. To get her blood circulating she stands stamping her feet and clapping her hands for a while. Then she looks at all his paintings, one by one. Each imparts a lively memory of its execution. It takes courage to create something new in the world. She has learned this and would like to tell him. She dwells on moments when there was affectionate complicity between them. She is avid to recall times when she made him smile. This is when she feels closer to the true spirit of their bond. Or so she tries to convince herself. She remembers how vulnerably boyish he always looked after he had washed his hair, like a deity constrained to submit to human vanities. His paintings are her responsibility now. As is his reputation as an artist. She wills herself to find evidence of genius in the brushwork, the scumbling, the play of light behind the varnish in his work. One painting is turned to face the wall. She turns it round. It is the painting of Fausto as Saint Anthony. She studies it closely, trying to understand why he didn't want to look at this particular painting.

50

"Look at all those stars. You know some of them ceased to exist thousands of years ago? We're looking at a gathering of ghosts. Mind boggling, isn't it?"

"You should save this kind of talk for a pretty girl," says Fausto. He needs no invitation to look up at the great swarm of stars. There's little else to look at. He thinks they look like prayers sent up into the sky. He and his companion are walking from an outbuilding to the farmhouse high on a ridge. The hard packed snow is slippery underfoot.

Outside the town of San Donà di Piave, he and Cesare were blindfolded by two bearded men carrying rifles. They were bundled up and down slopes of difficult terrain. He heard rushing water; he smelt pine needles. The air was alive with an encompassing quality of stillness. The sense of towering trees and looming rocky heights made him feel smaller and smaller. The air got thinner and colder. They spent a night in a charcoal burner's hut. He and Cesare were treated with hostile mistrust. He told some lies and discovered the telling of lies no longer made him feel cleverer and more intrepid than his companions. The men read his notebook which he carries in his rucksack. They made fun of him while sitting cross legged and warming their hands over the fire. They called him "the philosopher".

In the isolated farmhouse on the high ridge partisans come and go frequently. They are all bearded. Fausto cannot grow a beard. He feels less manly than his companions but lacks the energy to charm and play the comedian. Cesare was taken away one day but nobody will tell him why or what has happened to him. The building itself is oppressive with an atmosphere of unanswered prayer. There are rosary beads hanging from a rusted nail and prints of saints on the walls of the room where he sleeps. After a week up in the mountains, often in sub-zero temperatures, it feels like his life consists of nothing but the collection of rags that clothe his body.

Then he is told he has been given a mission to prove himself. He is to take the broken wireless to a repair shop in San Donà di Piave and get it fixed. He is blindfolded again. The humiliation of continually stumbling rankles. He is no longer able to laugh anything off. When the dirty bandana is removed from his eyes he stands in front of a ragged collection of stone houses flanked by a chestnut forest. A couple of old women in woollen housecoats and shawls stare at him from a doorway with no trace of sympathy.

"You're on your own now," says his companion. He hands Fausto the suitcase that contains the wireless set.

Fausto suspects this is some kind of game they're playing with him. But he is glad to be ridding himself of the humourless bearded men with their red neck scarves and righteous self-importance. He is not cut out for this rugged elementary lifestyle. For the deprivation and mortification of the flesh. Perhaps he can hide out the remainder of the war in San Donà di Piave. It's February of 1945. Surely the war can't go on much longer.

He detects a note of sympathy in his companion's eyes which he quickly hides when they say goodbye. It worries him as he walks away. He considers dumping the wireless set. It's a dangerous liability. But it has always been a dream of his to one day hear his voice on the wireless so perhaps it's a good luck charm, a sign he hasn't irrevocably been parted from his former world.

When he sits against a tree, needing a break from the glare of the white world, he is strangely conscious of it belonging to the soil in which it is rooted. He is reminded of a childhood feeling he had of being intimately connected to the two trees he could see through the window from his bed. He spent hours studying them when he was unable to sleep. Like they were messengers from another world. Depending on the nature of the wind they either seemed to be serenading or arguing with each other. As he recalls them now they make him feel he has always had two distinct lives – one of superficial bustle and chatter, the other, over which those two trees preside, timeless and infinitely more full of meaning and fate. He is not sure if he is frowning or smiling to himself when a strange insect lands on his raised knee. It almost immediately flies off, then returns. It looks at him and he looks back at it. It's like this grotesque flying thing with the spindly legs and papery wings has come to meet him. Like it is trying to open his eyes to an unsolved mystery. It looks like a death head with gossamer wings. There are men, he knows, who with a quick deft slap would reduce it to a pulped stain on their breeches. Perhaps because it makes them feel ignorant. Fausto has no desire to kill it. He feels an affinity with it, a deep respect for it. It holds fast to its secrets. And it has wings. Wings are what he has always wished for in life.

He has been trudging down towards a meadow of virgin snow when two figures on skis appear slaloming down the slope to his right. They seem to draw most of his gravity and light to them, leaving him unsteady on his feet and his mind plunged into darkness. They both wear woollen berets, tattered trousers held up with pieces of string, goggles and a red bandana tied around their necks. They have rifles slung over their shoulders.

He is tired down to his bones. There is little strength left in his mind or body. Defeat is less undesirable when you are exhausted. He attempts a smile.

"I recognise that gold tooth. When they told me they had a suspicious character with a gold tooth I knew it had to be you. The princess. You don't recognise me, do you? Your pals beat the shit out of me at Ca' Littoria while you watched."

Fausto needs to swallow to ease the dry scratching in his throat but his spit has turned to paste. He knows the man is going to shoot him. He can see the mental preparation for the act of murder take place in his eyes.

"You know why we've come to meet you."

The damning realisation arrives that it makes no difference in the world whether he lives or dies. Until he remembers the girl he got pregnant. For a moment he can't recall her name.

"I've got a young son," he says. "Why not just let me vanish? Who would know? I'm a nobody. Just a nobody person. And that way you wouldn't have a pointless death on your conscience."

"Has anyone ever told you you don't have a trustworthy face?"

Fausto thinks momentarily of his notebook. It is inside his rucksack. He wonders what will happen to it. Then he drops the wireless set and begins to run. He can think of no other option. There's more dignity in dying in movement, in action. He hasn't got very far when he hears the pitiless click of the rifle.

51

Grief is a prison. Walls have closed in around her. In her narrow cell memories become more vivid and gain new significance. With every new day in the prison of her grief she feels she is closer to understanding herself. She has little will to escape her prison, to clothe the nakedness of her grief. Her sentence is warranted. Her reward perhaps will be to know herself better. She feels guilty the moment she ever finds she's enjoying herself. It seems an act of betrayal against her father. As happens now in the foyer of the Teatro Goldoni where there is an atmosphere of high glamour and the anticipation of sophisticated pleasure. The air sweetened by a trail of perfumes, astir with chatter and laughter.

The funeral service in the basilica was grotesque in its vulgar propaganda and pomp. It angered her. Ever since she has been constantly picking arguments with her husband whose humanity she no longer wants to see. The things she and her husband said to each other have always generally been of little or no account. There is never anything of importance to be settled between them. But she has been unable to maintain the polite formality of their relations. Earlier this evening she took exception to the news that the fascists have now begun to employ women, but only in jobs previously occupied by crippled and war damaged men. "What clearer evidence do you want of how these men you work for view women? In their eyes, we're the equivalent of a crippled or a mentally distressed man."

"You want women to join parachute regiments?"

"How I hate that self-satisfied look on your face. You look like a little boy that's just learned how to ride a bicycle."

She still feels irritation towards him in the foyer of the theatre. But she is also curious to learn about his professional life, to discover what kind of fascist dignitaries his job brings him into contact with. She never sees him in public. Already he has greeted an SS officer as if they are regularly in contact. And several uniformed Italian fascists bloated with a sense of their own importance. These are the kind of men, worldly, ruthless, who intimidated her father. They intimidate her too. Make her feel like a child. Her mind shuts down when called upon to speak to them. She has no access to the quick clever wit expected of her. She spots among the milling crowd one or two cinema actors she recognises but whose names she can't recall. And there are many uniformed representatives of the Venetian branch of the GNR. Medals and ribbons pinned to their proud chests. She once heard someone say – was it Fausto? – that the principal appeal of fascism was its glamorous uniforms because they appealed to the vanity of the Italian male. There is gratified vanity on display everywhere she looks. A stark contrast to the poverty and the desolation evident outside on the streets of the city where refugees continue to arrive and there was no running water for a month after the Allies bombed the pipes of the aqueduct. Earlier this week she passed a mound of rubbish which twitched with the movements of white maggots writhing in its midst. It was a spectacle that still makes her flesh crawl.

The production she is here to see is Pirandello's *Clothing the Naked*. She is disposed to dislike Pirandello because he contributed his Nobel Prize medal to the collecting of gold organised by Mussolini to finance the war on Abyssinia. She remembers Luigi bringing up the fact the first time he came to dinner.

Half way through the first act there is a disturbance in the theatre. The house lights unaccountably blaze on. Three masked men wearing red bandanas and armed with pistols appear on the stage. The actors shuffle towards the wings, looking frightened.

The masked men appear to have a hostage. Following the example of others around her she turns her head and sees other gunman are positioned at all the red curtained exits. There is a stunned silence in the theatre. The man next to her in the uniform of the fascist militia slides his hand down to his holster. For a moment she has a vivid premonition of a gun battle in which she is caught in the crossfire. It's the first time during the entire war she has felt herself in immediate danger. She digs her nails into her knuckles.

"Venetians," says the man on stage, "the end of Hitler and all fascist traitors is imminent. Join us in the fight for the liberation of our country and the final annihilation of Nazi fascism. All anti-fascist parties are united in our fight for democracy and the rebuilding of a fairer, more free-thinking Italy. Now is the time to rally around the National Liberation Committee and the flags of the heroic partisans who are fighting for the liberty of our country. Death to fascism! Freedom to the people!"

She realises she, like everyone else, is spellbound. The man is allowed to finish his short speech uninterrupted. It seems almost like an act of magic after all the years of strict censorship. One of the other masked men throws out leaflets into the crowd. The speaker bows to the huddle of actors at the side of the stage and then the masked men are gone.

The stunned atmosphere in the auditorium lingers on. Barely anyone speaks. It's like this man on the stage has woken everyone up from a long deep sleep. Two fascist militia begin snatching the leaflets from members of the audience. They appear like sulking children who, having failed to get their way, take out their grievance on weaker children. She knows everyone feels exactly as she does. That the masked man on the stage has announced the end of fascism and the end of the war.

52

Hampshire 2021

She grows more and more tense as the time of the video call approaches. The Italian woman has insisted they speak face to face. Kate has never been able to assert her will against opposition. She doesn't, she has reasoned, possess the necessary self-importance. There is a dreaded moment now that is on a loop in her life. The moment a person registers the anomaly of her face. The moment when the overspill of fear and embarrassment in the eyes seeking not to stare at her palsied features performs its demoralising act of transfusion in her consciousness. The moment she is forced to own her ugliness all over again. She has come to learn people want tidiness, conformity, repetition from everyday life. They want the reassuring equivalent of ordered ranks of manicured front gardens. Her face has the effect of the overgrown garden of a haunted house. It is an unnerving summons into a darker more unruly world.

The UK, like Italy, is under lockdown because of the Covid pandemic. There are aspects of this new life that Kate much prefers to the old world. She likes the quiet. The absence of cars on the road outside her home. The ringing clarity of birdsong of a morning. The natural world has edged closer. She feels more intimately connected to the roots of her being. And she no longer has to feel guilty for her reluctance to go out into the world. And especially that when she does have to go out she can cover her face with a mask. She can hide her disfigurement. It's a blessing for which she is grateful. Covid has made her life easier to bear.

For a moment she stands looking at the portrait of her painted by Elisabetta Del Monaco. Her true face, as she likes to believe. The face posterity will remember her by. Then she sits down at her computer. A striking young woman with long black Medusa curls appears on her screen. The anticipated troubled look on her face is there for an instant but there is sympathy rather than naked embarrassment or shock in it.

"Hello Kate. *Buono*. It sounds awful but what I want is for us to rummage through your memories together."

Kate smiles, trying not to look down at the thumbnail image of her twisted mouth at the foot of the screen.

"As I said in my email I'm Venetian and I'm writing a dissertation for my PhD on Elisabetta Del Monaco. Barely anyone has heard of her and I want to make a case that she has a place, albeit a minor one, in the art history of Venice. Since we messaged I've spoken to a couple of her other former students. Including Phoebe Castlereagh-Dolan who told me you once had a plan to buy all Elisabetta's paintings."

So Phoebe *had* read her email but disdainfully decided not to answer it!

"Yes, but unfortunately I didn't have the funds. Do you know what happened to them?"

"Scattered to the four winds so far as I can ascertain. Phoebe also told me that Elisabetta painted you while you studied at her atelier."

"Yes. She did paint me. I bought that painting and also a landscape. That was all I could afford. I was worried about her paintings because they were being stored in a damp basement. Can I ask you what has led you to take an interest in her work?"

"Well, it's a family story. It began with my father. He worked for the railways, but he always wanted to be an art dealer. He spent all his free time attending auctions and rummaging about in antique stores. He bought two paintings by Elisabetta's father at an auction. Not a grand auction. Anything but. The kind of auction where all kinds of junk is up for sale. Anyway, when he took off the frame of one of the pictures, a depiction of Saint Anthony, another painting was hidden behind the board. A painting of a young man and woman. It's signed by Elisabetta. My father sold on the two paintings by her father but he kept Elisabetta's picture. It still hangs in our living room. I can't say I took much notice of it until my father died. He loved it. I suppose my dissertation is my way of honouring my father and his love for that painting."

"Can you let me see this painting? It sounds to me like the picture Elisabetta thought was lost. She once told me she had the horrible feeling it had ended up at the warehouse in Auschwitz. If it's the painting I think it is it's of a Jewish boy called Marcello and his sister."

"Yes, they look like brother and sister. How about, after the call, I send you an image and in return you send me an image of the portrait Elisabetta did of you and the landscape?"

Kate answers all Melissa's questions. It is rewarding to have someone take so much interest in her memories. She finds herself feeling fortunate she has made it through to this moment in her life. But she is impatient to see the painting. She concludes the call by saying, "There's something to admire in anyone who can make their presence felt as a force for good when they are physically absent. Sometimes that seems to me the finest achievement any of us can attain. Elisabetta was and still is like that."

"Thank you, Kate. I can't tell you how much I've enjoyed listening to your stories. I'll send you an image of the painting now."

Kate sits staring at the image of Marcello and his sister. Marcello has a kind and attractive face. She feels he is on the verge of whispering a secret. She marvels at how beautifully her teacher has painted the convergence of slanting light which gives his face depths of sensitivity. There's a subtly painted tiny cut on his cheek. It's like a prophecy of the fate that awaits him. For a moment she can't help imagining the distortions undergone by his face when the gas entered his lungs. The painting compels her to experience the bewildering horror of the Holocaust with a more pressing intimacy than she has ever experienced it before. The grimacing twist of her own mouth has always looked to her like an expression of disgust. At this moment, thinking of the Nazi death camps, it is finally eloquent of something she feels. Before long she is deeming herself vain and stupid for attributing so much importance to her appearance. Then she is able to exult again that Marcello has been returned to the world.

"You were right," she tells the ghost of her teacher. "It is your best painting. And you'll be pleased to know it has survived and is in good hands."

Acknowledgements

For inspiration, sustenance and feedback, thanks to: Charles Cecil, Freddie de Rougemont, Georgiana Calthorpe, Christabel Brudnell-Bruce, Emily Pennock, Talitha Stevenson, VJ Keegan, Rupert Alexander, Justin Sparrow, Anna von Kanitz, Jessica St. James, Paola Rosà, Gina Monaco, Alex Preston, Judith Kinghorn, Annabel Merullo, Charlie Campbell, Hamid Khanbhai, Charlotte Raymond, David Flusfeder, Tim Atkins, Eloise Anson, Vanessa Garwood, Hugo Wilson, Antonia Barclay, Lucy Corbett, Chiara De Cabarrus, Kim Macconnell, Stuart Bridgeman, Paolo Cristellotti, Katie St. George, Bill Liesegang, Tiarnan McCarthy, Sarah Haybittle, Ebba Heuman, Cristina Zamagni.